NOR

PRAISE FOR REBEKAH CRANE

Only the Pretty Lies

"Inspired by a true event, Crane (*The Infinite Pieces of Us*, 2018) earnestly explores how silence perpetuates racism and what it means to be antiracist . . . With countless quotable lines like 'Love is a human right, not a reward for good behavior,' and timely antiracism discussion, this is a YA novel with love and substance."

—*Booklist* (starred review)

"A naïve girl is forced to reconcile truths she thought she knew with the reality of the boy she loves. A romance that tackles serious issues . . ."

—*Kirkus Reviews*

Postcards for a Songbird

"An earnest exploration of the demise of a family, this book captures the sense of disconnect a teen can feel when buffeted by changing winds . . . The characters are well-developed, complex, and intriguing. A finely crafted story of the healing that can happen when family secrets rise to the surface."

—*Kirkus Reviews*

"An enjoyable read. Wren's vulnerability and decision to no longer play it safe will engage readers."

—*School Library Journal*

The Infinite Pieces of Us

A *Seventeen* Best YA Book of 2018

"Crane has created an organic and dynamic friendship group. Esther's first-person narration, including her framing of existential questions as 'Complex Math Problems,' is honest and endearing. A compelling narrative about the power of friendship, faith, self-acceptance, and forgiveness."

—*Kirkus Reviews*

"Crane's latest is a breezy, voice-driven, and emotional read with a well-rounded cast of characters that walk that fine line between quirky and true to life . . . The novel stands out for its depiction of the American Southwest . . . Hand to fans of Jandy Nelson and Estelle Laure."

—*Booklist*

"[This] journey of self-discovery and new beginnings will resonate with readers seeking answers to life's big questions."

—*School Library Journal*

"*The Infinite Pieces of Us* tells a story of judgement, family, trust, identity, and new beginnings . . . a fresh take on teenage pregnancy . . . Crane creates relatable, diverse characters with varying socioeconomic backgrounds and sexualities that remind readers of the importance of getting to know people beyond the surface presentation."

—*VOYA*

The Upside of Falling Down

"[An] appealing love story that provides romantics with many swoon-worthy moments."

—*Publishers Weekly*

"Written with [an] unstoppable mix of sharp humor, detailed characters, and all-around charm, this story delivers a fresh and enticing take on first love—and one that will leave readers swooning."

—Jessica Park, author of *180 Seconds* and *Flat-Out Love*

"*The Upside of Falling Down* is a romantic new-adult celebration of all of the wild and amazing possibilities that open up when perfect plans go awry."

—*Foreword Magazine*

"Using the device of Clementine's amnesia, Crane explores themes of freedom and self-determination . . . Readers will respond to [Clementine's] testing of new waters. A light exploration of existential themes."

—*Kirkus Reviews*

"This quickly paced work will be enjoyed by teens interested in independence, love, self-discovery, and drama."

—*School Library Journal*

"First love, starting over, finding herself—the story is hopeful and romantic."

—*Denver Life*

"A sweet, funny love story that YA readers will fall for."

—HelloGiggles

"The setting in lush and beautiful Ireland adds charm to the tale as does the romantic brogue of the leading man. Teens who like romance, mystery, and a strong-willed female will like this quick, enjoyable read."

—*VOYA*

The Odds of Loving Grover Cleveland

One of Bustle's Eight Best YA Books of December 2016

"Now that the title has captured our attention, I have even better news: No, this book isn't a history lesson about a president. Much more wonderfully, it centers on teenager Zander Osborne, who meets a boy named Grover Cleveland at a camp for at-risk youth. Together, the two and other kids who face bipolar disorder, anorexia, pathological lying, schizophrenia, and other obstacles use their group therapy sessions to break down and build themselves back up. And as Zander gets closer to Grover, she wonders if happiness is actually a possibility for her after all."

—Bustle

"The true beauty of Crane's book lies in the way she handles the ugly, painful details of real life, showing the glimmering humanity beneath the façades of even her most troubled characters . . . Crane shows, with enormous heart and wisdom, how even the unlikeliest of friendships can give us the strength we need to keep on fighting."

—RT Book Reviews

JUNE, REIMAGINED

ALSO BY REBEKAH CRANE

Only the Pretty Lies

Postcards for a Songbird

The Infinite Pieces of Us

The Upside of Falling Down

The Odds of Loving Grover Cleveland

Aspen

Playing Nice

JUNE, REIMAGINED

A Novel

REBEKAH CRANE

▇▃▅ SKYSCAPE

Text copyright © 2022 by Rebekah Crane
All rights reserved.

Published by Skyscape, New York

www.apub.com

Amazon, the Amazon logo, and Skyscape are trademarks of Amazon.com, Inc., or its affiliates.

ISBN-13: 9781542036115 (hardcover)
ISBN-10: 1542036119 (hardcover)

ISBN-13: 9781542036122 (paperback)
ISBN-10: 1542036127 (paperback)

Cover design by Leah Jacobs-Gordon

Printed in the United States of America

First edition

For my family, always.
Slàinte mhath.

ONE

June Merriweather sat in Concourse B at Cincinnati International Airport with a backpack at her feet and an urn in her hands. Her foot tapped rhythmically on the metal chair, while her hands played an accompanying pattern on the urn.

June's flight was due to board in fifteen minutes. Outwardly, she appeared only slightly tense, while, internally, she felt like a criminal running from the police. In fact, June was trying to outrun something much more cunning and well ordered than law enforcement.

Her life.

Any passerby would be surprised to know that June was holding a cremated body. To an onlooker, it appeared she was cradling an obnoxious football trophy. And while it was most definitely odd for a traveler to be holding a sports trophy, it was exponentially odder because her brother was inside. Some might call it depressing, even morbid or gross or horrifying. Some might go so far as to say June had a problem.

Some would be right.

"I know what you're thinking." As if carrying a football-shaped urn wasn't odd enough, June now began to talk to herself. Or maybe she was talking more to her dead brother. Neither boded well for her sanity, but after a month of cloudiness, June was finally thinking clearly.

"It's better this way. You'll see." Cigarette smoke clung to her hair from last night's party. Maybe she should have showered before leaving for the airport at four in the morning, but all she had considered was not waking her parents. Luckily, they had attended the Hartfields' notorious New Year's Eve bash, known for copious amounts of champagne and decadent food. The first-ever invitation for the Merriweathers had come just weeks ago, and while June's father, Phil, had immediately declined the offer, June's mother, Nancy, had felt it would be insulting not to attend.

"I think we have a pretty good excuse not to go," Phil had said. "Just say thank you, but we're staying in that night."

"Maybe it will be good for us," Nancy had offered. She showed Phil the invitation. "It says here it's catered, with live music."

"I don't want to eat oysters Rockefeller and talk business with the likes of Bob Hartfield when I could spend the evening in my own home."

"I bet it's a jazz band. You love jazz."

"Unless they're resurrecting Miles Davis, I don't care what band it is. The only reason we're invited is Josh."

"That might be true, but it's a nice gesture, and I don't want to upset them by declining. It's one night, honey."

"You're telling me we have to worry about the Hartfields' feelings when it's *our* son who's dead? Who's being cared for in this equation? The last thing I want to do is attend a party right now."

Nancy burst into tears, a volcano of grief. For the past month, this had been her reality—one instant she was calm and collected in the meat section of the grocery store, and the next she was cradling ground chuck wrapped in plastic and Styrofoam like a precious baby, her face smeared with makeup, mascara-blackened bags under her already tired and saggy eyes, as she thought of how Josh loved peanut butter and bacon on his burgers, whereas most people loved American cheese and pickles. How he was always on the brink of being truly revolutionary.

And now he was dust.

Nancy didn't cry in drops. She cried in streams. "Well, the last thing I want to be is a grieving mother of a dead son, but here I am," Nancy had countered to Phil. "We're going to the Hartfields' New Year's Eve party, and that's the end of it."

June now checked the time in the airport. It was eight thirty. Her parents were most likely awake, with three Advil tablets and two cups of coffee in their systems to counter their hangovers. June imagined her mom at the kitchen counter, hugging her mug to her chest, and her dad seated at the breakfast nook, cradling his head in his hands, the red Christmas poinsettia in front of him too large for the small table, in the center of which sat the letter June had left them.

She pushed the thought from her mind. She couldn't concern herself with her parents. Now all that mattered was getting on the plane.

"Be happy I brought you with me," she said to the obnoxious-looking urn. "You could be sitting on the mantel right now."

The silence that followed seemed to indicate that a girl with an urn on her lap, holding a one-way ticket out of Cincinnati and talking to a dead person, was indeed a little bonkers.

But June had her reasons.

June felt the sudden urge to weep large, ugly tears and hugged the football to her chest until the tightness clawing at her throat subsided.

The perky gate attendant, smothered with foundation and red lipstick and dressed in starched blue slacks and a white button-down with a crisscrossed red necktie, announced that flight 823 was almost ready to board. June stood, feeling the sharp contrast between the attendant and herself: worn-out flared jeans with growing holes at the back pockets, Phi Gamma Delta winter formal T-shirt stained with late-night pizza, newly procured pointed black boots bought just a few days ago with her Christmas money, and an oversize green-and-blue windbreaker grabbed from the front closet as June rushed out the door to catch her cab. Fashion and cleanliness had not been on her mind, but with

3

no idea when her next shower and change of clothes would be, June realized that maybe she should have given her outfit at least a passing glance.

Just like everything in her life recently, the thought had come too late. Now she would have to travel as the personification of a particularly bad Walk of Shame—like after shacking up with the only ugly lacrosse player at Stratford College, in bedsheets that hadn't been changed in three months, while his dorm mates played video games.

June draped her backpack over her shoulder. Her hand holding the boarding pass shook. She found it nearly impossible to move forward. She considered whether there was a God, the canceling of *Party of Five*, the first time she had had sex in the back seat of Mike Brogan's minivan, and the possibility of heading straight back to the ticket counter and returning her ticket. The sound of her cell phone jolted her out of her panic. She must have thrown it into the bag on instinct.

"Shit." She dug in her backpack. "Damn it," she said, seeing the name of the caller.

Declining a call from Matt Tierney would only create more suspicion. After last night, he wouldn't leave a voice mail. He'd hang up, walk the one hundred feet between their two families' houses in his pajamas, and knock on the Merriweathers' front door. She needed more time than that.

June flipped open her phone and answered.

"OK, confession time," Matt said before June could utter a word. "Do you remember when Marty Hillsdale farted in Mrs. Rockhold's class in seventh grade, and everyone started calling him Farty Marty? Well, it was actually me. I've never told anyone that. God, it feels so fucking good to get that off my chest. OK, now it's your turn. Tell me one of your deep dark secrets."

The sound of Matt's voice relaxed June, like the first sip of beer on a Thursday night. "You know all my secrets." That was a lie. Matt knew *most* of June's secrets. "I can't believe you never told me about Farty Marty."

"I was weak and young and a total dick."

"You were kind of a dick back then," June agreed. "Remember when you threw a party at Dustin Andrew's house when his family was out of town?"

"That kid still hates me."

"You stole a picture of his mom and hung it up in your locker."

"It was a Mrs. Robinson thing."

"You called her a MILF to Dustin's face."

"And he punched me. I accepted the punishment. That kid suffered from a bad Oedipus complex."

The gate attendant announced the boarding of flight 823. June placed her hand over the phone's mic, trying to muffle the sound.

"Where are you?" Matt asked.

"A coffee shop. I had a craving for scones."

"Scones." He sounded unconvinced.

"I'm trying to decide between lemon blueberry and orange cranberry. Which one should I get? I'm leaning toward lemon blueberry."

"June, where are you really?"

"They have a poppyseed one, but I hate how the seeds get stuck in your teeth."

"Don't bullshit me, June."

"Did I tell you about the poem I saw in the bathroom at Herb's Tavern the other night? You would have loved it. 'When you sit to take a shit / No longer should you fear / We all poop loud so just be proud / Don't worry what we hear.' Brilliant, right? All the best poetry rhymes."

"Don't."

"Don't what?"

"Distract from the topic at hand by pushing my literary buttons," Matt said. "Just tell me where the fuck you are."

5

June cursed herself for answering the call. Matt was too perceptive for his own good, and she knew it. Neither of them had made a single important decision without informing the other since they were five years old—until now, and that guilt sat on June's chest like a dumbbell.

"You worry too much," she said.

"I worry about *you*."

"Well, don't. I'm fine."

"You're still not answering my question."

"Life isn't about answers, Matty. It's about asking the right questions."

"That's poetic. Now I definitely know something's wrong."

"What can I say? You're rubbing off on me."

"June," Matt said in a tone that begged seriousness. "We don't lie to each other. No matter how bad it is. That's the deal."

June hugged the urn to her chest, a reminder of her reality. "It's my turn to order. I gotta go, Matty."

"Wait. Can I see you later? After . . ."

After I scatter Josh's ashes, June thought. Even Matt had a hard time talking about her brother's death. People around Sunningdale generally seemed unable to finish their sentences when talking to her, since Josh's untimely departure from this world.

I'm so sorry to hear . . .

When these things happen . . .

If you need anything . . .

June was left to finish the unsaid. Even Matt, whose life was constructed on complex and compound sentences, was reduced to fragments.

"I'll call you," June said.

"Do you want me to come?"

"No."

"Why don't I meet you at the coffee shop? We can eat scones together. Though, if you ask me, scones are fucking pretentious. They're like Americanos. Just call it coffee, for fuck's sake."

"You're pretentious, Matty," June said. "You wear a scarf and have a picture of Hemingway in your bedroom. You're a walking Americano."

"Good point. That might be true. Then what are you?"

"I'm a white-chocolate mocha with whipped cream. I'm what you drink when you want to caffeinate but you hate the taste of coffee."

"I have so much to say about this. I'll be there in ten minutes."

June heard him fumble on the other end of the line. "You can't!"

"Why not?"

"Because . . ." June stumbled. "I'm not in Sunningdale. I'm at a coffee shop in Clifton."

"By the university? Why?"

"I just didn't want to run into anyone."

"Then I'll come there."

"Actually, I'm leaving."

Matt turned serious. "What's going on, June?"

"Nothing."

"Nothing is always something. Tell me."

"I can't."

"Why?"

June was losing her resolve. The plane ticket in her hand got heavier. "Because my problems are ruining your life, Matty."

"No. George Bush is ruining my life. The oil industry is ruining my life. Hell, my dad's girlfriend is ruining my life. But you, June, you may have been a thorn in my side, a pain in my ass, a benign growth on my face, a really bad cold sore, the person who let all the ants escape from my ant farm, but you could never ruin my life."

"The ants weren't happy in captivity."

"See? You've always been the better person," Matt said. "Look, I know the past month has been rough. But today is a new year, and 2003 is going to be great. Trust me."

June was the only person left in the boarding area.

"I do trust you," she said.

7

"What's the name of the coffee shop? I'm getting in the car now."

The gate attendant approached June, bringing with her the smell of Clinique's Happy perfume. June covered her phone's mic.

"Are you coming, sweetheart? The doors are about to close. After they do, there's no getting on the plane. You'll miss it." The attendant smiled with a kindness June didn't deserve, in her chaotic, wrinkled outfit, with the lingering smell of cigarettes in her hair overpowering the attendant's potent citrus-and-floral perfume. June had been reduced to items you find in an ashtray—random scraps of paper, chewed gum, and squished cigarette butts stained red with cheap lipstick.

"Happy New Year, Matty." June Merriweather hung up the phone. Then she tossed it in the garbage can. It wouldn't work where she was going, anyway. "I'm coming." She handed the gate attendant her ticket and passport. One day she'd make Matt understand why she did this.

"Have you ever been to Scotland before?" the attendant enquired.

"No. Any advice?"

The attendant surveyed June's belongings: roller bag, backpack, and the world's ugliest urn. "I just hope you've got a raincoat in there. You're gonna need it."

TWO

Mom and Dad,

I had to leave. I took Josh with me. Just tell every-one I'm spending time at Grandma and Grandpa's in Michigan. Also . . . I don't want to do this, but here it goes. If you come after us, I'll tell everyone in Sunningdale what really happened to Josh. I'll be in touch as soon as I get settled.

I love you,
June

June stood in front of the Thistle Stop Café. Rain dripped from her eyelashes. She had been in Scotland for three days. Or at least, she thought it had been three days. Maybe four. Or five? Jet lag had a disorienting effect. That and the fact that Scotland saw very little sunlight in January, making day and night hard to decipher.

The only thing June was absolutely sure of was the rain. It had fallen in multiple forms since her arrival. Big, heavy globs. Sprinkled mist. Sideways. June had even experienced a moment when she thought the rain had ended, but when she turned her face to the sun, a drop fell directly on her forehead.

In Scotland, it rained even when the sun was out.

But the sun was not shining as she stood at the café door, bags and urn in tow, staring at a CLOSED sign. June turned just in time to see the cab that had taken her from the bus depot head down a side street and drive away. She was stuck. She checked the sheet of paper in her hand. The name and address of the café were correct: *The Thistle Stop Café, 25471 High Street, Knockmoral, Scotland*.

June smelled coffee and bread. Her stomach growled. Had she eaten today? She peered through the café window. Inside, wooden chairs were stacked on wooden tables. Light came from the back of the shop, where June assumed the kitchen was located. The café was small, rustic, yet artistically decorated—bohemian charm mixed with old English style. Or was it old *Scottish* style? Since arriving, June had realized how little she actually knew about Scotland.

For example, the rain. June wasn't completely naive about the weather. Having watched *Braveheart* numerous times, she assumed even rain needed to breathe, collect itself, and begin again. Apparently in Scotland, the weather only exhaled, and that exhale was cold and damp and lasted for days.

June had not come prepared. Her large roller bag was filled with all the needs of a twenty-year-old sorority girl—toothbrush, toothpaste, makeup, thongs, velour jumpsuits, wind pants, silk camisoles, white tank tops, black pants, J. Crew sweaters, Tri Gamma T-shirts, a hooded Ohio State sweatshirt (Matt's), tennis shoes, pointy black boots, and flared jeans. She should have come dressed more like Paddington Bear—a raincoat, Wellingtons, a hat, and a pair of gloves.

She knocked, forcefully, but had no response. A chill ran down her arms. No wonder the plane ticket to Inverness had been the cheapest option. The airline sales agent hadn't been forthcoming about the dismal weather, and June had only cared, at five in the morning at Cincinnati International Airport, that her destination was an ocean away from Sunningdale. June imagined cobbled streets, quaint shops selling kilts and wool blankets, pubs and restaurants with cozy fires, all surrounded by the gorgeous rolling hills, lochs, and mountains of the Highlands. All of this *and* they spoke English.

But in January, the hills surrounding Inverness were covered in snow. And as for English, June wasn't sure what the locals were speaking, but it was not a language she understood. Since landing, she had kept her composure, but as she stood at the Thistle Stop Café, shivering, June's confidence began to falter. What was she thinking, running away to Scotland? In the winter! If she were back in the States, June would be curled up in her warm bed at the Tri Gamma house, slightly hungover, leftover pizza in her mini fridge, dreading her 9:00 a.m. childhood development class. And she'd have her stack of *Friends* DVDs and heat. Lots of heat. Her stomach growled again.

She had been crazy to answer an advertisement for a job in a town she had never even heard of. Inverness was at least recognizable, but Knockmoral? June wasn't even quite sure where she was. She had seen water on her way into town, but there was water all over this country. Had she seen a loch, or the ocean, or just a really big puddle? Was this hamlet seaside, lakeside, or just waterlogged like everywhere else?

When she had called the café to enquire after the job, she had spoken to a barely understandable man named Hamish. He told her to take the 61 bus toward Ullapool; from Ullapool, take the 809 north and get off at the Knockmoral stop (which she almost missed on account of a staticky microphone and the language barrier). Then walk across the street to the taxi stand and tell the driver to take her to the Thistle Stop Café.

"He'll know the place," Hamish had said.

"Are you sure?"

"You're in the Highlands now, lass. Everyone knows everyone in this town."

She had followed his instructions, but Hamish had neglected to confirm whether he would be at the café. June hadn't thought that necessary. She held her hand out to catch the rain drops, which were coming down even faster now. Since she had landed, June had been damp all the time. Her shirt, her socks, her bra, her skin, her hair. She felt constantly chilly. And there wasn't a clothes dryer in sight. How was she supposed to clean her clothes without a dryer? She certainly couldn't line-dry them. She had taken to blow-drying her clothes, just for the heat.

June felt like she was going to cry. She couldn't survive on her own. She had spent the past two and a half years at Stratford College, a small party school tucked away in nowhere Tennessee, living in a sorority house with a maid and a chef. Her only concerns had been attending enough classes and avoiding an STD. What had she expected—that traveling abroad would magically make her more capable? That the fog she had been living in would miraculously lift in Scotland? If anything, June was incapacitated, her mind altered by grief and regret, standing in the rain in the middle-of-nowhere fucking Scotland, with no plan forward. Jet lag had made it worse, and to top it off, she didn't even have an umbrella. As it turned out, windbreakers were windproof, not waterproof.

She was about to sit down on the sidewalk, curl into a tiny ball, and cry for Matt, when the café door opened, startling her backward.

"Can I help you?" A tall man with rosy cheeks and a long brownish-red beard stood before June, wearing an apron and a kind smile. He eyed the bag at June's feet. "Are you lost?"

"I'm here about a job. I called yesterday and spoke with Hamish."

"Right! That's me. I'm Hamish." He ushered June inside, June dragging her roller bag behind her. "Can't keep my own head straight these days. Can I get you a cup of tea? Warm you up. You're soaked through."

Hamish took down two stacked chairs from a table and went behind the counter. June shook out of her soaked backpack and windbreaker and hung them to dry on the back of a chair. Hamish pulled a cup and saucer from the piled dishes. "How about a wee plate of biscuits, too?

Can't have tea without the cookie. It's the best part. We make them from scratch here. My wife's secret recipe. Even after fourteen years of marriage, she still won't tell me what they're made of. Bleeding stubborn woman insists on making them herself." Hamish chuckled. "That lass went into labor three weeks ago and wouldn't hear of leaving the house until she'd frozen enough biscuit batter for three months. Thank goodness it's low season, or she would have given birth with a spatula in her hand on our kitchen floor." Hamish set a cup of tea and a plate of cookies in front of June and took a seat. "So." He leaned back and smiled.

June took a long sip of hot tea, feeling it all the way to her bones. "Your advertisement said you need an assistant."

"Right. You Americans, always getting down to business." Hamish sat up straighter. "My wife, Sophie, and I usually run the place ourselves in the winter. Business is slow, only locals coming in. Not many tourists. Only a crazy person would want to come to Scotland in the winter. I should ask . . . Are you crazy?"

June gave an appropriate response. "Only as much as the next person."

"What's an American doing in Scotland in January, anyway? It's dreadful here. Why aren't you on a beach somewhere in Mexico?"

June thought of spring break in Cancun and sipped her tea. It was not as tasty as a margarita, but much warmer. "The beach is overrated. Too much . . . sunshine . . . and sand." God, sunshine sounded nice.

Hamish chuckled. "You're a masochist, then, are you? Well, you'll fit in fine 'round here. Knockmoral has its fair share of hermits, misanthropes, and broken hearts."

"Which one are you?"

"I'm a sucker. I can't stand to see any of them starve, so I stay open all year when most places 'round here shut down."

Between the food, tea, and warm smile, there was something incredibly nurturing about Hamish, who looked like a young Santa Claus, minus the huge belly. June felt as though she could trust him.

"Our little man hasn't stopped crying since he took his first breath three weeks ago, so it's been just me at the café. Sophie's up all night, and I'm up wishing I could do something, but seeing as there's only one set of breasts between the two of us, I'm useless. Then I come here all bleary eyed, messing up orders and burning toast. I need another set of hands."

June held up her hands. "I have a pair."

"Grand." Hamish ran a hand down his beard. "Café opens at nine and closes at four. I do all the cooking, so you'd be in charge of taking orders, making coffee, bussing tables, and the like."

"Great," June said. "I have a lot of restaurant experience."

"And you have a work visa."

June's heart sank. "A work visa? No. I don't have one of those."

Hamish's smile deflated. "I'm afraid I can't hire you without one."

"Are you sure? We do it all the time in the States."

"Aye," Hamish said. "I could lose the café. And I can't go doing that. Who would feed all the misanthropes?"

June sat back in her seat, still feeling damp. Rain lashed at the windows. Had she flown all the way to Scotland only to turn around in less than a week?

"I really need a job," she said. What June needed even more than that was time. A month, maybe, to get her head on straight. Then she could return to the States, apologetic and composed. Her family would understand, because she would no longer feel as though she might crack open and spew toxins all over the people she loved. She'd plead with her professors at Stratford College. Claim bereavement. Promise never to miss another class. She'd make up missed assignments and tests, and by the end of spring semester, it would be as if June hadn't missed a step. She would be back to her old self.

But time cost money. June had some savings, but the hostel in Inverness charged forty pounds a night. Add to that her airfare, food, and the money she'd need to spend on weather-appropriate clothes, and

June's bank account was shriveling up quicker than an old man in a cold pool. There was her college scholarship money from the Women's Club of Sunningdale, but the account was monitored and strictly reserved for Stratford College. If June was caught spending those funds on anything other than designated costs—tuition and classroom expenses— the scholarship would be immediately revoked, imploding June's return plan. If she lost her scholarship, June could no longer afford Stratford's out-of-state tuition.

"Are you sure you can't hire me?" she pleaded with Hamish.

"I hate that you came all this way only to be disappointed," Hamish said, pushing the plate closer to June. "At least have the biscuits before you leave."

Leave to go where? June hadn't considered not getting the job. She had dragged her belongings with her under the assumption that she would be staying in Knockmoral. Now she'd have to go back to the hostel in Inverness with her roommate, Kasper, from Norway, who smelled like BO and wore tighty-whities as if they were appropriate dinner attire. Not to mention, June had no idea when the next bus left Knockmoral toward Inverness. For all she knew, she could be stranded overnight.

She took a large bite of a biscuit, defeated, not knowing when her next meal would be.

Hamish smiled. "Why don't I put some in a baggie for you, too."

June nodded and swallowed; too quickly, she noticed a long-forgotten taste in her mouth. She placed the biscuit back on the plate and grabbed her backpack.

"Everything OK?" Hamish asked.

June scoured her bag as if her EpiPen would miraculously appear inside, knowing full well it was sitting on her dresser back at home. She had packed thongs and not her EpiPen. She had bought a ticket to Scotland without considering there might be work restrictions. June was more messed up than she thought.

15

She coughed, moving her jaw and swallowing, as if that might clear the problem slowly presenting itself.

At that, Hamish understood the severity of what was occurring right before his eyes. "Bloody hell. You're allergic to peanuts, aren't you?"

June felt her blood pressure drop as her body went oddly warm.

"Don't move." Hamish stood up in a panic. "I'll be back." He ran out of the café into the dark, rainy evening, leaving June alone again.

Her money problems no longer mattered. As it turned out, June had flown all the way to Scotland to die.

THREE

To: j_merriweather42@hotmail.com
From: Matt.F.Tierney@yahoo.com
Subject: WHERE THE FUCK ARE YOU?

June,

First, you hang up on me, then you turn off your cell phone, then I call your mom and she says you're taking a fucking break from school and visiting your fucking grandparents in Michigan indefinitely. I thought you were at a coffee shop in Clifton! What kind of horseshit is that? Nan's obviously lying. It's like the time she told me you had the stomach flu for a week when you'd really started your period. I'll say the same thing I said then. Whatever's going on, I can handle it. You don't need to hide. I'll buy you metaphorical tampons. Get you a metaphorical heating pad and some aspirin. Eat metaphorical chocolate and watch *Titanic*, for fuck's sake! Just tell me where you are!

—Matt

To say that June had not expected to die in Scotland would be a gross understatement. While death had made a sudden and unwelcome appearance in her life, June still functioned under the common and blissful young-adult mindset that *her* death was intangible. She could smoke weed, drink, have sex, and still wake up in the morning with only a slight hangover, easily cured by greasy fast food, two Advil tablets, and a day of *The Real World* reruns. June's death was a hypothetical concept to be ignored, not a reality to be considered.

As she struggled to breathe in a strange café an ocean away from home, June's thoughts should have been on her parents. Just yesterday she had visited an internet café in Inverness to check her email, only to find a very pointed message from Nancy Merriweather reminding June of her innate lack of foresight and the inevitable repercussions of her rash decisions. Her mother may have had a point there, though June was unwilling to admit it, even while dying. Nancy ended the email, as ever, by reminding June of her forthcoming responsibilities: the Women's Club of Sunningdale was expecting 115 thank-you cards, personalized and handwritten by June herself, to be sent to the club's benefactors and silent auction winners by February 15.

Thank-you cards be damned. Soon enough, Phil and Nancy Merriweather would have, unbeknownst to them, two dead children hiding out in Scotland.

But June's thoughts were not on her parents. Only one person had great influence on June Merriweather. If she was honest with herself, which at this point in her life she most definitely was not, Matt Tierney had an indelible power over June, though she refused to name it. Definitions are fixed. Permanent. Once set in place, one must act on them. And June wasn't ready for that sort of commitment.

Now, as she rubbed at her itchy arms and felt her bloated lips, June had one thought: she had taken a bus for the first time and hadn't told Matt Tierney. He would want to know about the trip, every detail.

Where did you sit?

June, Reimagined

In the back.

Did it smell?

Like diesel and dirty armpits.

Are the roads as narrow as they look on TV, and is it weird driving on the other side?

June had been certain they were going to sideswipe every hedgerow they passed. A few times she even gasped. But there was so much more to tell Matt—how she sat by the window, mesmerized by the gray clouds that hung low over the mountains like a blanket; how the older couple sitting across from her held hands the entire ride; and how the bus had to stop to let sheep cross the road.

June hadn't responded to Matt's email, which she regretted now as she sat dying in Knockmoral from a peanut allergy. Matt didn't even know Knockmoral existed, let alone that June was in it.

For the first time in her life, June was decidedly without her best friend. The thought of never seeing him again made her already pinched breath even tighter. A montage of their lives together flipped through her mind, like slides in the old-fashioned projector she'd found in her grandparents' attic, next to boxes of Kodachrome film.

Matt and June as children, burning leaves with magnifying glasses, eating highly processed icy pops that stained their tongues blue and purple. The first time June and Matt stole, and drank, beers at the Tierneys' annual Halloween party. The time Matt kicked Billy Carson in the balls after Billy said June was flat chested and called her Tortilla Tits. June teaching Matt what the word "virgin" meant. The two of them secretly watching *Fatal Attraction* and seeing boobs for the first time on-screen.

If Matt were here, none of this would be happening. Whereas June was reckless, Matt was meticulous and his life was mapped out. He always chastised her for constantly forgetting her EpiPen, so much so that in high school he carried an extra one in his backpack, just in case.

In the end, though, June's carelessness got the better of her. Her body was too focused on the allergic reaction to emit tears, but if she could have, June would have been blubbering. Matt Tierney wasn't just her best friend. He was a physical place—the safest June had ever known. Safer than her own house or bedroom. Safer than herself. And she had run away from that. But she had a good reason. Matt had said June could never ruin his life, but he was wrong.

The door flew open as Hamish reemerged, out of breath and drenched from the rain. "The lass is in here!"

What happened next felt as if June were out of her body. Behind Hamish came someone else. The man rushed to June's side, a familiar object in hand.

"I need to unbutton your jeans. It's more effective that way," he said in a Scottish accent that was, thank God, understandable. June noticed the man's shirt, which clung wetly to his chest: *Knockmoral Fire and Rescue Service*.

"It's a bit early in our relationship, don't you think?" June said, though the swelling in her mouth muffled the words. "We just met."

"A comedian. Should you really be joking at a time like this?" He unbuttoned June's jeans and pulled them down just enough so that her outer thigh was exposed.

"A nut that bears a striking resemblance to testicles is about to kill me," June joked again. "Now is a good time to laugh."

"You're not going to die," he said.

"How do you know?"

"Because I won't let you. There's only one thing I hate more than death." He pressed the EpiPen hard on June's leg, activating the auto-injector and sending epinephrine into her system.

"What's that?" June asked.

"Paperwork." He brushed his hands together, satisfied. "The ambulance is just 'round the corner," he said to Hamish.

"Good. I'll follow in my car."

The man nodded. "I'll let Sophie know what happened."

"You're a lifesaver, Lennox Gordon," Hamish said. "I owe you."

"No, you don't, Hamish. You know that."

Lennox lifted June out of the seat, gently pulling her pants back to their rightful position, and set her back down. The café doors opened then, two men came in with a gurney, and June was loaded into the back of the ambulance.

"I'll bring your bags!" Hamish yelled as the doors closed.

On a positive note, June didn't have to wait in the rain for the next bus out of Knockmoral.

~

June had not considered free medical care when she had bought her ticket to Scotland. Ushered to the closest hospital in Bonar Bridge, she saw a nurse and a doctor, who cleared her of any further issues and released her with a prescription for a new EpiPen and instructions to keep it on hand at all times. There was no payment. Just help for someone who desperately needed it.

In the waiting room, Hamish slouched in a chair, June's belongings next to him. He sat upright at the sight of her.

"You're alright." Spared from death, June barely managed a nod as Hamish rubbed a hand over his face, smooshing his wrinkles and making the bags under his eyes more pronounced. "This is all my fault. I'm too distracted and tired. Why the hell did I convince Sophie to have a third bairn? I thought we were young enough for this. We're not young! I'm a middle-aged Big Friendly Giant with a scraggly beard and a Peter Pan complex!"

June sat next to Hamish, exhausted. "You want to compare poor choices with a person prone to anaphylactic reactions who just ate a peanut-infested biscuit while attempting to get a job she can't have in a country where she doesn't live?" She patted Hamish's knee. "I win."

"I should have told you about the peanuts."

"And I should have . . ." June's head fell to her hands. "I should have done a lot of things differently."

In the past month, June had come to appreciate a clean death. When Josh died, two hundred miles from home in an apartment in Marion, Ohio, he had left behind more questions than answers. June grew to envy people whose loved ones left the world in an organized manner, politely. With wills in place. Orderly desks and closets. Financial planners and email accounts with easy passwords. A life mapped out precisely so the people left behind didn't have to wonder about important matters like whether to cremate or bury the body and what songs to play at the funeral. June's parents had argued over these decisions, each invoking a son that the other didn't know, as a defense.

"Josh would want 'Amazing Grace,'" Nancy had said.

"No, Nan, *you* want 'Amazing Grace,'" Phil countered. "Josh would want something by the Beatles."

June knew Josh would hate both. "How about 'Another One Bites the Dust' by Queen?" she had offered. Her suggestion had been met with tears from her mom and a reprimand from her dad, which sent June retreating to her room in anger. She had meant it honestly. She could hear Josh's boisterous laugh in her head, congratulating her on the idea.

A sad funeral isn't new! Make 'em laugh, June, that way they'll remember me. And for Christ's sake, no crying.

In the end, the Merriweathers had played "I'll Be Seeing You." The standing-room-only congregation wept loudly, gasping for air, a few grievers wailing. June sat in the pew fuming, dressed head to toe in black, another of her mother's instructions, supposedly in Josh's name. Josh hated to see people cry.

Hamish put his arm around June. "Cheer up, lass. The day wasn't a complete disaster. At least I didn't have to explain a dead body in the café to my wife."

Not dying was only baseline living. June hadn't accomplished anything. She was still jobless and homeless, with a dwindling bank account and an ever-growing fear that she might not be cut out for this, whatever this was.

Hamish patted her knee and stood. "Let me give you a ride back to where you're staying."

But where was June staying exactly? She had left the hostel in Inverness thinking Knockmoral would be her new home. It was pitch black outside. June had literally no idea where in the world she was.

She couldn't get up from her seat. She grabbed Hamish's arm and yanked him back down next to her. "Look, I know you can't technically hire me because of the work visa and all. And I know I must seem totally irresponsible for not having my EpiPen on me, but I promise, I'll be the best damn café assistant you've ever hired."

"You'd be the *only* assistant I've ever hired." Hamish chuckled.

"I'll be on time. I won't drop plates or spill coffee on the customers. I'll clean the bathrooms. Whatever it takes."

"I know you'd be just grand. Hell, at this point, I'd hire my six-year-old if she could make coffee, but I'm just not sure how we can make it work."

"Maybe we can come up with a compromise," June offered. Her thoughts raced as she put the impromptu plan together. "Maybe we can work out . . . an exchange? You need help at the café, and I need a place to stay for a little while. I could stay with you, and in exchange, I'll *volunteer* at the café. You won't be paying me, so technically I won't be working for you."

"One small problem," Hamish said. "My house is madness as is."

"I could sleep at the café," June suggested. "Or in a tent in your backyard? Or a closet! I could be like Harry Potter! I'll stay in the cupboard under the stairs. You won't even know I'm there."

"A tent in the dead of winter in the Highlands. You're more of a masochist than I thought."

June thought of her house in Sunningdale, of Matt's house next door, the thin strip of lawn separating the two. Some spring and summer mornings, with the windows open, June could smell Matt—a stack of old books next to a cup of hot black coffee—from her bedroom. Vintage and alive. She couldn't go back to that. Not yet.

They sat in silence in the waiting room. A doctor was paged over the intercom. Hamish chewed his lower lip, his brow furrowed in thought. June had put him out so much already. Could she really ask a practical stranger such a favor?

"It's alright." June patted Hamish's leg. "You saved my life tonight, and here I am asking for more favors. You don't owe me anything."

"*Me* save you? Lennox did that."

June may have been out of it, but she remembered the man with the EpiPen. His arrogance had cut through her stupor like a knife. She snorted. "Clearly one of the town's misanthropes."

Hamish chuckled so hard his shoulders shook. "You have no idea, lass."

June liked Hamish's barrel laugh, and being called "lass." Was it possible to miss someone you'd just met?

Hamish smacked June's thigh. "I need to ring someone. Mind if I step out for a wee moment?" He stood and left.

Alone in the waiting room, June tapped her foot on the metal leg of her chair, counting seconds, just as she had at the airport.

Hamish returned a few minutes later with a bright smile. "Stand up, lass. It's time to go. I found you a place to stay."

"You did?" June stood.

Hamish grabbed her roller bag and started dragging it toward the exit, June close behind him. "I'll warn you. Your neighbor . . . he can be a wee bit of a bawbag, but I have a feeling you're not a lass who backs down from a fight."

June didn't know what a bawbag was, but she could handle a grouchy neighbor. Hell, she'd put up with an entire neighborhood of curmudgeons if it meant she didn't have to leave. "I can handle him."

"I was hoping you'd say that."

They walked out into a misty rain, but June barely noticed. She had a place to stay, and that's all that mattered. She beamed. "I'll just make sure to stay off his lawn."

FOUR

June stood at the door of the Nestled Inn, a stately property situated just blocks off the high street in Knockmoral. *Is it considered a house or a manor?* June wondered. The stone exterior, large windows, and medieval-looking architecture made the place appear more like a small castle than a home. Hamish lifted the grand brass knocker and let it fall against the wooden door, three times.

June couldn't believe her luck. She had gone from a cold, damp hostel to being homeless to living in a mansion. Or manor. Or estate. She could smell the fire inside and grinned, imagining herself curled up next to it under a wool blanket with a hot cup of tea. Now, this was finally Scotland.

The large front door opened, light pouring onto the stoop where Hamish and June stood.

"Told you you'd survive." Lennox leaned against the doorjamb, casually.

June gaped at him. "*You* live here?"

"Not that it's any of your business, but no."

"Oh, thank God," she said, relieved.

"I live next door."

June turned to Hamish. "*He's* the bawbag?"

Rebekah Crane

"Is that how you Yanks thank people who save your life?" Lennox enquired. "By calling them a scrotum?"

"Please," June mocked. "You were simply avoiding paperwork."

Hamish laughed heartily and clasped his hands in excitement. "She's just what this place needs. A little spark plug to light the dark months."

"Poetic," Lennox deadpanned. "But I don't follow."

"June is moving in!" Hamish announced. "I already cleared it with Amelia."

"No," Lennox said.

"You don't live here, so it's not up to you," June countered.

"Not that it's your business, Yankee, but I own the place."

"Co-own," Hamish corrected. "With his sister, Amelia."

"Thanks for the reminder," Lennox said. "Uncle."

June was shocked. "You two are *related*?"

Hamish ran a hand over his messy hair. "I know I look like Shrek, but I was quite dashing in my younger years."

"No, you're wonderful," June said to him kindly, touching his arm. Then she scowled at Lennox. "He's just so . . ."

Lennox was intimidatingly broad and tall, like Hamish. He blocked most of the light from inside. And he was not much older than June— maybe twenty-four, she thought—with shaggy dark-brown hair, with hints of red, that hung in short, loose curls.

"Mind what you say, lass," Lennox said. "I *did* save your life today."

"Grudgingly," June reminded him, and herself.

"Now, Len, I got it all figured out with Amelia." Hamish handed June's roller bag to Lennox, who took it, confused. "June is staying in room eight. Amelia already made up the bed and left fresh towels for her."

Lennox dropped the bag. "She can't stay in room eight. It's under construction. Leaky ceiling."

"Angus fixed that three weeks ago," Hamish said. "Now, be a good host and give June a tour of the place."

"As you know well, Uncle, I'm not a good host."

"Then why do you own an inn?" June asked. "Isn't that a job requirement?"

"My parents owned the inn." Lennox crossed his arms. "I didn't have a choice in the matter."

June mimicked his stance. "So why aren't they running the place?"

"Because they're dead," Lennox said curtly. "Any other questions?"

June bit her lip. She couldn't expose the fact that she was accompanied by another tenant, albeit a dead one.

Lennox leaned forward. "Sorry, lass, there won't be any tours. The inn's closed. And what the hell do you have in your bag, anyway? It's heavier than shite."

"None of your business," she said.

"Actually, it is my business, considering you're about to move into my house."

"So, you'll take her then! Grand! Let's get her all settled, shall we?" Hamish picked up June's bag and stepped forward to enter the house.

Lennox's muscle-sculpted arm barred the doorway. "I said no such thing."

"Now, Len," Hamish said, stepping back, "you'd be helping the lass out by taking her in."

"Hamish, I already saved her bloody life today. Haven't I done enough?"

"Then do it for your old uncle."

Lennox cocked an eyebrow at Hamish. "And how, might I ask, does this situation help you?"

"I'm working at the café," June stated proudly.

Lennox narrowed his gaze on her. "Are you sure you want to hire her, Uncle?"

"Why shouldn't he hire me?" June snapped.

"You could be a murderer."

"A murderer!" June threw her arms up in disbelief. "That's ridiculous. I don't even look like a murderer."

"You don't look like much of a worker either. How do we know you're not a thief?" Lennox offered. "Did you check her references?"

"I've never stolen anything in my life," June said to Hamish. "Except for a tube of Bonne Bell strawberry lip balm when I was seven, and my mom made me return it the moment she found out."

"So, you *have* stolen something." Lennox sounded satisfied.

"Didn't you hear what the lass said?" Hamish countered. "She gave it back!"

"Instincts are instincts, Uncle."

"I believe you know well, lad," Hamish said seriously, "that people can change those instincts if they work hard enough at it. Come on, Lennox. My brother always helped people when he could, especially a bonnie wee lass."

"My da was a better man than I'll ever be. You know that. She's a liability, Hamish."

"You don't even know me," June snapped.

"Where was your EpiPen this afternoon?" Lennox asked matter-of-factly.

June had no argument. She *had* forgotten a lifesaving tool thousands of miles away in the States. And while she had good reason for leaving hastily, she wasn't about to explain that to a stranger. She doubted he would take pity on her, anyway.

Lennox again leaned against the doorjamb and crossed his arms, satisfied.

Rain that had been mist just minutes earlier fell harder on June's shoulders. She envied how warm Lennox looked in his flannel shirt, how clean he smelled, like cedarwood and mint. And whatever spiced meal had been cooked for dinner wafted out the front door and right into June's nose. Her stomach growled. What she wouldn't give for a long hot shower after the day she'd had. But the longer she stood there, the colder she got. Her teeth began to chatter. She tried desperately not to look weak, but a chill had settled in her bones.

June forced her teeth to stop chattering and gently touched Hamish's arm. "Let's go." She extended the handle on her roller bag and hiked the backpack up on her shoulder. Then she met Lennox's eye with as much fire as she could muster. He may have been bigger and loads stronger, and June may have been about to crumble, but she'd be damned if she let him see that. "Thanks for saving my life. I'm sorry it was so taxing for you." She turned away with a straight back and shaking hands, noting the panic weaseling its way into her system.

Lennox grunted. "Fine. She can stay in room eight."

June stopped, her back still to the door.

"Grand! I knew you'd come 'round!" Hamish threw his hands up in celebration.

June turned enthusiastically and started back toward the house, but Lennox stopped her with his arm. "On one condition."

"What?" June and Hamish asked simultaneously.

Lennox pointed a long, strong finger at June, distrust written all over his face. "No more life-threatening emergencies. I deal with enough of those as it is. Do you think you can handle that, *Peanut*?"

June wanted to grab his annoying finger and twist it.

"Sure, she can!" Hamish announced. "Right, well, I better be gettin' home to Soph and the kids. She'll be at her wits' end, wondering where the hell I am." He told June to take the next day to settle into her new accommodations and acquaint herself with the town. Then he pulled her into a hug and whispered, "Let's not tell Lennox about our little *exchange*. If he asks about money for the room, tell him Amelia specifically said not to bother him with that. And do yourself a favor, buy a proper raincoat and some wellies." He released June and winked. "Work at the café starts on Monday, nine o'clock sharp."

And before June knew it, she was standing alone with Lennox, the lights of Hamish's car dwindling down the driveway.

Lennox turned and walked into the house. "This way, Peanut."

"My name is June."

"I'm aware, Peanut."

"Are you always this infuriating?" She rolled her heavy bag behind her, its wheels echoing off the stone floor of the foyer.

"Are you always this combative?" Lennox asked.

June wanted to strangle him, but she took a breath and ignored the question altogether.

A large fire burned in the living room's sizable stone fireplace. A deer head with huge antlers hung above the mantel. The ceiling was lined with thick wooden beams. The furniture was dated—worn-out red-and-blue tartan couch, faded leather chairs, paintings of the Scottish countryside dotted with deer. Peeling green paper covered the walls, which were hung with smaller taxidermy deer and sheep heads.

"And you think I'm the murderer," June stated. "Kill all these yourself?"

"I don't hunt," Lennox groaned.

"Well, between you and that couch, it's *so* vintage nineties in here." June gestured to Lennox's well-worn brown-and-dark-blue flannel shirt. "Is flannel the official tartan for the Clan of the Bawbags?"

Lennox narrowed his eyes. "Yanks aren't usually funny."

"My first compliment." June put her hand over her heart, mockingly feigning gratitude.

"I was making an observation, Peanut. You're consistent with the trend." He headed toward the large staircase, with faded green carpet, that split the lower level of the house into two sections. Opposite the living room was a large dining room, wallpapered in navy-blue-and-green tartan and covered in more animal heads, and what June assumed was the door to the kitchen.

She would have to wait to find out as Lennox was already climbing the stairs. June lifted her suitcase and heaved it up the first few steps. She paused. Her day had exhausted her—that morning she had boarded a bus from Inverness toward Ullapool and then Knockmoral, was then taken in an emergency vehicle to a hospital in Bonar Bridge (wherever that was), and was now back in Knockmoral. June had no idea what time it was, but it felt *late*. She leaned back on the ornate wooden banister, letting her fatigue wash over her.

At the top of the stairs, Lennox turned and groaned again.

June pressed a hand to her clammy forehead. "You sound like a caveman when you do that." She imitated Lennox's guttural moan. "Me not like you. Ugh."

Lennox stomped down the stairs to retrieve her bag. Too easily, he picked it up and carried it to the top. June followed, proclaiming that she was perfectly capable of carrying her own bag.

"Aye, you're in great shape," Lennox jested, pointing to the sheen of sweat on June's brow.

"I've had a rough day." *A rough month,* June thought. *Or year . . .* If she was honest, June could barely remember a recent time when her life wasn't choppy. "Can you just take me to my room so I can sleep?"

Lennox gestured to his right. "Eva's, David's, and Angus's rooms are down that hallway. Amelia stays on the main floor. Your room is this way." He started to his left, dragging June's bag.

"Where is everyone?" June asked.

"The pub."

"Why aren't you there?"

"Not your concern."

"Did they go without you? Shocking, considering how social you are."

Lennox approached room eight, but before he opened the door, he turned to June. "How bad is it?"

"How bad is what?"

"Don't lie. I know a disaster when I see one."

"First I'm a murderer, and now I'm a disaster."

"Don't deflect the question. Tell me about the mess you left behind in America."

June avoided Lennox's gaze. "I don't know what you're talking about."

"Look, lass, as you can see by the empty rooms, people don't tend to come to this part of Scotland in the winter, unless they've got something to hide. Best to tell me now what it is."

June hoped Lennox hadn't caught her eyes darting to her suitcase. "Well, I'm not like everyone."

"Yes, you're a unique peanut, Peanut," Lennox mocked. "Just keep your shite to yourself."

"You keep *your* shite to yourself." June sounded ridiculous saying "shite."

A feather of a smile pulled on Lennox's lips. He opened the door to the room and handed June the key. "Laundry is downstairs. Food left in the kitchen without a label is fair game, so I suggest you put your name on anything you don't want Angus to eat."

"What about a phone?" June asked.

"Missing someone, are you? Let me guess, he looks like one of those homoerotic boy-band lads on MTV with bad cornrows and a purple fur jacket."

June hated that her eyes filled with angry, vulnerable tears. She ached for Matt, down to her deepest core. None of this would have happened if Matt had been here.

"Phone's all yours," Lennox said, annoyed. "Just use a calling card. You can buy one at the co-op." He stood at the doorway, waiting impatiently.

"What?"

Lennox rolled his eyes. "I assume you're planning to pay for the room. This isn't a charity house."

June forced confidence. "Amelia said she'd deal with it."

"Fine. Better her than me." He turned to leave.

"Wait!" June had her own questions for Lennox, like why was he on Fire and Rescue if he hated people? And what happened to his parents? How did they die? And if he hated being an innkeeper, why not just sell the place? "Why do you live next door and not here, with everyone else?"

"I would never live in the same house as Angus." Lennox started to go.

"Wait!" June should thank him. As rude and insufferable as he was, Lennox had saved her life, and for that she *was* thankful. But she couldn't get herself to say the words. "What's with the tattoo?"

Lennox's sleeves were rolled to just above the elbow crease, exposing five tally marks, the fifth crossing the other four.

"Let me guess," she quipped. "One for each of the dogs you had growing up? Or the number of countries you've been to? Or, I know . . . one for each woman you've loved?"

"Wouldn't that be sweet." Lennox mustered a saccharine smile. He rolled down his sleeve, covering the tattoo. "If you knew what it was for, lass, you'd hate me even more than you already do." With that, he walked away.

And once again, June Merriweather was alone.

FIVE

To: j_merriweather9802@stratfordcollege.edu
From: Registrar@stratfordcollege.edu
Subject: Spring Semester Schedule

Below is the spring semester schedule for JUNE MERRIWEATHER. Classes start January 6. If you require schedule changes, please contact your advisor. Thank you.

ECEE 3100 Introduction to the Science of Reading MWF 9:30-11:30 211 Morton

ECEE 3810 Play & Creativity in Elementary Education TTH 10:00-12:00 312 Jefferson

ECEE 3002 Junior Clinical Experience in Elementary Setting TBD

GEOL 1010 How the Earth Works MWF 2:00-3:00 112 Tiffin

PHYS 1001 Canoeing TTH 1:30-3:30 Bing Recreation
Center

June awoke the next day groggy and disoriented from a heavy night's sleep, dried drool on her cheek. Last night she had flopped onto the creaky bed like a dead fish, her shoes and clothes still on, all the fight gone from her body, from sparring with Lennox Gordon.

His own quaint cottage, she could now see, was separated from the inn by a wide pebbled driveway and large hedgerow. Unfortunately, from her window June had a perfect view of its slate roof, white shutters, and stone exterior.

Her room was sparse and as dated as the rest of the house: bed and nightstands, lamps from the 1970s that resembled her grandparents' vase-like lamps in off-white, wooden dresser, electric kettle with a basket full of English breakfast tea and honey packets, and attached bathroom, with white pedestal sink and small box shower.

After taking a long shower, changing into fresh clothes, and unpacking, June hid Josh's urn in the back of the closet and closed the door. Then she padded quietly down the stairs and retraced her steps from the night before.

Multiple tables were scattered about the dining room. June imagined that in the summer they would be full of tourists chatting about their itineraries, examining maps and guidebooks, making notes for their vacation days. Now the room was quiet. The seats looked as though they hadn't been moved in months, the tables empty of place settings. June pushed open the kitchen door slowly, hearing voices on the other side.

A guy and girl stood at a stove with their backs to June, the guy, shirtless, only slightly taller than the dark-brown-haired girl.

"Get your disgusting paws away from me, Angus MacGowan." The girl shoved the guy in the chest. "How many times do I have to tell you? I don't eat animals."

"You'd change your mind if you took a bite out of this one," Angus said. "I'm tasty, Amie. I promise."

The girl, Amie, had the same hair color and domineering height as her brother, Lennox—Amelia Gordon. June knew her instantly, even from behind.

"You're a filthy pig," Amelia said.

"I do have quite the hog," Angus said, and oinked in Amelia's ear. Then he grabbed her hips and pulled her close. "Come on, Amie. Let's make piglets together."

"The only thing I'd get from you is a venereal disease." Amelia shoved Angus away again. "If it were up to me, I'd get rid of all the animals in this house. Dead or alive."

"This is a pleasant breakfast conversation." A girl sat on the kitchen counter hugging a cup of tea, thick black-framed glasses perched on her nose, her short blond hair pulled into a half ponytail. Last night Lennox had mentioned a female tenant named Eva, and June deduced that this must be her. "I'm not sure what's making me feel worse, my hangover or this conversation about dead animals," she said in an English accent.

"This hog is very much alive." Angus ate a spoonful of eggs from the pan and immediately spit them out in the sink. "What the hell did you put in this, Amie?"

"Just salt." Amelia took a spoonful for herself and gagged. She reached for the saltshaker, shook a sprinkling into her palm, and tasted the grains. "Fuck."

Angus then tested them himself. "Bloody hell. You put sugar in the eggs."

Simultaneously, a burning smell permeated the kitchen, and bread the color of night popped up in the toaster.

"Fuck!" Amelia pulled out the smoking toast and tossed it in the sink. Then she took the pan of ruined scrambled eggs and dumped them into the garbage. "I can't even make bloody breakfast! It's toast, for Christ's sake. Everyone can make toast. I can't spend the rest of my life in this godforsaken town cleaning toilets and changing sheets, talking to the bloody dead animals on the walls."

Angus wrapped his arm around Amelia. "How about we get naked and I give you the best damn orgasm of your life? That will cheer you right up."

Amelia detangled herself from his grasp as Eva jumped down from the counter and went to the fridge. "I'll make breakfast."

"Can I help?" June offered from the doorway. "I'm pretty good with toast."

Amelia brightened immediately and bounded toward June, a smile now on her face. "You're awake! After yesterday, I wasn't sure what state you'd be in. But look at you, all healthy and rested. I'm so glad you're here."

June was startled by the warm welcome, after Lennox's greeting the night before. "You are?"

"You have no idea," Amelia whispered in June's ear. "Coffee or tea? I'll try not to fuck it up."

June requested coffee as Angus approached with a lazy smirk that showcased a small, endearing gap between his two front teeth. Despite his size, with his tightly buzzed light-brown hair, he looked almost innocent. *Almost.*

"It's good to see you again, *Peanut.*"

Then June realized why Angus looked familiar. His chest had been covered yesterday, in a Knockmoral Fire and Rescue jacket, but she remembered noticing his bright-blue eyes when he loaded her on the gurney.

"June," she said, her cheeks heating. "You work with Lennox?"

"Volunteer." Angus flexed his muscles. "They only call me in for the dangerous assignments."

Amelia laughed. "You drive the ambulance, Angus."

He winked at June. "Anytime you want a ride, just say the word."

"Put a shirt on," Amelia said. "You're scaring the new girl."

Angus brightened. "I have a better idea. Why don't we all take our shirts off? Then no one will be singled out."

"Go back to the sty you came from." Amelia threw a towel at his head, and Angus caught it deftly, with a rosy-cheeked smile.

"But then who would unclog the toilets? Or change the light bulbs? Or fix the leaky sinks?" Angus crept closer, until he was standing right next to Amelia, his lips a breath away from her ear. "Just admit it. You need me, Amie."

"What I need," Amie said with a shove, "is to not be surrounded by animals all bloody day and night."

"Can't help you there, lass," Angus said. "You know how Lennox feels about the place."

"I'm well aware of what he *prefers*," Amelia groaned.

Eva O'Neill properly introduced herself to June as she whisked eggs in a bowl. "So you're the American plot twist that showed up yesterday. Just when things were getting dull around here."

"Plot twist?" June asked.

"Watch out for that one." Amelia gestured toward Eva. "She's too observant for her own good."

"It's a prerequisite for being a writer," Eva said, pouring eggs into a sizzling pan. "That and a penchant for cigarettes, diet soda, and insomnia. Are you sure you want to stay here, June, now that you've met the inmates?"

There was something oddly familiar about the scene, from the food to the disheveled look of the housemates. A Sunday morning at the Nestled Inn resembled a Sunday morning at the Tri Gamma house: everyone slightly hungover, tired, and starving.

"You should see breakfast at my sorority house," June answered. "By now someone would have mentioned blow jobs and puking . . . potentially in the same story."

Angus perked up. "Details, please."

Just then a man burst into the kitchen, dressed head to toe in traditional Highland apparel: kilt, Jacobite shirt, sporran, kilt hose, and ghillie brogues. His shoulder-length brown hair was pulled into a loose ponytail at the nape of his neck. Eva introduced June to David Corrigan. English like Eva and an actor by trade, David was quick to inform June that he had played Hamlet in the Oxford School of Drama's production of the play to rave reviews just two years ago and now led tours at the Highland Museum, impersonating a Scottish Jacobite for eight pounds an hour—a fact he could not get over to this very day.

After the detailed monologue, David asked the group, "Whose fucking idea was it to do fucking shots last night?"

"Yours, idiot," Angus said.

"'O, what a rogue and peasant slave am I.'" David gagged. "I have the mouth sweats."

Angus smacked him on the back. "Cheer up, mate. You might be a loser, but at least you're still ugly."

"Forgot your shirt again this morning?" David asked. "Or did it run away when it saw your pint-size penis?"

"There's nothing pint size about my hog." Angus flexed his pecs. "Who would ever think a scrawny bawbag like you is Scottish?"

"Thanks to Mel Gibson, everyone outside Scotland." David turned to June. "You must be the American plot twist. Heard all about you at the pub last night. First piece of advice: take everything Angus says and cut it in half. He struggles with delusions of grandeur, especially when it comes to size. He was never any good at maths."

Angus grabbed David, who was considerably smaller and skinnier, in a headlock and gave him a noogie. "How does your head feel now?"

"I'm having flashbacks to primary school," David said with a strained voice, his face growing redder. "Don't you have to nail in a screw somewhere?"

Angus let go. "You don't nail a screw, idiot."

David fixed his disheveled ponytail and poured himself a cup of tea.

Just then Amelia's mobile phone started to ring. She grumbled, seeing the caller, and picked up. "Yes, Brother? How may I help you today? Aye. I told Hamish she could stay . . . No, I don't care what you say. I have every right to take her in. I'm part owner. I put up with the bloody animals on the walls. You can put up with her!" Lennox's raised but muffled voice was audible as Amelia held the phone away from her ear and rolled her eyes. "Ack, wheesht, Lennox! Calm down!" She scurried out of the kitchen to take the rest of the call in private.

"I've always found Lennox to be such a charming fellow," David said.

"You don't bloody know him, so keep your comments to yourself," Angus snapped back, serious for the first time that June had seen. But then he grinned slyly at her. "Let me know if you need anything screwed later, Peanut. I'm also trained in mouth to mouth . . . if you need further medical assistance." And then he left.

David stood. "I better crack on, too. Another day of tourists, bagpipes, kilts, haggis, and fried Mars bars. It was a pleasure to meet you, June. My advice: keep your door locked when Angus is home. He conveniently needs to 'fix' something in your bathroom when he hears a shower running." He left with a dramatic bow.

Amelia reentered the kitchen then, sliding her phone back into her pocket, and looking exhausted. "Wanker," she complained.

This was all June's fault. If she weren't here, Amelia wouldn't be fighting with her brother. June couldn't justify tearing a brother and sister apart, especially when their parents were dead. She knew that kind of regret, and she wouldn't wish it on anyone. "I should just leave," she said.

"No!" Amelia protested. "You have to stay."

"But I'm causing problems between you and your brother."

"No, you're not. What Lennox can't understand is that I'm trying to solve a problem. I'm trying to bloody well help him, but the stubborn arse won't ever listen." Amelia took a mug down from the cabinet and poured herself some tea. "Just make me a promise, June. Don't leave."

"But why would you put yourself out for me?" June asked.

Amelia waved away the question and took a sip of her tea. "No need to worry about that. Just promise me you'll stay."

June nodded. After all, she had nowhere else to go.

"Good." Amelia filled up a plate with eggs and toast for June. "Now, eat up. You're gonna need all the energy you can get."

SIX

To: j_merriweather42@hotmail.com
From: hotgirl14@hotmail.com
Subject: crabs

OH MY GOD! trevor garrison has crabs!!! and now half
the phi gamma delta house has them, too! thank god i
didn't hook up with him last weekend.

so . . . apparently u r in michigan at ur grandparents??
BORING. school is in session. get your ass back here! i
called your cell but it went straight to voicemail. i need
my roommate!! who's gonna watch 90210 reruns with
me and make fun of donna's boobs?

BTW . . . my parents gave me their gas card. i already
stocked our mini fridge with diet dr pepper and natural
light. best christmas gift ever!

—Al

J une clutched the calling card and cordless phone in her hands. Nerves like she had never felt threatened to paralyze her. She had been in Scotland for a week. She now knew her way from the inn to the café. She had labeled groceries in the fridge. Her clothes occupied drawers, and her suitcase was packed away in the closet.

The deer heads lining the living room walls stared at her in judgment. June couldn't delay this moment anymore. She started dialing the long number on the calling card as she sat on the worn-out tartan couch in the living room. She immediately stood, unable to sit still. With every second she considered hanging up, until a voice answered.

Matt sounded out of breath.

"Are you running?" June asked.

"June! What the fuck? Is that you?"

"Answer my question."

"No, I'm not running. You know how I feel about endurance sports. I couldn't find my damn cell phone and I panicked. I just tore all the cushions off the couch."

"Why are you panicked?"

"Why the hell do you think, June?" he yelled. "You Harry-fucking-Houdinied on me!"

June bit her lip. "I'm sorry."

"For what? Leaving? Not answering my emails? Shutting me out of whatever the hell is going on with you?"

"I didn't mean to scare you."

"It's not about me, June. I'm not worried about me. I'm worried about *you*. How am I supposed to take care of you if I don't know where you are? Is it me? Did I do something wrong? Is that what's going on here?"

"No! It's never you. You're perfect, Matty. It's . . ." June put her head in her hands. "Me."

"Then tell me what's going on."

His voice was coated in fatigue and worry, and June hated that she had done this to him. But she also knew that a full confession would only make it worse. "Are you back at school?" she asked, feeling like a coward. "Is it freezing in Columbus?"

"You know what it's like. It's winter in Ohio. Stop avoiding my questions."

June could picture Matt walking across Ohio State's campus, a scarf around his neck. She loved that Matt wore a scarf. It made him look academic and metropolitan in a midsize city like Columbus, where the college-student uniform was a hooded Ohio State sweatshirt and jeans. The scarf was a reminder that Matt Tierney was destined for more than some midsize town in Middle America. Ohio was not his future. It was simply his now, a stepping-stone to balance on before leaping to a bigger rock.

If anyone would understand her need to get away, it was Matt. He had been dreaming of a life outside Sunningdale since they were kids. Whereas June's brother, Josh, had hung posters of swimsuit models on his walls, Matt had the skyline of New York City. He memorized the buildings and their locations, stayed up to date on Broadway shows and exhibits at the Met, obsessed over the subway system. Matt talked so frequently about New York that, by the time his dad took him there in high school, June had forgotten that Matt had never been before. And when he came home, wearing a Strand Bookstore T-shirt, June's best friend had changed. It was as if Matt had grown, not physically but in every other way. He had become too big for their small town.

"OK. Don't freak out, Matty."

"Fuck," he said. "Now, I'm freaking out. Where are you, June?"

June willed herself to speak the word. "Scotland," she whispered. The line went quiet. June thought he'd hung up, and she panicked. "Matty, are you there?"

"I'm here," he said in a low, serious voice. "I knew your parents were lying. What the fuck, June? Scotland? How did this even happen? Why didn't you tell me you were planning this?"

"Because you would have come with me!"

"Damn right I would have. And that's a bad thing?"

"Yes!" June said. "I won't derail your life because mine's a mess."

"But Scotland? Why did you run so far away from me?"

June started to cry. "Because you can't fix this."

"I know I can't bring Josh back, but I can make you happy. If you would just let me try, June."

She didn't respond. Matt always assumed he knew all of June's problems because that's how it had always been. For over a decade, they had shared everything, and then a few years ago, that bond had changed. Now she was too far in. Her lies were compounding, and the more she was around Matt, the more she set him up to suffer.

"I just need some time away from everything," she said.

"Me included?"

June couldn't answer that. She didn't want space between her and Matt, and yet staying close to him was impossible. If she cared about him at all, which she did with all her heart, the only way to protect their friendship was distance.

"At least tell me how in the hell you ended up in fucking Scotland," he said.

June confessed to buying the cheapest ticket she could get, describing her first few days in Inverness, the advertisement for work at the Thistle Stop Café in Knockmoral, her new room at the Nestled Inn. She omitted her near-death experience, and Lennox. Revealing the trip to the hospital would only scare Matt more. And as for Lennox, if Matt knew some asshole was giving June a hard time, he would be on the next plane out of the US.

"You took a bus?" Matt asked. "Public transportation scares you."

48

"That's because some ex-cop terrorist might hook a bomb to the bus."

"You're deflecting again," Matt said. "And you got a job? What does that even mean? When are you coming home?"

"Think of it like . . . I'm studying abroad."

"But you're not, June. Does Stratford even know about this?"

She let her silence answer his question. Matt had grown more and more tense, and June braced herself for the onslaught she knew she deserved for her recklessness.

"It's OK." Matt about-faced. "I understand."

"You do?"

"Remember the time you jumped the railroad tracks at full speed and you popped two tires on your dad's car?"

"How could I forget? I was grounded for a month."

"Or the time you smoked weed with those strangers at the Phish concert? Or the time you used your mom's cleaning bleach to dye the front of your hair, to look like that chick from *My So-Called Life*, and you burned your scalp?"

"Rayanne," June said. "Of course, I remember. What's your point, Matty?"

"You're rash, June. You jump before you think. I should have seen this coming. Your brother just died of some bizarre, undetected heart condition. The whole situation makes life feel so fucking unpredictable. Makes sense you did something impulsive. It's what you do. At least you didn't shave your head."

"You don't think I'd look good bald?"

"I think you'd look beautiful, but you'd regret it immediately. You'd make me buy you a million wigs. Remember how paranoid you were at the Phish concert? Barely ten minutes after you smoked, you were sure the weed was laced with something. You made me hold your hand all night and tell you if things were real or not."

June had been so afraid at the Phish concert. It was the closest she'd come to a panic attack. She sat on the couch, the cushion so thin she felt the coils. "You're saying I'm going to regret this."

"I'm just saying I wish I was there to fix things if it goes sideways," Matt said. "And June . . ."

"What?"

"You're not going to die like Josh. That was a freak accident."

"I know." June bit the inside of her cheek and refused to cry again.

"I have to say, I'm surprised you picked Scotland. I would have thought you'd go someplace flashier, like France."

"As it turns out, flying to France is more expensive than flying to Scotland. Apparently, people like visiting there no matter the season." A pregnant pause followed. June would have done almost anything to take away Matt's pain. "How about we go to Paris together, Matty? You and me. I promise."

"Only if you promise you won't complain when I drag you to all the museums."

"Then you can't complain when I drag you into every cheesy tourist stop and make you buy souvenir spoons and snow globes."

"Don't forget the key chains and coffee mugs," he said.

"And berets," June added.

"No. I draw the line at ridiculous hats."

"Come on! You have to. And scarves. I love you in a scarf."

"My neck is very sensitive to the cold."

"Whatever. You wear it because the ladies love it. I bet men in Paris wear scarves."

"If they want to get laid, they do."

"Can we eat snails, too?"

"No," Matt said. "I'm not eating snails."

"You're already wearing a beret. What's a few snails?"

"Fine, I'll eat snails," Matt conceded, too quickly. June knew he was still worried. "But I draw the line at dressing like a mime. And you can't complain when we go into bookstores."

"No one complains in Paris, because they're *in Paris*," June said, hugging her arms tightly around herself as if she could mimic the intimacy of Matt holding her, there in the capacious living room. "Just because you're not here doesn't mean you're not with me, Matty. You're *always* with me."

"Yeah, yeah. It's just different."

"Maybe different will be good for us."

"I like us the way we've always been."

They sat in silence for a time, neither willing to end the conversation.

June eventually said, "I better go, Matty, before I use up all the minutes on my calling card."

"Wait. First, confession time . . . I miss you."

"I miss you, too."

"Meet you in Paris?"

"Meet you in Paris," June said.

After she hung up, she felt no more relieved than when the call had started. Now she missed Matt more than ever. And yet going home and seeing him would only make her lies worse. Over the past few years, June had justified her actions, but when she examined them closely and honestly, it was clear she didn't deserve Matt's compassion and friendship. Because June was a liar.

She stood quickly, went up to her room, and changed into wind pants, a T-shirt, her windbreaker, and sneakers. She needed to get out. She pushed open the front door of the inn and left, determined to run until she was numb.

SEVEN

The fields around Knockmoral were rolling green and brown, dotted in snow, sheep, and a hairy cow or two or five. June blinked rain from her eyes and turned in a slow circle. She was sure she knew her way home. At least, she was sure a few miles back, but running had possessed her, and now she stood soaked, shivering, and lost.

At the beginning of the run, she had almost given up. Every step felt as if her shoes were made of lead. Every breath, fire in and fire out. She almost cried. In high school, June had run a six-and-a-half-minute mile for the cross-country team. Not the fastest, but definitely not the sloth-like pace she was pushing now. The most recent exercise June had had was the Tri Gamma sloshball tournament, which was just kickball with a keg at second base. Every player who made it to second had to chug a beer before moving on to third. What did she expect?

She had almost given up, but stopping would have been too easy. Pain was penance, and June needed her legs to ache and her breath to burn. She didn't deserve relief. The harder she ran, the more it hurt, the better. When the rain started, it was a welcome reprieve from the sweat collecting on her forehead.

But now, as she panted on the side of the road, hands on her hips, catching her breath, June questioned a slew of poor decisions. Damp clothes that had kept her hot skin cool now turned chilly. Blisters ached on her heels. She was alone with no phone, no directions, and no idea what to do next. Her stomach grumbled.

June turned back as her teeth began to chatter. Why in God's name did she not bring her new rain jacket? Had she not just spent an entire week getting so intimate with rain that it knew her body better than her high school boyfriend had? It had been dry when she left the inn, but Scotland was a country of unpredictability that demanded preparation. Yet again June had failed the test. She attempted to run, but her legs seized with rippling cramps, and she fell to the wet ground. She cried. She thought about digging a hole, crawling in, and never coming out. She wondered what dirt tasted like.

June rubbed her calves, like her cross-country coach used to do. She got to her knees, forced herself to stand. At the rate she could limp, she would make it back to the inn by tomorrow morning, if she could find her way in the encroaching dark. But what other choice did she have?

"Pretend it's a warm shower," she whispered, tasting rain on her lips. "Pretend it's a warm shower." But that just reminded June how *not* warm she felt. Her fingers were wrinkled. Goosebumps covered her skin.

As she considered that maybe the best option was to befriend a hairy cow and hide underneath it, car lights approached down the road. The vehicle was headed into town. June stuck her thumb out. Then she waved. Then, mustering all the energy she could, she simultaneously jumped, waved, and flailed. The car stopped. June crossed the road, dragging her left leg, which had seized up again. The driver's window rolled down, and June immediately regretted dancing in the middle of the road, begging for a ride.

"Hitchhiking?" Lennox asked.

June straightened herself, hoping to seem confident. "Actually, I was out for a run."

"You're an athlete?"

"Don't sound so surprised."

"You just seem . . ."

"What?" June snapped.

"Delicate."

"I am so *not* delicate. I broke my wrist once, falling out of a speeding golf cart, and didn't go to the hospital for five days."

"So, you're delicate and stupid."

June burned with a desire to punch Lennox Gordon right in the nose. What did he know of what she'd been through? She had come to realize, in the past few months, that emptiness had a sound. The absence of Josh in the house was louder than when he had played Tupac at full volume to get amped up before his Friday night football games. A hollowness overwhelmed her. Tears stung her eyes. Damn it—of all the times to cry. June pivoted, fists clenched, and walked away from the car, refusing to let Lennox see her weakness.

"It's six miles to town, Peanut," he hollered from his dry seat in his warm, dry car.

"Don't call me that."

"Why not?"

"Just go away."

"I thought you wanted a ride."

"I'll wait for another car."

"Not many people come down this road. Might be a while."

"I'll take my chances."

"Why in God's name would you run all the way out here in the first place? There's a perfectly good running trail in town, down by the water."

June didn't need his condescension. She raised her index finger. "I believe you requested that I keep my *shite* to myself. Isn't there a cat stuck in a tree somewhere?"

"Right now, I'm trying to help a woman suffering from acute hypothermia, but she's being a pain in the bloody arse. Get in the damn car, Peanut, before I drag you in here myself."

"Don't call me Peanut!" June stomped her foot and screamed. It was that or break down and weep, which she refused to do.

"I'm trying to help you," Lennox said, too evenly.

This only stoked June's anger. "I don't want your help," she snapped. She wanted Matt. She wanted Matt's hand-me-down brown Lancer to pull up next to her, the front seat covered in library books and peppermint gum wrappers. June would move to put the books on the ground, but Matt would stop her: "Just because they're beat up doesn't mean you can treat them poorly. How would you feel if someone tossed you aside because of a few torn pages or a broken spine?" June would apologize to the books before setting them gently in the back seat. Matt bought only used or borrowed books. He liked them covered in fingerprints and smudges and notes. He once said that books weren't just about the words on the page but the people who had turned the pages. Matt would offer her a stick of Trident, and she'd put a well-worn Dave Matthews CD in the player. Matt would play air drums to "Ants Marching." The sun would shine, the windows would be rolled down, and when they returned Matt's books to the library, he'd say, "Until next time, friend," gently dropping each into the bin.

Lennox Gordon was the last person June wanted to see right now. Revealing her emotions to him was a bad idea, let alone her guilt and shame. He would only weaponize them against her. "Just leave. I'll wait for the next car."

Lennox groaned. "Don't be an idiot. Do you even know what hypothermia does to a person?"

"First, I'm delicate. Then, I'm stupid. And now, I'm an idiot. Your foreplay skills are impressive. Women must love you."

"They rarely complain."

June hated his confidence. No doubt women fell at Lennox's feet. His ridiculous good looks and hooded, pensive hazel eyes only made him more annoying and mysterious. She shivered and sulked down the road.

"Damn it, Peanut," Lennox yelled. "Your body temperature is getting low, which means blood won't flow to your skin. It'll go to your organs and start to slow them down."

"Sexy," June mocked. "Talk dirty to me some more."

"Jesus Christ! Is everything a joke to you? Pretty soon your body will shut down. Now, would you get in the damn car before you collapse and I have to take you back to the hospital?"

Every fiber of her being wanted to resist, to piss him off more, but June couldn't go back to the hospital. What would Hamish think? She had told him to trust her. June couldn't threaten her current situation. And she had promised Amelia she would stay. Lennox couldn't win by proving that June was weak, a liability. But she refused to sit in the front seat. She climbed into the back and slammed the door.

"Do I look like a bloody chauffeur?" Lennox asked.

"You got me in the car. Now, take me home, *Jeeves*." She crossed her arms like a petulant child and stared out the window.

"Jeeves was a valet, not a chauffeur," Lennox mumbled.

June ignored the comment. Warm air flowed from the vents, and she cupped her hands to her mouth and blew on her cold fingers. Her whole body shook, try as she did to stop it.

Lennox pulled the car over to the side of the road, went to the trunk, and returned. "Here." He threw a blanket at June. She caught it before it hit her face. "Take off your clothes and wrap yourself in that." He produced a granola bar from the center console. "And eat this." He tossed it at June.

The snack landed on her lap. "I am not taking my clothes off in front of you. And I'll eat when I get home."

"I didn't ask," Lennox said sharply. "Now do it."

June didn't move.

"Jesus Christ, Peanut! Don't be an idiot!"

"Stop calling me an idiot!" June's face burned hot with shame. She shouldn't even be in Scotland, let alone in this car with a man she despised, thousands of miles from the best friend she loved. But she had done this to herself. She wasn't an idiot, like Lennox thought. That would be a step up. She was worse. She was a liar.

"I'm sorry," Lennox said unconvincingly.

"You could at least turn around." June started to peel off her clothes. She wrapped the blanket tightly around her shoulders, and Lennox started down the road again. Hills passed through the rain-streaked window, blurred and slightly distorted, as if seen through tearful eyes.

June eased into the seat, heat finally making its way to her fingers and toes. She rested her head back, exhausted, and pulled the blanket snug around her body. Something poked at her back. She shifted and felt it again. She reached back and lodged in the thick wool of the blanket was an earring. She pulled it free and examined the silver hummingbird stud. She spun it between her fingers, making the bird appear as if it were in flight. A lost item from a lover, perhaps? Lord knows how many women had been wrapped in this very blanket.

"What do you have there?" Lennox asked, looking into the rearview mirror.

June hid the earring. "Nothing."

They made it back to the Nestled Inn. Lennox pulled into the driveway and threw the car into park. He turned and glared at her. "Don't lie. What is it?"

"Calm down. It's just an earring."

"Give it to me," he said, firmly.

She hated his demanding tone. Hated his confidence, when she felt so weak. Hated that Lennox, of all people, had to be the one to see her so vulnerable. Again. June clutched the earring tightly. "No."

Lennox grunted. "Give it to me, Peanut."

June wasn't going to bend. He would have to take it from her. "It's clearly not yours."

"It's in my car."

"So what? You have no more right to it than I do."

"I know who it belongs to."

"Great," June spoke evenly. "What's her address? I'll make sure she gets it."

Lennox slammed his hand on the steering wheel. "Goddammit, Peanut, give it to me!"

The intense anger in his voice startled June. Scared her almost. Lennox took a breath, and in that moment, June saw grief wash over his face. She knew the look well, having drowned in the same emotion for weeks. Choked on it, really. She set the earring on the center console and collected her clothes. She needed a shower and a hot cup of tea and her pajamas.

When Lennox spoke again, his voice softer, June didn't want to hear it. She couldn't look at Lennox any longer. She didn't need any more sadness in her life. She slammed the door on her way out.

EIGHT

To: j_merriweather42@hotmail.com
From: sienaravenhorse@yahoo.com
Subject: Josh's stuff

Hi June,

I know you're probably surprised to hear from me, seeing as we haven't seen each other in four years (except for that brief minute at the funeral).

Anyway, I have a box of Josh's stuff—pictures, a few t-shirts, his old high school football jersey, a Weston College sweatshirt. I thought you might want them. I don't feel right keeping any of it. I'm getting married next year, and I don't think my fiancé wants my old boyfriend's stuff in our house.

I know my relationship with your brother was . . . complicated. But all the bad times don't seem to matter now. What I remember most are the good times. When Josh was so kind. Like the time I got my wisdom teeth out and he took care of me all weekend. He never left my side. And there was another time senior year when he offered to carry Lydia Reading's books for her when she broke her leg. He followed her from class to class for a week. I was sure he was cheating on me (because I was insecure and needy back then). But Josh just knew what it was like to be hurt and he wanted to help. He didn't want people to be alone with their suffering.

I'll never forget the game when he dislocated his shoulder. I swear the entire stadium went completely silent. It gives me chills to think about. Coach Ricky said it was the worst "hospital ball" he'd ever seen. I never thought Josh would play again. I should have known better, though. Josh never liked sitting on the bench. Not when other people were having fun.

Anyway, sorry to rehash. I'll put his stuff in the mail next week. Now that I'm writing this, I might just keep the jersey. Don't tell my fiancé. ;)

I hope you're doing well.

Xoxo,
Siena

Anderson's Pub smelled of rain, barley, and people. June finished a pint of beer and licked her lips clean of foam, her body humming. The uncomfortable weight that constantly pressed on her chest had finally dissipated, thanks to the beer. She had one goal tonight: get bloody drunk.

Earlier that day, June had come home from the café, taken Josh's remains from the urn, and held the plastic bag out her bedroom window in the rain. "Siena thinks you actually gave a shit about her stupid wisdom teeth," June had said to the ashes. "What a fucking joke."

She had laughed like a lunatic. She could hear how crazy she sounded, and yet she couldn't stop herself. For a second, she thought she might actually release the ashes. Let the wind and water carry Josh away, so she could finally be relieved of the burden. The ashes would turn to mud and mix with the soil. Josh's remains and the ground would slowly amalgamate, no difference between him and the earth. But June had stopped herself.

After the maniacal cackling subsided, her body went heavy. She sat on the floor of her bedroom, Josh's ashes across from her, as if they were young again, face to face for an intense game of Uno. June, younger than Josh, had a hard time holding so many cards in her small hands and would inevitably display her cards.

"You're not supposed to let me see your hand, June," Josh would complain. He'd take her cards, organize them, and fan them out perfectly to fit her tiny grasp. "There. Hold them just like that."

But not three turns later, June would pull a card from her hand, spilling the rest on the floor, and Josh would help all over again.

"Uno," she said to the ashes. "I'm the only one left alive."

June didn't deserve the relief of letting Josh go, hadn't earned it. As mad as she felt at the lies that people believed about her brother, he was her burden. The desire to relieve herself of it was selfish.

She had stuffed her brother's ashes back into the urn and returned it to the closet. Amelia knocked on the door shortly thereafter, insisting that June come out for a night of drinking at the pub, and June was all for drowning her sorrow.

The table was now full of pints. Eva sat across from June, glasses perched on the tip of her nose, notebook in hand, intently writing. Amelia and David were at the bar procuring another round. June reached across the table and took Eva's barely touched pint. When Eva noticed, she adjusted her glasses. Her blond hair was worn sleek tonight, parted in the middle and falling bluntly just beneath her chin. Eva would seem severe with her pale skin if it weren't for her warm brown eyes, always intrigued.

June slugged down more beer. "What are you writing, anyway?"

"I'm collecting characters."

"You're what?"

"Look around. This place is full of stories." Eva gestured across the crowded pub. She pointed to an older gentleman in a booth by himself, a half-drunk pint of beer and a glass of whisky his only companions. "What do you make of him?"

"He looks lonely," June said.

Eva bit on the end of her pen. "D-list Scottish porn star whose recent release, *Mary, Queen of Cocks*, in which he played the Prince of Wails, was panned. And his agent just called. He didn't get the lead role in *While You Were Sheeping*."

June laughed so hard she had to cup a hand in front of her face to prevent beer spilling from her lips. "Who knew we were among royalty?"

Eva pointed to a young girl, maybe fourteen, who sat with her pudgy, rosy-cheeked family of five. "Britain's deadliest assassin, whose unique form of torture is playing Chumbawamba on repeat until her victims go insane."

June was impressed. Her own creativity amounted to changing her eyeshadow from Creamy Beige to Tough as Taupe.

"What makes stories interesting isn't what you see on the surface," Eva explained. "It's all about what characters are desperate to hide. Then they have something to lose."

"And here I thought people liked stories for the happy endings."

"And filthy sex scenes," Eva added.

David set a tray of fresh drinks on the table and took the seat next to Eva. Amelia sat next to June.

Eva took a fresh pint and sipped foam from the top. "June and I were just collecting characters."

"Oh, I love this game," David said. "Who's next?"

Eva pointed to a young woman at the bar, probably in her early twenties, well put together, wearing slightly too much makeup for a Thursday night at the pub. Her drink of choice—a glass of white wine.

David offered his interpretation first. "She's waiting for a blind date. They met in a *Lord of the Rings* chat room. Her handle: 'Drinking Is a Nasty Hobbit of Mine.' His: 'Now That's What I'm Tolkien About.'"

"You've been in a *Lord of the Rings* chat room, haven't you?" Amelia said.

David shrugged. "In my early AOL days."

Eva laughed. "What was your handle?"

"Pippin Ain't Easy."

After the laughing died down, Amelia offered her story. "Heiress to a billionaire whose sex tape with Robbie Williams leaked on the internet and landed her a starring role on a new reality dating TV show set in Scotland, called *Kilt by Love*. Working title, of course. But secretly she's in love with her best friend, Dahlia, from boarding school."

"Unrequited love," David said. "Always a good option."

Eva tapped her pen on the side of the table. "I think she's an Amish girl in Rumspringa. This is the first time she's ever worn makeup, and she's not sure if she did it right. She wants to snog a boy for the first time tonight. Tomorrow she'll wake up hungover, and miss the smell of hay and freshly baked bread, and the feel of her mom's hands on her scalp as she braids her hair. And she'll wonder what freedom really means."

David threw a coaster at Eva. "Unfair advantage. You're a writer."

"Now I feel bad for the lass," Amelia added. "Should we invite her to sit with us?"

"Nah. She's clearly number fifty-four," June said, thoroughly confusing everyone. "Angus told me yesterday he's shagged fifty-three girls. She's number fifty-four."

David nearly choked on his beer. "Bloody brilliant," he said. "And highly likely."

"Now I don't feel bad for her at all," Amelia quipped.

Not two minutes later, Angus walked into the pub, followed closely by Lennox. Together they looked almost ridiculous, both oversize and tattooed, like two men pulled from paperback romance novels.

"I'll be damned," Amelia whispered as she stood. "I can't believe you're here, Brother. You haven't been to the pub in—"

Lennox cut her off. "I know how long it's been. You don't have to remind me." He shrugged out of his jacket, shaking rain from his hair, and his gaze briefly fell on June. "Nice to see you're alive, Peanut."

"I wish I could say the same to you." June took a long gulp of her beer and angled herself away from Lennox. His clean scent of cedar and mint infiltrated her mind. She hated how well she was coming to know it, but his blasted blanket had been the warmest item she had in the chilly inn, and she had needed to wrap herself in it, her nose pressed to the fabric.

"Sorry we're late," Angus said, pulling a chair from a table, spinning it backward, and seating himself next to Amelia. "We had some important business to attend to."

"Getting your eyebrows waxed again?" David said.

Angus grabbed the pint from David's hand and drank half of it in one gulp. "I'm surprised to see you out. Don't you usually masturbate to *The X-Files* on Thursdays?"

Lennox sat opposite June, wedged between Eva and Angus. When David offered Lennox a pint, he declined. "I'm driving."

"Of course," June said, under her breath, she thought, but in her inebriated state, it came out much louder.

Lennox leaned forward, his elbows on the table. "What's that supposed to mean, Peanut?"

"I'm just not surprised," June mumbled. "God forbid you have a drink and loosen up."

"You think I need to loosen up?" he asked.

"Wouldn't hurt. I promise you'll feel so much better once you take the stick out of your ass."

Eva and Amelia gasped.

"Really?" Lennox queried.

"Really," June said. "You might actually be fun."

"Fun like risking anaphylaxis, hypothermia, and alcohol poisoning all in one week?"

"Whatever." June took a swig of her beer. "At least I'm not a control freak."

"Would you mind speaking a little louder," Lennox chided, "so I can hear you when you insult me?"

June was ablaze. "I just said that you're a control freak. That's all."

"Is that right?" Lennox crossed his arms over his wide chest.

"Yes, that's right." June's beer-fueled confidence grew.

"You know me well enough to say that," Lennox stated.

"Please." June rolled her eyes. "I know all I need to know."

"You're saying I should be more like you? Self-destructive and dangerous?" Lennox asked.

"I am not dangerous." June pointed at him. "Don't pretend like you know me."

"I've seen your knickers, Peanut. I know a little."

Angus sat up straighter. "Details, please."

Lennox smiled devilishly. "And you've been naked in the back of my car."

"When were you naked in his car?" Amelia asked, shocked.

"That was circumstantial," June explained, "and it wasn't enjoyable."

Lennox leaned back casually in his seat. "I don't know, Peanut. You seemed pretty hot and bothered to me."

June gaped at him. Her blood was boiling. She had come out to the pub to drown her anger and sadness, not have it brought to the surface by a cocky Scotsman with a Superman complex. June stood, swaying, pint in hand. "I'm getting a shot."

"Try not to get hurt on your way to the bar, would you?" Lennox said. "It's my night off."

June wanted to launch herself over the table and strangle him. Liquid courage coursed through her veins. "You're just a big old bully. And you know what they say about bullies. They pretend to be tough, but they're more scared than everyone else."

"Now, Peanut," Angus began, "I'll have you know our lad here—"

"Save it, Angus." Lennox's hazel eyes didn't move from June's.

"It's why you make everyone afraid of you," June spat, "so they can't get too close and see the truth." She held the table so she wouldn't sway too much. "But I'm not afraid of you. You're just as scared as the rest of us, you just control it better."

A shadow descended over Lennox's eyes. "I think you've had enough to drink, Peanut."

But June pressed on. "What are you so afraid of, huh, Lennox?"

Everyone at the table was frozen stiff, but June was too drunk to care. She wasn't going to let Lennox off, not after all his judgment. June felt like a fighter in a ring, gloves up near her face, waiting for her opponent's jab.

But Lennox broke unexpectantly, his whole demeanor awash with sadness. Gaping, endless, and utterly familiar. A desperate hand reaching through the darkness. June felt it in her core, that identical sadness that lived in her. Like a magnet that had finally found its mate.

"Forget it." June stumbled to the bar, wanting to wipe clean the connection she felt with Lennox. She despised him. Abhorred him. She needed more alcohol. She needed to drown the unrelenting shame that gnawed at her like a hangnail. June put ten pounds on the bar. "A shot, please."

The bartender examined her money. "Whisky?"

June could barely see the bottles lining the wall, let alone the labels. She nodded. She didn't care. When the shot glass was before her, she slammed it back, feeling the burn. She placed the glass back on the bar. "I'll have another."

NINE

June awoke to a body next to her in bed. She felt its pressure on the mattress. The body shifted. June peeled back her eyelids but quickly closed them against the penetrating light that threatened to explode her delicate head.

She moaned. The body shifted.

Oh God, she thought. *Please say it's not Angus.*

June lay absolutely still. The body inched closer, forcing June to the edge of the bed. She squeezed her eyelids as something large and wet made contact with her face. Slobber covered her cheek, and she rolled over to face a very large brown dog. She sat up in bed, her brain throbbing in her skull. Then she almost threw up.

She was in a bed with a dog, a disturbing fact. But more disconcerting was that June had no idea *whose* bed. Angus didn't own a dog. No one at the inn did.

The room was unfamiliar. June searched her brain for pieces to the puzzle of where she was, and how she got there, but her last memory was of the bottom of an empty shot glass.

June grabbed her aching head. Where the hell was she, and what had she done?

Clothes were folded neatly on top of a wooden dresser. A chair sat in the corner of the room. The clock on the nightstand read seven in the morning. June rubbed her forehead. She was definitely not at the inn. Wherever she was, she needed to get out of there. She had work in two hours.

A bright spot—June was fully clothed.

I'm never drinking again, she thought as she stared at the strange, incredibly cute dog. Was that a smile on its droopy face? Was the dog in on the joke? June scratched behind its ears, and the dog nuzzled into her, laying its head on her lap and gazing up at her affectionately. When the bedroom door opened suddenly, June pulled the sheets up, as if covering herself now could renew her dignity.

"Aw, shite. Get off the bed, Max." Lennox hurried into the room. June wasn't sure what surprised her more, the fact that she was in Lennox's room or the fact that Lennox had a dog. "Sorry. He knows better than to get on the bed."

Max lumbered out the door, his large ears swinging.

"You have a dog?"

"Why so surprised, Peanut?" Lennox held out his hand, displaying two pills. When June hesitated, he said, "Aspirin. I take them to dull the pain of the stick up my ass, but they work for headaches, too."

June cringed, remembering what she'd said to Lennox the night before. She took the medicine and swallowed it down with the glass of water sitting on the nightstand. "Do you have anything that will restore my dignity?"

Lennox actually chuckled.

"Is this when you lecture me about the perils of alcohol, and the fact that you saved my ass once again?"

But Lennox didn't reprimand June. "No, Peanut. I'm the last to judge."

An awkward silence followed. He was different this morning. Softer. Tired, maybe. June should have scurried out of the bed and headed back to the inn, but something kept her rooted. She told herself it was the hangover, and Lennox's comfortable bed, but it was deeper than that. The truth was that June felt awful for what she had said at the pub.

She should apologize. She had been drunk and sensitive and looking for a punching bag, but when it actually came to saying the words, she couldn't get them out.

"Do you want breakfast?" Lennox asked.

June needed to get out of his house before the two of them ended up in a fistfight over pancakes. She stood up from the bed. "Does breakfast come with coffee?"

~

Lennox placed a plate of fried eggs, thick-cut bacon, and toast in front of June. The delicious smells of warm butter and hot coffee filled the kitchen. She restrained herself from lunging at the plate face first.

"You got the cooking talent in the family."

"Along with my stunning good looks and huge . . ." Lennox paused, smiling. June gaped, waiting for the next word. "Feet."

"Right." She chuckled. "I bet the girls just love your . . . feet."

"I'm happy to show you."

June choked on her coffee. Was Lennox flirting with her? He laughed and set his tea on the counter. "I better get ready for work."

"Wait." June took his arm as he walked toward the stairs. Now was the time for her to apologize for needling him last night. To thank him for bringing her safely home from the pub. She bit her lip, trying to find the words. His skin felt warm against hers. The tally-mark tattoo on his arm seemed darker today—more defined, like it had been carved deeply into his skin instead of etched on the surface. June wanted to run her finger over it.

"Finish your breakfast, Peanut." Lennox pulled away. "I'll just be cleaning my . . . feet upstairs."

He left, and soon June heard the water running in the bathroom. She tidied the kitchen, washing the dishes and running a sponge along the countertops, delaying her departure. What was she doing? For a week, all June wanted was to avoid this man, and now she didn't want to leave.

With the water still running upstairs, June meandered into the living room, where a couch was made up as a bed. The room smelled slightly of the old logs and ash in the fireplace. Max lay on his dog bed at the foot of the worn fabric couch. He got up to greet June as she walked into the room, brushing against her leg, and she bent to pet him.

Other than the couch, the room housed an oversize canvas chair and an end table. There was a cabinet with an eight-disc CD player and a tall rack of CDs. On display in another corner, three guitars, two acoustic and an electric, were propped on stands. Not a single picture was displayed on the mantel or anywhere, just like at the inn.

June started to fold the blankets on the couch. It was the least she could do. She made sure to be neat, taking her time. The couch would have fit June fine, but Lennox must have slept with his legs hanging off the end. When she was done, June investigated the CD collection. She ran her finger down the rack, reading the album titles, until she came to Pearl Jam's *Ten*. It had been a few years since she'd listened to the album in its entirety, but back in high school, she had played it on repeat.

She put the CD in the stereo, skipped to track three, and pressed play. Then she sat on the floor, "Alive" humming through the speakers, remembering late nights in Matt's Lancer, windows down, a bag of Skyline Chili Coney dogs between them, screaming the lyrics at the top of their lungs. She had felt young, infinite, in that moment, like nothing would ever come between them, nothing would ever complicate their relationship to the breaking point. How naive she had been, and yet she would do anything to get that feeling back now.

June lay back and closed her eyes. Her fingers dug into the rug beneath her as if it might morph into Matt's smooth hand. He'd grab ahold of her, pull her from the floor, and say, *OK, confession time. If I had to make out with a man, it would be Eddie Vedder.*

OK, confession time, she'd say. *If I had to make out with a man, it would be Eddie Vedder.*

Matt would act offended and make June promise to never let a man come between them.

"Are you lost, Peanut?"

June startled. Lennox stood in the doorway, a large cardboard box in his hands. He set it on the chair, his hair still wet from the shower, his woodsy scent filling the room.

"You didn't need to clean the house," Lennox said.

"It was the least I could do." June suddenly felt sheepish again for her behavior the previous night. She should have left after breakfast, but even now, she wasn't racing to the door. In fact, she was angling for a reason to stay. She pointed at the guitars. "Do you play?"

"Not as much as I used to."

"Why not?" She walked up to one and strummed the strings, more noise than music.

"Just leave them," Lennox said. "They're horribly out of tune."

But June picked up the acoustic. "Then tune it." She held it out to Lennox. When he hesitated, June strummed it dissonantly again.

"You're maddening, you know that, right?" Lennox groaned, but he took the guitar from June and began to tune it. When he was done, he gestured to the couch. "Sit."

She did as instructed. Lennox knelt down in front of her, placing the instrument in her hands. Then he arranged her left hand along the neck of the guitar. "Now press down."

He took June's right hand. "Relax, Peanut. It's just a guitar, not a person. It won't dump you if you don't touch it right the first time."

But it wasn't the instrument making June tense. She hadn't been this close to Lennox before, hadn't noticed the smattering of freckles on his nose, the small crinkles around his eyes, the scar just below his right eyebrow.

"How'd you get that?" June resisted touching his face.

Lennox ran a finger over the scar. "I was young, arrogant, and stupid."

"You?" June jested. "Arrogant and stupid?"

A whisper of a smile pulled on Lennox's face. "I'm sorry I called you an idiot, Peanut. I'm the last person who should be throwing stones."

June didn't want to rehash the past week. "What do I do now?"

Lennox took her right hand and gently made her strum the strings. A beautiful G chord rang out, vibrant and clean. June squealed at the accomplishment. Lennox moved her fingers, made her strum a C chord, and then shifted her fingers to an E chord.

"Now, try it on your own." He sat back as June fumbled from choppy chord to choppy chord. She messed up more than she did it correctly, and Lennox chuckled at her clumsiness.

June stopped. "I know. I'm horrible."

"It's not that." A spark lit Lennox's eyes, making their hazel color glow greener. "You stick your tongue out of the side of your mouth when you play."

June covered her face. Ever since she was little, it had been a tick of hers, any time she was heavily concentrating. She handed the guitar to Lennox. "Your turn."

"No."

"Come on. You can't be worse than me."

"My four-year-old cousin is better than you, Peanut."

June shoved him playfully. "Just one song."

"I can't," Lennox said.

"I don't believe that."

"Believe it," he said seriously.

"No," she said stubbornly.

"You're not going to stop until I play, are you?"

"I promise, I won't judge you, Lennox," June said. "You can trust me."

With a groan that June was starting to find endearing, Lennox took a seat next to her on the couch and positioned himself with the guitar on his lap. He was a natural, and when he began to play, it was as if the guitar became an extension of his being. His fingers moved deftly along the neck, manipulating notes and chords with ease, plucking strings swiftly, effortlessly. But more than his skill, June was mesmerized by the way Lennox became the music. He didn't just play the song; he lived it, too. June couldn't take her eyes off him. She found herself leaning in, aching to touch him.

She sat speechless when he was done.

"I told you. I haven't played—"

June put her hand on his. "You're wrong about yourself. You're the opposite of bad." They sat in awkward silence yet again, until June forced herself from the couch.

Lennox put the guitar back on its stand. "Can you give this box to Amelia for me, Peanut?" He handed it to June. "It's just some things I should have let go of a long time ago."

Inside were Christmas ornaments, a wool sweater, a pair of slippers, a pipe, and a camera. But not just any camera—a 35mm Nikon.

June set the box down. "You're giving this away?" She retrieved the camera, pulled off the lens cap, and put the camera to her eye, fiddling with the features. Nothing was broken. The lens was even clean.

"Do you want it?" Lennox asked.

"Are you serious?" Photography had been June's favorite class in high school. All her other subjects had been a rush of material, a crunch to get in as much information as possible in the time allotted, but June's photography teacher, Ms. Flores, spent days with her students, just sitting.

"Don't rush," she would say. "Just wait to be inspired."

The class took frequent slow walks around the school, cameras dangling from the students' necks, just observing.

"I can give you a fancy camera," Ms. Flores once said to June. "But no matter how good the equipment, it still only takes pictures. It can't *see*. Only you can do that. That's the job of an artist."

For a time during her senior year, June had considered art school. She knew she wasn't good enough for highly competitive programs like the Rhode Island School of Design or the California Institute of the Arts, and the Merriweathers could never have afforded such schools. But she had quietly requested college brochures from the Art Academy of Cincinnati and the University of Dayton, in-state colleges with less flair but good programs.

But when Josh reinjured his shoulder playing college football during the fall of her senior year, he had to move home for a semester, and everything changed. The Merriweathers had a front row seat to the disintegration of a dream. Josh's life had been football, and he would never play again.

Watching him lie in bed and lose weight, fading into oblivion on pain killers, his anger toward his circumstance festering, had made June want to escape and forget her dreams of being the next Annie Leibovitz. All she wanted was a college far from home. She didn't want to bear any more witness to Josh's life. So June found the Women's Club of Sunningdale scholarship, awarded to a girl planning to major in education and looking to attend an out-of-state school, and she applied. Until then, it hadn't even occurred to June to major in education.

The Merriweathers had visited Stratford College in Tennessee once before, when the college was interested in recruiting Josh to their football program. Nancy had fallen in love with the southern charm and grand Greek houses. She had even bought a sweatshirt.

During her senior year, June accepted the Women's Club of Sunningdale scholarship in front of a room full of women dressed in Talbots clothes and smelling of Charlie Red perfume. She spoke to the women about her love of children, her passion for learning and the gift of sharing that passion with others, and of course her favorite teacher, Ms. Flores. What June really had a talent for was running. Nine months later, she was safely tucked away in Tennessee.

"I can't take your camera," June said to Lennox.

"It's not my camera. And either you have it or someone else does."

June pushed it away. "I can't." It was too generous an offer after everything Lennox had already done for her.

"Look, I know it's not a nice, new digital one."

"You think I care about that?" she balked.

"Why do you have to make everything into a bloody argument?"

"I just find it interesting that you think I'm shallow."

"I never called you shallow," Lennox huffed.

"You didn't have to."

"For God's sake, would you take the damn camera?" He shoved it into June's hands.

"Fine!" June bit the inside of her cheek. Lennox was being kind, and here June was fighting with him. Again. "Thank you," she said.

Lennox nodded.

June gave Max one last good scratch behind the ears. "See you later, Max." But as she walked to the door, box in hand, her new camera dangling from her neck, the dog followed.

"Leave the lass alone," Lennox said, pulling him back. "Sorry. He's a needy bugger. Sometimes, I worry I'm gone too much."

June paused. "I could take him on runs with me."

"You'd do that?"

"Why do you sound so surprised?"

"Don't start again, Peanut. I didn't mean anything." Lennox thought for a moment. "He actually might keep you out of trouble. At the very least, I'd know you're not alone."

He said it like he cared. Like he worried about June. Like he thought about her when she wasn't there. A warmth spread across her chest, the sudden lighting of a match in the dark. "We have a deal?"

"You have a deal, Peanut."

Lennox leaned against the doorjamb as June walked away. She forced her eyes forward, forced her body to move away, forced herself to forget how it felt when Lennox was close. She couldn't let the spark between them grow. Being here was easier if she hated him. If she planted no roots in Scottish soil, then goodbye wouldn't hurt. The plan was never to stay. Scotland was just a break from a future she was determined to get back to in America. June had had enough of painful goodbyes recently.

TEN

To: j_merriweather42@hotmail.com
From: nanmerriweather@aol.com
Cc: Merriweather_Phil@aol.com
Subject: Break

Dear June,

Any time you wanted to cross the street when you were little, I made you hold my hand. You want to know why? Because you always moved too soon. You were so focused on getting where you wanted to go as fast as you could. I needed to hold you back or you might get hurt.

Just please tell me you're looking both ways in Scotland.

Mom

To: j_merriweather42@hotmail.com
From: Matt.F.Tierney@yahoo.com
Subject: Paris

I did some research. I know, you're shocked. Me in the library? There's a new girl at the front desk. I checked out Faulkner and asked her to coffee. She said yes. Works every fucking time.

Did you know there are more dogs in Paris than there are children? That's a lot of fucking shit. And there's only one stop sign in the whole city. Also, there's a Hemingway walking tour. Don't roll your eyes. I'm wearing a beret for you.

Confession time: I cried when Joey and Pacey broke up on *Dawson's Creek*. I know. I'm such a pussy. But they're soul mates and it was fucking sad.

OK, your turn. Tell me a deep dark secret.

—Matt

The deer heads disappeared from the Nestled Inn two weeks after June arrived. She left one morning for work and came home to empty walls, no taxidermy in sight. Circles where the wallpaper hadn't faded marked where the animal heads had been. When asked why they had been taken down, Amelia said, "It was finally time to rid the walls of death."

Now, a month in, June sat in a quiet corner of the café after closing, a pack of fifty thank-you cards spread out on the table before her, along with a cup of tea. It was just past four in the afternoon, but night had already fallen on Knockmoral. June yawned into the back of her hand. The February deadline for sending the cards was approaching. If June allowed herself to go back to the inn, she would not write a single letter. She would push the chore to another day and spend the rest of the evening watching reruns of *Absolutely Fabulous* with Angus. Yet another day would slip by, just as the previous three weeks had, the job left undone.

June wiggled the pen in her hand. Today she was determined to tackle the annoyance head on. She would not leave her seat until she had crossed off and completed at least half of the list sent by the Women's Club of Sunningdale. It was an easy enough task, and one that secured her scholarship, which June desperately needed if she intended to return to Stratford College. And she did. She reminded herself daily.

June eyed the camera among the other items on the table. The roll of film was half-used, practice pictures June had snapped around Knockmoral. Each shot she'd taken over the past three weeks had refined her vision, old instincts remembered, as if her eyes were seeing her world more clearly. She had forgotten how much she enjoyed capturing people on film—an older gentleman sitting serenely on a seaside bench or Hamish singing into a spatula, beard braided, a red bandana holding back his long hair. She had even started to pick up the daily newspaper on her way to work, to inspect the photos, trying to glean something of the art form from them, a task Ms. Flores had assigned to her years ago. A few of the photos she had even cut out and taped to her bedroom wall for inspiration.

June wanted to take pictures with her free time, or run with Max, not write thank-you notes. But what she wanted mattered little when it came to her future. She would buckle down . . . after another cup of tea. June went into the kitchen, filled the kettle, and opened the fridge, looking for a snack while she waited for the water to boil. Hamish's office light was still on.

As she approached the door to let him know she had stayed after hours, she heard not one but two familiar voices inside. Amelia, who must have come in through the back door, was in Hamish's office. June was about to interrupt when she noticed the cautious sound of their voices. She peered through the cracked office door.

"He said I could take down the wallpaper, Hamish." Amelia sat on her uncle's desk, her long legs dangling. "In five years, that's never happened. This might actually be working."

"God willing." Hamish looked to the ceiling. "It's been too long as it is. We can't live like this forever."

"*I* can't live like this forever. I'm wasting away here."

"Go on, Amie." Hamish patted his niece's knee. "He'd understand."

"I can't. What if it happens again? What if he . . ."

"It's been years," Hamish said.

"But you remember how awful it was?"

"Aye. Can't forget something like that."

"I can't leave 'til I know he's alright." Amelia pulled a long blond wig from her purse and put it on Hamish's head. "I have a plan."

"What are you up to, Amie?"

"Just trust me, Uncle."

The kettle whistled, startling June. She ran to turn the burner off and acted casual when Amelia and Hamish emerged from the office, Hamish still wearing the wig.

"I didn't know you were here," Amelia said.

"I had some extra work to do." June's heartbeat was in her throat. She examined Hamish. "I had no idea you were moonlighting as a Vegas showgirl."

Hamish chuckled and pulled the wig from his head. "Ack, it's for Up Helly Aa."

"Is Up Helly Aa the local strip club?" June teased.

"Have you never heard of it?" Amelia asked.

June had indeed never heard of the Highland fire festival, a day in early February when, for twenty-four hours, the small, quiet town of Knockmoral was transformed into a Viking festival.

Hamish held up a finger, then disappeared into his office. He returned with a large coffee-table book and placed it on the kitchen counter before June. A group of men dressed as Vikings surrounded a galley on the book's cover. Hamish pointed to the man in the middle, the clear leader. "That was my da when he was Guizer Jarl twenty years ago." Then he pointed to another, similar-looking, younger Viking. "That's me. Barely had a beard back then. Grew it out for an entire year."

As she flipped through the book, June learned that the Guizer Jarl was the head of the Up Helly Aa celebration, which the town spent an entire year putting together, from costumes to torches to the gigantic wooden galley. The lucky few appointed to the Up Helly Aa committee wore proper Viking clothes, crafted by hand, while the rest, broken into squads, were relegated to other, usually hilarious themes—hence, Hamish's wig.

After winding the large ship through the streets, singing and chanting and carrying torches, the men burned the galley to the ground. Celebrations followed at different halls around town, where every squad was required to put on a show as an expression of gratitude for the party. The festival sounded to June a little like Greek Week at Stratford College, but with more costumes and a huge fire hazard.

"It's a celebration of our heritage," Hamish explained. "The Viking heritage of getting drunk and lighting things on fire."

"And speaking of the festival," Amelia said, "I've been meaning to talk to you about something." Her hesitant tone worried June, which was justified, as Amelia explained to June that she had double-booked her room.

"What?" June gasped.

"It came in months ago, long before you showed up. The room was empty then, so I booked it. It's one of the only times we get tourists in the winter. The whole inn is completely full. But it's only for a few days. Then you can move right back in."

"A few days?" June started to panic.

Amelia clarified. "Five, actually."

"Five days! When do I have to leave?"

Amelia bit her lip. "Friday."

June uselessly attempted to remain calm. She didn't have enough money to rent another place for five whole days, especially at the prices rooms would be going for during the festival—assuming there were even any rooms available. June would have asked Hamish if she could crash on his couch, but he had already done so much for her.

"Don't worry." Amelia touched June's arm. "I've already solved the problem."

"Oh, thank God," June said, clutching at her heart.

"Well, don't thank me yet," Amelia added. "The double-booked room wasn't the worst part."

June asked tentatively, "Where am I staying exactly?"

Amelia glanced at Hamish, who looked as surprised as June felt, and said, "At the house next door."

After the night at the pub, it was no secret how June felt about Lennox, or at least how people assumed she felt. She had kept her budding feelings under wraps since that night, with no intention of revealing them, ever. Now she had to hold on to the counter to stay steady. Five nights at Lennox's. There was no way he agreed to this willingly.

"And he said yes?" June asked.

"Not exactly . . ." Amelia said. "But he didn't say no either. He just kind of . . . grunted, which is as good as a yes, as far as I'm concerned." Then she quickly added, "He'll be busy with work and getting ready for the festival anyway. You'll barely see him."

Over the past three weeks, June had come to realize just how often Lennox was gone from his little house next to the inn. Exactly what he was doing, June had no idea. The lack of interaction between them was a good thing, allowing the flicker of heat she'd felt to fade. June had planned to keep it that way. She *had* to keep it that way.

But now Lennox would be unavoidable.

"It all worked out in the end," Amelia said with a smile. "I have a feeling this year's festival will be one to remember."

June's throat was dry. She hoped Amelia was right, that Lennox would be busy. And the festival *did* look amazing. A boon of photo-worthy moments. With such a spectacle, and the amount of people attending, June could, at the very least, busy herself taking pictures.

She flipped through the coffee-table book and stopped on a page with a collage of images: people in costume, tourists lining the streets watching the galley parade, the Knockmoral pipe band leading the charge. But what captured her attention most was a picture of a man and his son, dressed identically as Vikings.

"Is this . . ." June pointed at the picture.

"Lennox and our da." Amelia grinned. "I was just a wee bairn that year."

The dark curls. The hooded hazel eyes. Even the freckles across their noses. All astonishingly the same. Lennox's father's face was radiant, bursting with life. "Your dad's so handsome."

"He was, wasn't he," Amelia said with a longing smile.

A million questions arose in June's mind. She wanted more informa-tion, but the passing of her brother had taught her that conversations about death were invitation only. How many times had June been cornered into a discussion about Josh that she'd wished she could evaporate from?

"Aye, Liam got all the good looks and left none for me," Hamish quipped. "God duct-taped the scraps together and sent me down to the earth six years later." He closed the book. "Now, go on home. It's getting dark."

Amelia offered June a ride back to the inn. June collected her unwritten thank-you cards for another day. She snapped a picture of Hamish in his blond wig; uninhibited, he struck his best pose.

"So, what are you dressing up as?" June asked.

"I can't reveal any secrets. It's against the rules," Hamish said, wagging his finger at her. "You'll have to wait and see. But I can promise you this. You've never seen anything like it in your life."

"That good?" she asked.

"Just when you think you've seen it all"—Hamish grinned—"that's when the fun starts."

ELEVEN

June held the house phone between her ear and shoulder as she pushed herself up on the kitchen counter. A half-eaten grilled cheese sandwich sat on a plate next to her. "I signed up for a dance class," Matt said.

"Matty, you're the worst dancer I've ever seen."

"I know. I'm terrible. I haven't improved one bit. It's a gaping hole in my résumé as a romantic male lead. Thank God for my sarcastic wit, in-depth knowledge of *Gilmore Girls*, and complete memorization of David Gray's *White Ladder* album, or I might never get laid."

"Don't forget your powerful rendition of 'Your Body Is a Wonderland,' played on the recorder."

"John Mayer did every man a favor when he wrote that song."

"Please tell me you don't still make the constipation face when you dance." June vividly recalled Matt with his freshman-year homecoming date, Vanessa, who, while Matt was wildly convulsing to the tune of "Come on Eileen," asked if he was having a seizure and whether she should put a spoon in his mouth.

"Yes. It's awful and completely uncontrollable. Dancing just makes me clench."

"That's not healthy, Matty. You're not supposed to hold it in. You'll get a butt cut."

"Butt cut." Matt laughed. "Is that a medical term?"

"Yes," June said with authority. "It's in the textbooks with wiener and hoo-ha."

"Don't forget tatas, funbags, and my personal favorite, lunchables."

"My gyno always asks how my jubblies and vajayjay are doing."

"Well, she's a good, professional doctor. She cares about you."

June giggled as the warm feeling she always got when she talked to Matt spread across her chest and down her legs—like she had curled up under the world's most perfect, fuzzy blanket. "Why in the world would you sign up for a dance class? Are you looking to commit GPA suicide?"

"Do you know how important flexibility is as we age?"

"This is about your health," June summarized doubtfully. She knew Matt better than that.

"It's all very medical. Yesterday I saw a girl put her leg behind her fucking head. While she was standing. I think it's my job as a student of the arts *and* sciences to conduct a thorough examination into the correlation between dance and . . . what was the technical word you used for it? My wiener."

"Now the truth comes out." June set down her sandwich and brushed crumbs from her hands. "How did you even get into this class?"

"Turns out guys don't really take dance class because most of us are fucking idiots, so they're always in need of guys to hold up the girls and twirl them and stuff."

"You mean lifts and turns."

"I told the professor I have really great upper-body strength from working construction all summer."

"Construction?" June balked. "You were traffic control for the City of Sunningdale. You stood in the street for six hours a day flipping a **STOP/SLOW** sign."

"On a construction site," Matt emphasized.

"This sounds a lot like the time you got a job at Twin Peaks."

"That was a great résumé builder."

June smiled. "You had to threaten to sue the owner to get the job."

"It's illegal to discriminate in hiring based on gender, even if your restaurant is called Twin Peaks and all the servers happen to be women who are required to wear crop tops and tiny jean shorts."

"You looked ridiculous in that uniform," June said.

"That owner underestimated me. I'm not afraid to make a fool of myself in pursuit of a goal. And I have great fucking legs. You should see them in my dance onesie."

"Leotard, Matty. Dancers wear leotards. You better know the lingo if you're taking the class."

"Whatever. It's all dirty laundry on my bedroom floor."

"I thought you were into the girl at the library," June stated.

"I was, and now I'm not."

"What happened?"

"She was a fan of Beckett. I mean, I'm a fucking snob, but I draw the line at Beckett."

"You know I have no idea who or what you're talking about, right?"

"Of course," Matt said.

June pictured him in his flannel pajama pants, worn-out Cincinnati Reds T-shirt, a cup of black coffee in his hands, sitting on the pull-out sofa in his apartment, the *Today Show* muted in the background, the morning overcast as it often is in the winter in Columbus. The scene was as familiar as her own bedroom back home, and June felt as though she were practically sitting next to her best friend.

"OK," Matt said. "Confession time."

"I'm still reeling from the *Dawson's Creek* revelation. I can't believe you cried over Joey and Pacey," June said.

"This from the girl who had a crush on Danny from New Kids on the Block. Have some self-respect."

June giggled, jumped down from the counter, and went to the fridge. She grabbed a lemon soda, took off the label that claimed it as Angus's, and poured herself a glass.

"What are you doing?"

"Eating." June took another bite of the sandwich. "I needed a little something before my run."

"You're running again? When did that start?"

"Probably around the time you signed up for dance class."

"Why are you running?"

"You say that like running is a bad thing, Matty. It is actually good for my health."

"I know," Matt said.

"But . . ." June could hear hesitancy in his voice.

"You're just telling me now," he qualified.

"You just told me about the dance class."

"That's different."

"How?"

"Because, for the most part, my life at college is exactly the same as before. *I'm* exactly the same. But I have no idea what your life is like over there, or what you're doing, or who you're doing it with."

"Honestly, Matty, my life here is pretty boring."

"Just promise me you're not going to come home with some lame-ass eyebrow ring, or a Chinese-character tattoo, or a venereal disease you caught from a weekend bender in Amsterdam."

Matt didn't realize how changed June was. She had morphed over the past few years, her lies slowly becoming her, occupying her body and mind, all while she kept up the appearance of her old self.

"What if I do?" June asked, poking at the sandwich on her plate. "Come home different."

"Why would you?"

"I don't know. People change."

"Is there something you're not telling me?" Matt said. "Has something happened?"

"No," she lied, and then deflected. "Unless you count the boob job as something."

"Call them by their medical term—shirt potatoes."

June laughed, relieved to have dodged Matt's suspicion. She was just about to take a sip of soda when Angus walked into the kitchen, shirtless as always, wearing only jeans. After having removed the tartan wallpaper in the dining room, he had spent most of the day painting the room Calming Cerulean. He looked tired and thirsty, covered in blue streaks from face to fingers. June froze, the glass of soda in her hand, her shoulder holding the phone to her ear.

"What the hell have you got there, lass?" Angus asked.

June set the glass down on the counter. "I only took a little, Angus."

Matt's voice came through the receiver. "June? Who the hell is Angus?"

Angus crept toward June like a stalking cat. "That soda had my name on it. You know there's a penalty for stealing food."

"This isn't food." June held up the glass. "It's a drink." But Angus only circled her closer. June backed away. "I just took a little."

"That's not a wee nip." Angus pointed to the sizable glass June had poured. "What you've got there is a pint. And it's time to pay the barman."

Matt spoke again. "June, what the hell is going on? Who is that?"

Right as Angus lunged at her, June yelped and dropped the phone. She sprinted for the kitchen door and had almost made it when Angus caught her around the waist. He hoisted her over his shoulder, June dangling helpless and laughing.

"Put me down, Angus! I'm gonna puke!" Her body bobbed as he jumped up and down, which only made her laugh harder.

"That's the point! I want my soda back!" Angus laid June on the counter and played her stomach like a keyboard as he sang, "I love a lassie, a bonnie Hielan' lassie."

"You have a terrible voice!" howled June. Angus only sang louder and played her stomach harder. June writhed and wiggled, but it was no use. Angus belted the chorus at the top of his lungs, finishing with a flourish of hands and a bow. June's stomach hurt.

"Steal my soda again and I'll be forced to do even dirtier things to you." Angus winked and left the kitchen.

June sat on the counter, still laughing. Angus might be a self-centered meathead, but he was a funny self-centered meathead. A faint voice came from the phone on the floor. June jumped down from the counter and grabbed it. "Matty!"

"June, what the fuck is going on? Do I need to call for help?"

"No! I'm fine." She was out of breath and still giggling. "I just got distracted for a second."

"Distracted? It sounded like you got attacked."

"It was just my housemate, Angus. He's harmless."

"Who the fuck is Angus?"

"Calm down. He lives at the inn with me. He's a friend."

"A friend. Is that it?"

"Weren't you the one who just confessed to taking a dance class strictly to get laid?"

"That's different."

"How?" June asked, not caring to explain Angus's infatuation with Amelia and his asexual relationship with June. The line went quiet. June waited, her laughter gone.

When Matt finally spoke, his tone was darker. "You're lying to me, June."

Everything inside June dropped toward the floor. She was frozen scared. "I'm not lying to you." But her quivering voice betrayed her.

"If your life is so boring in Scotland, then why stay? Huh?" Matt was full to the brim with patience, but there was no more room for nonsense. He overflowed now, unable to hold himself back. "Jesus Christ! This is getting ridiculous."

"I thought you were on board with this, Matt."

"I thought you'd be home by now, June. I thought you'd get home-sick or bored or come to your senses. Or, God forbid, miss me."

"Come to my senses? I thought you understood."

"I understand going a little crazy after what happened to Josh. I understand needing a break, but you've been in Scotland for a month."

"You think I've gone a little crazy?"

"June, you're not acting like yourself."

"And how should I act, Matty? Is the problem that I'm not acting like myself, or is the problem that I'm not taking orders anymore?"

"When the fuck have I ever ordered you around?"

June pictured him standing from the couch, coffee clutched so tightly in his hands that his knuckles were white. She squeezed her eyes closed. Matt may not have directly bossed June around, but he had influenced everything she did, everything she even considered. Because Matt sustained June like water.

"Just tell me what's really going on," he pleaded. "I know it's been rough lately, but was your life here really so bad you want to throw it all away?"

She held back a verbal vomit of confessions. Matt didn't understand because he couldn't; telling him the truth—that June left *because* of him—would hurt Matt more than it hurt June to keep it from him.

"You know I just want you to be happy, right?" he said. "I'd do anything for you."

But Matt's protection was the problem. His good deeds made June's lies even worse. His loyalty made her betrayal more gut-wrenching. His bravery made her cowardice even more intolerable. Matt's insistent love only made June less deserving of it.

"Maybe that's the problem." She paced the kitchen. What she was about to say would hurt Matt, but June saw no other way. June Merriweather had always existed in tandem with Matt Tierney. He was a shield for her, down to the EpiPen he kept in his backpack. Now

June had to shield Matt, from herself. She was the poison he needed protection from. She had thought putting some distance between them would be enough, but it wasn't. "I should be who you want me to be, right? I'm just supposed to follow instructions like some neutered puppy?"

"I didn't say that. You know that's not how I feel."

June was sick to her stomach. "I have to go."

"Wait. Don't hang up. We can fix this. We never hang up mad at each other."

"Well, then I guess we have changed." June ended the call and steadied herself on the counter. If she let go, she might crumble. Did she really just do that to Matt? She felt as though she had just cut the umbilical cord, a lifeline she had survived on for as long as she could remember. She could barely breathe. Who was June Merriweather without Matt Tierney? Could she even live without him?

But this was not about what June needed. She didn't deserve Matt, or his kindness or his protection or his love, because June was a liar. And as afraid as she was to live without Matt, she was more afraid to watch her lies destroy whatever remained between them.

~

June sprinted to Lennox's house, spare key in hand. He had given her a copy so she could let herself in to get Max when he was gone, which was often. Her hand shook as she put the key into the lock. She needed to run. She needed air and space and quiet after what she had just done to Matt. More than anything, she needed absolution.

But as she opened the back door and entered, June stopped. Lennox was home. The last thing she needed right now was him. She felt frail and broken and vulnerable. She had no energy to spar with him. One wrong word from Lennox and she might drop like a weak child.

She started to back out the door, but Max came into the kitchen and bounded toward her excitedly. June bent down, hushing the dog and petting him in hopes he wouldn't bark and reveal her presence.

"It was good to see you today. I needed you, Isobel." Lennox's voice came from the other room. June was caught. She flattened herself against the wall, biting the inside of her cheek. "I couldn't have survived without you. You're my angel."

Who the hell is Isobel? June remembered the hummingbird earring, and the intensity with which Lennox demanded she give it to him. And the way he spoke now—intimate, gentle, vulnerable—was so unlike anything June had heard from him, the opposite of misanthropy.

Her gut twisted. June hated that Lennox incited involuntary reactions in her. She either loathed him or craved him. But what she really wanted was to be indifferent, a stone sculpture he was unable to crack or change.

"Aye, I'll come see you right after the festival," he said. "Amelia has me doing charity for one of the guests. Lord knows what would happen if I left the lass alone in the house for too long. She'd probably burn it to the ground and then call it an accident."

Charity? The word was practically a synonym for pathos. June needed to get out of the house, but just as she turned to go, Max barked. Seconds later, Lennox came into the kitchen, flip phone in hand.

June grabbed the leash off the table. "I'm taking Max on a run. I thought you'd be at work."

Lennox set the phone on the counter. "I had something else to do today." He didn't expound.

"I'll go." June turned toward the door.

"Wait." Lennox came closer and examined her face.

June wondered at the state of it. No doubt her eyes were puffy after her conversation with Matt, but she didn't want to admit that to Lennox. It was all just too . . . pathetic. Too weak.

"Are you alright, Peanut?"

"I'm fine." She dodged his large frame, not wanting to meet his eyes, and hooked the leash onto Max.

Lennox scratched the dog's ears. "Make sure you bring her back in one piece, Max."

But Lennox's request was impossible. June was already shattered.

TWELVE

To: j_merriweather42@hotmail.com
From: shs@sunningdaleboosters.org
Subject: Mark your calendar!

You are formally invited to the Josh Merriweather
Invitational Golf Tournament and Gala!

WHERE: Sunningdale Country Club

WHEN: May 31, 2003

The schedule of events is below. Golf tournament begins
at 7am. Gala to follow that evening. To donate items to the
silent auction, please contact Sheila Smith. All proceeds go
to the Josh Merriweather Athletic Scholarship Fund pre-
sented by the Sunningdale Boosters in conjunction with
Nancy and Phil Merriweather and their daughter, June.

Please RSVP by clicking the link below.

We hope to see you there!

When the police had called the Merriweathers the day after Thanksgiving, June's house had still smelled of roasted turkey and stuffing. The night before, the weather had dropped to bitterly cold temperatures. June had sat at the island in the kitchen, home from Stratford College for the long weekend, hugging a mug of coffee in her hands, the hood of her Ohio State sweatshirt pulled over her head for warmth. She had stolen the hoodie from Matt. The cuffs were tattered and worn. A small cut had been made at the neckline, so the hood didn't hug too tightly around June's neck. The fuzzy cotton inside had long since pilled. And with the hood pulled tightly around her head, June could smell coffee and old books, as if she were wrapping herself in a Matt Tierney cocoon. June had washed the hoodie so many times that she knew the smell was most likely in her imagination, but either way, when she snuggled herself in that sweatshirt, it was like she was hugging Matt. It was June's most treasured piece of clothing. She never traveled anywhere without it.

When the house phone rang that morning, June didn't move from her seat.

"Don't pick it up," she said to her dad.

"This could be your brother. I'm not missing his call." Phil Merriweather poured his cold coffee into the sink and reached for the phone.

June pleaded with him. "Josh would call your cell."

"No, he wouldn't. He knows I can't get used to the thing. I never even turn it on."

"Then he'd call Mom's phone."

"She's worse than me," Phil protested.

"It's not him, Dad. Please let the answering machine get it."

"June, what has gotten into you? It's your brother."

The bad feeling that had become rooted in June when Josh didn't show up for the holiday intensified. She thought about tearing off the hoodie, but each ring of the phone was like an electric shock to her system. She couldn't move.

Nancy ran into the kitchen then, her hair still damp from the shower. "Pick it up. It's Josh."

June pulled the hood more tightly around her head, muffling the sound of her father answering, the weighted pause as he realized it wasn't Josh, the scream of her mother when Phil looked at his wife with a quiet sob and then said, "Josh is dead." June breathed in and out, slowly, but the smell of Matt was already fading.

In the weeks that followed, as funeral arrangements were made, flowers were sent to the house, people were called, and lasagna was delivered by neighbors, June would blame Josh for many things—the constant putrid smell of rotting lilies in the house, the five extra pounds she put on from so much pasta, the awkward interactions with old schoolmates she hadn't seen in years—but the most superficial was the hoodie. It was ruined. She could never wear it again without thinking of that morning.

The police had found Josh's body on the bathroom floor of his apartment. The sink was still running. The television was on. The fridge contained only Hot Pockets and Mountain Dew. He had been dead for three days.

June and her father went to Marion to speak with police and collect Josh's personal effects. Nancy refused to go. Instead, she made phone calls.

Josh Merriweather had died of a rare and undetected heart condition. The faster Nancy could spread the news around Sunningdale, the more real it felt until, a week later, it had become the truth. June marveled at how a lie could morph into fact, simply by a confident delivery. In all of June's life, what else had she been told with such earnestness that she didn't even think to question it?

June hadn't worn the Ohio State hoodie since the morning the Marion police had called, but she had brought it with her to Scotland, because, like with Matt, she could never let it go. She held it in her hands now as she stared down at the half-packed suitcase on her bed, Josh's urn next to the bag.

"You know what I did when the phone rang that morning?" June stared at the ridiculous urn with Josh's name engraved at the base. "I prayed." She sat on the bed and spoke as if Josh were actually by her side. "I didn't pray for you," she confessed.

That morning June had said a silent prayer to God, begging not to lose Matt Tierney. She knew that it was fruitless, even then, but she pleaded nonetheless. Until then, she had convinced herself that all the lies she'd told Matt could dissolve away if Josh changed. One turn of direction and everything June had fabricated for three years to cover her brother's choices became worth the risk. Instead, with his death, her lies turned to concrete.

It had been three days since June and Matt's last phone call, and while she might not be speaking to him, her mind was obsessively occupied with her best friend. She didn't know what was worse—losing someone who was already dead or losing someone who was living. She pressed the sweatshirt to her nose and took a deep breath, searching for Matt, but all she smelled was roasted turkey and stuffing.

"I should have prayed for you, Josh." June wrapped the urn in the hoodie and placed it in her suitcase. She finished clearing the room of her belongings for the new occupants, who were due to arrive in Knockmoral later that night, and grabbed the letter addressed to her parents off the dresser. Inside were pictures from around Knockmoral, snapshots of her life in Scotland.

June dragged her bag and backpack down the hallway, camera slung around her neck. She wasn't sure what was heavier, her luggage or her being. Not only was she mourning and missing Matt, but now she had to spend five days under Lennox's roof. Not wanting to leave just yet, she detoured down the long hallway toward Eva's room on the other side of the house. She stopped and knocked on the door, and Eva beckoned her in.

David was sitting on Eva's bed, still dressed like a Jacobite and sipping whisky.

June leaned against the doorframe. "Whisky sounds nice right about now."

"An artist is never low on two things—booze and anxiety." Eva held up the bottle and clinked David's glass.

"And insecure conceit," he said and slugged down a gulp.

Eva's black glasses matched her black turtleneck and jeans and made the writer look like a proper beatnik poet. She handed a full glass of whisky to June. "Cheer up, love," she said. "Will staying with Lennox really be that bad?"

"Is getting eaten by a lion one joint at a time really that bad?" June countered.

She lumbered into the room and sat next to David, who put his arm around her and said, "'There is nothing either good or bad but thinking makes it so.'"

"At least he's a hot lion," Eva offered. "You'll have a good view as he eats you."

At that, June actually smiled.

Eva's bedroom was scant, not unlike June's: a bed, a dresser, a simple bathroom. A desk with a laptop sat at the large window overlooking the backyard. But the most interesting aspect of Eva's room were the sheets of paper, fifty-two in total, lining her wall like a mismatched quilt of white rectangles and black words. Each was the last written page of one of Eva's unfinished stories. The wall was a homage to ideas never seen to completion. With a few of them, Eva had gotten so frustrated she had stopped midsentence, printed the page, hung it on the wall, and never looked at it again—like a dangling conversation cut short.

June was mesmerized by the wall. So many unfinished stories on display would have paralyzed her. But to Eva, they were a reminder of a commitment to seeking out stories that meant something to her, and to not being owned by them out of obligation or fear that another might never come along. As June sat with her whisky in hand, the room came into focus. The light through Eva's window cast the perfect highlights and shadows.

"Don't move," June said.

She saw the image in her head before she snapped the picture. Just yesterday she had bought a roll of black-and-white film, perfect for the shot. She moved around the room, capturing Eva and the wall of unfinished stories from multiple angles.

"Another artist in the house?" David said.

June felt she wasn't skilled enough. "No. I'm just playing around. Lennox gave me the camera."

"He did, did he?" Eva's tone was too suggestive for June's liking.

"He was getting rid of it," June explained. "He would have given it to anyone."

Eva turned to David. "What is the number one motivating factor for men?"

David said, "Sex."

Eva looked at June with a smirk. "See."

"Lennox does *not* want to have sex with me." June put her camera back in the case and took a long pull of whisky.

"Lennox wants to have sex with you," David said matter-of-factly.

June spit out a bit of her drink. "Did he tell you that?"

"No," David said, "but one thing is true for all men. We want sex. Anytime. Anywhere. I'm just saying he's considered the *possibility* of having sex with you. He's probably imagined it, too . . . a few times."

June slugged down the rest of her drink. Maybe it was *possible* Lennox had considered it, like he considered his wardrobe in the morning. A passing glance at a shirt hanging in a closet full of other shirts. No doubt the thought ended quickly and with a twinge of regret. June refilled her glass and tried to sound nonchalant. "I think he might be with someone already."

That caught Eva's attention. "Why?"

June shrugged. "I found an earring in his car."

"So what? That's nothing," Eva stated. "It could be Amelia's."

"Believe me, it was not nothing."

"In the six months I've lived here," Eva said, "I've never even seen a woman come out of his house."

June wasn't about to tell Eva and David about her eavesdropping, but Isobel, whoever she was, meant something to Lennox. June was sure of that. "Maybe he only goes to her place," she offered. "He *is* gone a lot."

Eva bit her lip. "No. Doesn't feel right. Something doesn't fit."

None of this was June's business, anyway. The less she knew about Lennox, the better, but she couldn't deny how intrigued she was, and his clear desire for privacy only captivated June that much more. She swirled the remainder of her whisky around the glass. "Do you know what happened to their parents?"

"They died in some sort of car accident is all I know," Eva said. "Amelia won't talk about it."

The inn, the café, and Lennox's house were bare of pictures or any remnant of their parents. The most June had seen of them was in the Up Helly Aa book, and Hamish had put it away and quickly ended the conversation. It was as if the three of them were erasing the past. But why?

Maybe five days at his house would answer that question. June shot back the rest of her drink in one gulp and handed the glass to Eva. Eva opened her desk drawer, pulled out a handful of condoms, and shoved them in June's pocket. "In case you're wrong about Lennox."

"Don't worry. You won't need those," David offered. "I'm sure Lennox has plenty of his own. Like Hamlet said, 'It would cost you a groaning to take off mine edge.'"

Ten minutes later, June stood at Lennox Gordon's door, feeling just as she had the night she appeared at the Nestled Inn, her roller bag at her side, backpack on, rain drizzling on her uncovered head. This was going to be her home for five days. She knocked.

Moments later, Lennox leaned against the doorjamb, examining June critically, making her even more nervous. The wind picked up, blowing a freezing gust through June's hair.

"You best get inside, Peanut," Lennox said. "There's a storm coming."

THIRTEEN

Knockmoral had seen its fair share of snow. The surrounding hills were almost always white in winter, the rain at that altitude often starting as snow and then warming as it fell. Occasionally, June would wake up to a thin blanket of slushy white that would melt over her shoes as she walked to work. But by afternoon, the snow was forgotten, her tennis shoes drenched in melted rainwater.

When June woke up on Lennox's couch Saturday morning, a thick layer of snow covered the yard. She stood at the window, a blanket over her shoulders, watching large snowflakes spill from the sky, adding to the accumulation.

The previous afternoon, June had barely made it into the house before the first snowflake fell. At first, it had been awkward. Lennox's house was by no means large, but as June stood in the living room, it felt teeny-tiny. And when he'd insisted that June take his bed, she had politely refused and placed her bags on the living room floor, prepared to take the couch for the duration of her stay.

"I'm not making a woman sleep on the couch." Lennox groaned, already exasperated. "I'm not a barbarian."

"When you grunt like that, you kind of sound like one."

He ran a hand over his unruly dark hair. "Take the damn bed, Peanut."

"You don't even fit on the couch."

"I'll manage."

"Fine." June started setting up on the floor of the living room.

"What the hell are you doing?"

"I guess we're both not sleeping in the bed."

"Why are you so obstinate?"

"You know what obstinate means? You're smart for a barbarian."

Lennox paced the room as June organized blankets on the floor. "You're not going to give in, are you?"

"I guess you'll have to wait and see." She picked up a pillow and threw it at him.

He caught it easily. "Fine. I'm going to bed. *In my room. Alone. Max, let's go.*" As if in protest, the dog lay down on the blankets and looked at Lennox with a sorry expression. Lennox grabbed an acoustic guitar. "Traitor."

June was satisfied with her win, determined not to be pathetic in front of Lennox. She turned her attention to making up her bed on the couch, but as soon as she heard music from upstairs, she began to soften. She sat on the couch, blanket around her shoulders, and soon she was downright aching for Lennox, desperate to watch him play again. The music was a cruel form of torture, a gigantic thorn in the side after her win. She covered her ears with the pillow and willed herself to sleep.

In the morning, Max came up beside her. He had stayed at the foot of the couch all night. June scratched behind his ears. "No run for us today. Sorry, buddy."

"No work either." Lennox stood in the doorway, guitar in hand. "Hamish just called. Café's closed because of the storm. I doubt anything in town will be open today."

June felt bashful in her velour pajama pants and T-shirt. She pulled the blanket tighter around her shoulders. "Does it snow like this very often?"

"I haven't seen a storm this big in years." Lennox put the guitar back on the stand.

June had always loved snowstorms at home. The entire city came to a halt. Schools closed. Roads emptied of cars and busses. Everything fell silent. It felt like the whole world paused to watch the snow fall and drink hot chocolate.

She stretched, arching her back. It popped loudly.

"Jesus Christ," Lennox said. "I knew you should have taken the bed. You're sleeping there tonight."

"I'm fine on the couch."

"I swear, Peanut. You're driving me mad. Why won't you just do what's good for you and take the damn bed?"

"What about you? You don't even fit on this couch."

"I'm twenty-four goddamn years old. I don't need looking after. I can handle myself."

"Well, so can I."

"Really? Eat any peanuts lately?"

June stepped toward him and pointed. "That's not fair. I was jet lagged." She could smell the scent of Lennox's soap on his skin. He had already showered and dressed, whereas June was still in her pajamas. "Are you going somewhere?"

"Not that it's any of your business."

"Fine. Be that way." She went to her bag and started rooting around for clothes. She had no idea what she was going to do, seeing as she didn't have to work, but better to feign like she had somewhere to be. If June didn't want to be treated like charity, she needed to start acting as if she was worth something.

"There's coffee and tea in the kitchen." Lennox turned to leave.

"Wait." June took a CD out of her bag and held it out. When Lennox hesitated, June pushed further. "It's just a mix CD. It's not going to kill you. I made it as an apology for the other night. I was a drunken . . . idiot."

"That was weeks ago, Peanut."

When he didn't take the CD, June grew embarrassed. It was a stupid idea. He'd probably hate her taste and mock her for it. Worse, June had spent hours on Hamish's computer after closing the café, curating the list and rearranging songs for the best flow. Worst, deep down she had done all of it to impress Lennox, to prove she was capable of doing something nice for someone else, too. "You'll probably hate the songs anyway."

Lennox took the CD. "Get dressed. Wear something warm. You're coming with me."

"Where are we going?"

Before he disappeared to give June her privacy, Lennox said, "Do you think we can make it a full day without killing each other?"

June welled with satisfaction. "What fun would that be?"

~

They managed to visit three houses without arguing. The snow did not slow all day, piling up by the hour, but Lennox brought firewood to the Nicholsons and checked the old radiators at the Fergusons', and he and June had just finished shoveling the long driveway at the Brody farm when they got back into Lennox's car.

June shook snow from her hat and gloves. Heat blasted from the vents, and she reached her hands forward to warm them. Lennox put the car in reverse. The tires spun, and the vehicle slid sideways slightly. He braked and then put the car in drive, the wheels finally catching on the snow.

Lennox appeared to relax. He drove slowly, the windshield wipers slapping back and forth. June let out an exaggerated breath.

"What?" Lennox asked.

"Nothing."

"For the love of God, out with it."

June turned to face him. "It's just . . . we're not having any fun."

"You sound like my six-year-old niece."

June perked up. "Snowstorms are supposed to be fun. You know, snowball fights, sledding, hot chocolate."

June recalled the one time Stratford College got five inches of snow, an unheard-of event for that part of Tennessee. Students skipped class and went sledding with dining-hall trays. A gigantic snowball fight broke out on the college green. Anyone attempting to walk the gauntlet to class was penalized with a bombardment. The storm had transformed the students into innocent eight-year-olds again.

"You want me to find you some hot chocolate, is that it?"

"No," June whined. Lennox just didn't get it. He was always too serious, too strict. She sat back and looked out the window.

"Then what do you want, Peanut?"

June wanted to feel young like that again. The magic of snow days wasn't just the weather. The magic came from the unexpected freedom, the break from monotony, the chance to be a little irresponsible because responsibility had called in sick. The snow day gave June permission to bury what happened with Matt—all her lies, all her guilt—under inches of snow, to pretend it didn't exist until tomorrow's melt. She rolled down her window.

"What the hell are you doing?" Lennox asked.

"Calm down, old man. Just drive." June leaned out the window, cold wind and snow lashing at her face.

"Bloody hell, Peanut. Sit your arse back down in the car!"

"Don't you ever just want to be a little reckless?" she yelled. She closed her eyes and let the snow dampen her eyelashes and face. "Drive faster, old man!"

"No." Lennox gripped the steering wheel.

"Fine. Then I'll be forced to take off my clothes." June moved to unzip her coat.

"Damn it, Peanut." Lennox pressed on the gas. "Is this fast enough for you?"

June unzipped her jacket further, teasing him. He growled and sped up more. The cold on her face and the wind in her ears were welcome distractions. She tipped her head skyward, arching her back, letting the wind blow over her. Her ears were too fogged with noise to hear the voice in her head that constantly nagged at her, the shame that dripped like a leaky faucet in the back of her mind. It all went quiet. June lifted her arms toward the sky.

Lennox watched in awe, a need in his eyes, a hunger unsatiated. That look clung to June, hooked into her and demanded her attention, her closeness, her desire. She sat back in her seat, snow melting on her eyelashes and cheeks, drawn to Lennox from the center of her chest, against her better judgment and all the effort she had put into resisting this man.

Just as June's resolve was about crumble, Lennox slammed on the brakes, jerking her forward. Standing not one hundred feet from the car was the biggest, hairiest cow June had ever seen. Lennox swerved to avoid it, but the back tires acted more like ice skates, and their momentum pulled and pushed at June until they spun off the road and landed in a ditch with a thud.

"Are you hurt?" The gravity was back in Lennox's voice.

But June only laughed. "I'm fine."

"Damn it, June." Lennox banged on the steering wheel. "You distracted me."

"Don't get your panties in a bunch."

"You could have been hurt or worse."

"Don't be so dramatic. Nothing happened."

Lennox clenched his jaw. "This time. Nothing happened *this time*. But what about the next or the next? Is nothing serious to you?"

"Is everything serious to you?"

He didn't respond. He attempted to drive out of the ditch, but the car didn't budge. "Fuck. We're stuck."

"Look at you. You're a poet and you didn't even know it."

"Seriously?"

"What? 'Fuck' and 'stuck' rhyme."

"Now is not the time for bad American humor." Lennox got out of the car.

June followed him. "Well, seeing as we're stranded in a snowstorm in the middle of nowhere, now seems like a good time for a little humor."

"We are *not* stranded."

June leaned back on the car as Lennox paced, examining their position in the ditch. "Those wouldn't happen to be snow tires, would they?"

"You don't need snow tires in Scotland."

"Apparently, you do."

"This is all your fault."

"No, it's the cow's fault."

"No," Lennox countered. "If I was paying attention like I ought to have been, instead of watching you, I would have seen the damn cow in time." He walked to the back of the car and instructed June to steer while he attempted to push it out of the ditch. "Now gently press on the gas, Peanut."

June did as she was instructed. The car didn't move.

"Give it a little more!" he shouted over the motor. June pressed on the pedal, revving the engine. "Stop! Stop!"

Snow dripped from Lennox's face as he attempted to shake his clothes clean. June met him behind the car, gasping with laughter, and began to wipe at his shoulders and chest, her lips tight as she tried to contain her giggles. But when a glob of snow fell into Lennox's eyes, she burst into hysterics.

"You think this is funny?" he asked.

"I do, actually. I think this is all very funny."

Lennox nodded and licked his wet lips. "Right." He made a snowball and cocked his arm to fire before June could even consider running.

She turned quickly with a yelp, but it was too late. A thud hit her back. With a pivot, she pointed at Lennox. "This means war."

For years June had played endless games of catch, running bases, and battling Josh and Matt in snowball fights. She could pack a firm weapon, dodge incoming fire, and throw with the best of them. But Lennox was tough competition, agile on the slick snow, swift and determined. Snowballs rained down as the two of them dodged each other. June ran across the street and ducked behind a stone fence for cover. She sat against the wall and caught her breath.

"Surrender!" Lennox shouted.

June crawled on her hands and knees, her pants now soaked, her hair full of snow.

When Lennox next spoke, he sounded slightly concerned. "Peanut? What are you doing back there?"

He crossed the street, where she pressed herself against the wall and then stealthily slithered to the other side as Lennox looked for her.

"June, where the hell . . ."

She leaped onto his back. Lennox startled and grabbed her, spinning them around. He lost his balance as their bodies tangled, and snow and gravity forced them to the ground with a thud, June landing on top.

"Jesus, Peanut. Are you OK?"

But June was laughing too hard to respond. She took a handful of snow and smeared it on Lennox's face. Clumps clung to his nose and eyelashes, increasing June's hysterics. But her laughter stopped when Lennox's large hand wiped snow from June's hairline down to her chin. She blinked, shocked. Lennox took another handful and casually started eating it.

"I hope there's dog pee in that," June said.

"It's more likely to have cow piss, where we are."

"Admit it. I win."

"I don't think so."

"Look who's on top," June said.

"Who says I'm not letting you pin me? If I wanted you off me, I'd make it happen. But I just so happen to like a woman on top."

The fire that June had fought hard to squelch caught quickly. She pushed the feeling away and stood, wiping snow from herself. "What do we do now, Mr. Responsibility?" She gestured toward the car and the empty country road. "Got a miracle in your trunk?"

Lennox retrieved his cell phone out of the glove box. "It's not a miracle, but it might just work." But no one answered at the inn, and Amelia's phone went straight to voice mail. June rubbed her arms, hugging her limbs tightly into her core. Lennox left a message for his sister and shoved the phone into his pocket.

"Come on, Peanut." He started walking down the deserted road.

June stumbled to catch up. "Where are we going?"

"Can you keep a secret?"

FOURTEEN

June stood on the bow of a gigantic ship. The snow was gone from her hair now, just a slight dampness remained. She had never seen anything like this in her entire life.

The galley that Knockmoral would burn to the ground in just a few days was adorned with an ornate dragon's head at the front, a wide belly with a mast, and a rounded stern that came together to form a fish tail. June ran her hand along the carved details of the dragon.

"You actually built this?"

Lennox climbed on the boat. "Well, I had a little help from a few hundred other people, but yeah, I built it."

The details were astounding. The side paneling was painted red and white. The rim of the boat was gold, decorated with stenciled axes and shields. A platform of different blues to mimic the high seas cradled the base.

In the welcome warmth of the barn's portable heaters, June was eye level with the dragon's blue-and-white neck, its head a scaly crown of fiery red. It even had teeth in its open jaw. She couldn't believe that after working so hard on it, they would burn something so beautiful to the ground.

A horned helmet sat on the floor of the boat. June picked it up and placed it on her head. It was too big for her and immediately went lopsided. "Not a very ferocious looking Viking, am I?"

"Aye, but that's the most lethal kind. You look like a bonnie wee lass, but inside you're a warrior." Lennox rubbed his arm. "I think I have a snowball bruise. Where'd you learn to throw like that?"

June warmed further when Lennox called her a "bonnie wee lass." Her toes began to thaw. Feeling returned to her fingers. "My brother taught me," she said. "He had a wicked arm. It felt like catching a bullet when he threw you a football."

If Lennox noticed June's choice of "had" and "threw," he didn't let on. Speaking about Josh in the past tense still felt unnatural, made it sound as if her brother was no longer Josh, when to June he was ever-present, always infinitely himself.

Lennox righted June's hat, but it fell lopsided again. "You need a bigger head."

June took it off and stood on tiptoes to place the helmet on Lennox's head. It fit perfectly. She stepped back to admire him. "You look like your dad in that helmet."

A shadow fell over Lennox, and he took the helmet off. "What the hell do you know about my da?"

"Nothing." June stepped back. "I just saw a picture of you two in an Up Helly Aa book that Hamish showed me, that's all."

Lennox turned his back, his whole body tense. June shouldn't have said anything, but it just slipped out. She would take her words back if she could. Anything not to ruin the moment. Lennox stood at the far end of the boat, what felt like miles away, and she wanted him back, as much as she hated to admit it. Lennox was addicting. And like any addict, she was willing to bargain for a taste.

Confession time, she heard Matt say in her mind. *I want to tell you a secret, but you have to promise to tell one in return. Truth is only fair when it's even.*

The first time Matt had said those words, they were in high school, and unbeknownst to her, he had just found out his parents were divorcing, after his dad was caught having sex with a woman he worked with.

"My mom kicked him out of the house. I don't think he's coming back," Matt said. "Your turn."

June attempted to remain stoic, though inside she couldn't believe what Matt had just confessed. "OK," she said. "Remember when we went on the Demon Drop at Cedar Point, and I said I didn't feel good afterward, and I rushed to the bathroom? I peed my pants."

Matt had laughed. "I thought you smelled that day." And then he said, "Promise me, we won't fuck each other up with lies. We'll always tell the truth, no matter how bad it hurts."

June had agreed. Back then the idea of keeping anything from Matt Tierney seemed impossible. *Confession time, June . . .*

"You were right about me," she said now to Lennox, the words out of her mouth before she could take them back. "When we first met. I *did* leave a mess back home. A pretty bad one."

June sat down on the wooden floor of the galley and hugged her knees to her chest. Talking about Josh made June want to feel small and contained. Then maybe her secrets, and her tears, might not all come out at once.

Lennox came to June, just as she wanted, and when he sat next to her, stretching one long leg in front of him, she felt his closeness like the sun's reappearance from behind a cloud.

"I was a bloody wanker that night," Lennox said.

"Maybe. But you were still right." June rested her chin on her knee, fighting her instinct to run from the conversation. But then Lennox's leg brushed hers, sparking on contact, like static popping but without the pain, only the warmth. She couldn't run from that now. Didn't want to. "My brother died almost three months ago."

June saw Josh in her mind: his mousy brown hair and brown eyes, his long arms and skinny legs, the dimple on his left cheek. Most days it was hard to reconcile that all of Josh could fit into a silly football now. It felt unfair that no matter how big the life, we all reduce to the same small pile of ash.

"Tell me something about him," Lennox said.

"He collected baseball cards," June offered. "Hundreds of them. He always claimed he was going to sell them one day for millions of dollars."

"An entrepreneur."

June chuckled. "He only ate the middle of Oreos. Drove me crazy he wasted a perfectly good cookie." The tightness in June's chest eased a bit. "This one time in junior high, our mom was so sick of hearing us slam our doors all the time, she took them away. I was so mad I almost slammed my closet door just to piss her off." June released her legs from her tight grasp. "I was lying on my bed, pissed, and Josh was in his room directly across the hall, just as mad, and the next thing I know, a tennis ball comes flying into my room. And there's Josh, sitting on his bed, waiting with open hands, like 'Come on. Throw the ball back.' We played catch for hours. And then it kind of became our thing. Every night before bed, we'd play catch, Josh in his room, me in mine."

"Did you ever get your doors back?"

June nodded. "Our parents gave them to us as Christmas presents. I acted relieved, but . . . I was actually sad. I knew we wouldn't play catch anymore."

"And did you?"

"Not once." June curled back into a ball and rested her cheek on her knee. "Josh had a scar just like yours." Then in what felt like the riskiest thing June had ever done—more than smoking a stranger's weed at a Phish concert, more than jumping the railroad tracks in her dad's new car, more than upending her life and flying to a foreign country to stay in a foreign town—she reached up and touched Lennox's scar. He didn't back away. She ran her finger across the crease below his eyebrow, taking her time, savoring the contact. She wanted intimacy with his skin, to experience every pore, every crinkle, every texture.

"How'd it happen?" Lennox asked.

"Pillow fight. I knocked him over, and Josh hit his eyebrow on the corner of the bedpost. He had to get stitches. I thought my mom was going to kill us. I swear every time he was mad at me, he'd rub that scar just to make me feel bad." June's hand fell away from Lennox. "How about you?"

Lennox rubbed his scar as if he could scrub it away. "A stupid fight."

"No way. Mr. Responsibility, fighting? I don't believe it."

"Believe it, June." Lennox spoke as if his words were weighted, and in his eyes was the cavernous, gutting sorrow June had seen before, recognized in herself, because while every living, breathing human carried the weight of grief and guilt in some form, only a few created a permanent harbor for it.

June placed a hand on his shoulder. "Lennox . . ."

He shook her off and stood. "Don't tell me I'm a good person, Peanut. You don't know me."

June flinched at his condescension. Were they really back to this? She got up and walked away, wanting the boat's length between them, but Lennox followed her.

"I'm sorry."

June put her hands on the railing, looking out over the edge of the ship as if she were at sea, the salty air in her hair. "I hate those two words."

I'm sorry about your loss.

I'm sorry you're going through this.

I'm sorry this happened.

I'm sorry . . .

I'm sorry . . .

I'm sorry . . .

"I'm sorry" was never on time. It was always too late.

Those two words haunted June.

She didn't want to talk about Josh anymore. The barn felt claustrophobic, the heat too much. She missed the cold, the deafening sound of wind in her ears. What she wouldn't give for a snowball right now. A distraction. She saw a plastic sword leaning against the mast and grabbed it, pointing it at Lennox's chest.

He threw his hands up in surrender. "What are you doing, Peanut?"

She pushed the pointed end into his chest. "It's time you walk the plank."

Lennox cocked an eyebrow and stepped back. "Now, just take it easy. No need to get pushy."

June lifted the point of the sword to his throat. "How many times have I told you not to boss me around?"

Lennox backed up further. "How many times have I saved your arse when you haven't listened?" He grabbed a play spear from the ground so quickly that June barely registered what he was doing.

She crouched with the sword, ready for a fight.

"Are you sure you want to do this?" Lennox asked.

June whacked at his spear. "Why? Are you scared?"

"Of a bonnie wee lass the size of a Smurf?" She struck the shoulder she had bruised earlier with a snowball. Lennox flinched and grabbed at it. "Playing dirty, are we?"

"Is there any other way to play?"

A wicked grin grew on Lennox's face. "I hope not." He dropped the spear and lunged at June, who shrieked and threw up the sword, her only defense. She pivoted in an attempt to get away, but Lennox had her around the waist. He pulled her to his chest, licked his finger, and brought it to her ear.

June squirmed. "Don't you dare, Lennox."

"You're the one who started this. Now just hold still. This will only take a moment."

June hadn't had a wet willy since elementary school. She thrashed against Lennox's grip and laughed uncontrollably, begging him to stop, and before she knew it, they were face to face, not even a whisper between their bodies.

They both stilled. June's breath was labored, her hair a mess. Lennox tucked the chaotic strands behind one of June's ears, then rested his hand on her collarbone, so close to her heart. She didn't dare move. His eyes were magnetic. He bit his bottom lip.

"Lennox?" Amelia's voice echoed in the barn. "Are you—" She stopped when she saw them. Lennox and June immediately separated.

"We can leave if you need more time." Angus stood behind Amelia, crossed his arms, fully entertained. "Though Lennox isn't known for that."

"Fuck off, Gus." Lennox jumped down from the galley. "Why'd you bring the bawbag, Amie?" He helped June down, taking her by the waist and setting her on the ground. She felt wobbly and disoriented, as if she and Lennox had really been at sea and were now back to the reality of solid earth.

"He's the one animal I can't seem to get rid of," Amelia said. Angus growled in her ear, and she shoved him away, turning to June and Lennox. "Sorry I couldn't get here sooner. The roads are complete shite. What were you doing out in this mess anyway?"

"Long story," Lennox said, and then side-eyed June. "Right now, I just want to get home."

"Come here, lass, you look cold." Angus wrapped his arm around June as the four of them walked out of the barn.

Amelia leaned in close to Lennox. "You weren't at—"

"No." He cut her off. "I didn't go today."

"But you always go."

Lennox shrugged, his eyes falling on June. "I got distracted."

"What do you think of our ship?" Angus asked June. "I hear Scottish ships are bigger than American ones. Bigger than most, actually. Some of the biggest in the world."

"Subtle," Amelia said.

"It's my specialty."

As they walked back out into the snowstorm, June took one last look at the galley. It would burn to the ground. There was no stopping that. But June wouldn't forget this day. Not ever.

That night back at Lennox's, showered, dry, and warm in her pajamas, June was sitting on the makeshift bed of a couch when a ball fell into her lap. Lennox walked into the living room and put June's mix into the CD player. Then he sat on the ground across the room from her and opened his hands.

June tossed the ball back to him. And for the next few hours, they listened to music, played catch, and said nothing.

FIFTEEN

To: j_merriweather9802@stratfordcollege.edu
From: Admissions@stratfordcollege.edu
Subject: Attendance

Dear Ms. June Merriweather,

We have received notice of unexcused absences in one or more of your classes nearing 30 days this semester. Please contact the Admissions Office immediately. Should you surpass 60 days of unexcused absences, you will automatically be unenrolled from Stratford College.

Regards,

The Admissions Office
52 Court Street
Lyons, TN

T he snow stopped on Sunday, and by the Tuesday of Up Helly Aa, the sun was shining. Since June had arrived in Scotland, the weather had never been so fair, as if the storm had collected all the water and had exhausted itself making snow, leaving only clear skies and sunshine for the fire festival.

Hundreds of people lined the streets of Knockmoral to watch as the Guizer Jarl and his squad of fifty men—Lennox, Hamish, and Angus among them—marched through town. Amelia was busy helping Hamish's wife, Sophie, wrangle three children in the large crowd, leaving Eva, David, and June to view the festivities together.

The Knockmoral Pipe and Brass Band led the procession, filling the town with traditional music. As sleepy as Knockmoral had been for the prior month, it was wide awake this Tuesday. June felt the energy of every person on the street as she stood between Eva and David, bundled in jackets, hats, and gloves.

"Smile." June raised her camera. Eva and David struck celebratory poses as she snapped a picture.

June was mesmerized by the spectacle, nervous almost that it would be over too soon, and determined to document the day from start to finish. She snapped a picture of men in kilts with large bagpipes.

The Jarl squad appeared next. The Guizer Jarl walked regally in front of the galley, which was even more impressive today, surrounded by Vikings. The Jarl's silver helmet was adorned with large brass wings, and he carried a shield and hefty axe. The squad was in matching costumes, with white fur-lined cloaks and red knee-length tunics, silver armor layered on top. The men wore leather boots laced up to their knees. June noticed Hamish first, his long red beard braided into a pointy end. She captured his proud walk, her finger working quickly to get multiple angles and shots.

When June found Lennox among the men, she was struck still, camera to her eye, finger unable to move. He resembled a warrior, broad and tall, with weapons in hand, his stoic nature even more intimidating now. And while June knew the sword was plastic, she couldn't help but feel awe at how he looked like a real Viking.

"If you bite on that lip any more, it might bleed," Eva whispered. June released her lip, embarrassed. "I can see it now. Two gorgeous people locked in a house. Alone. For four days . . . and a Viking costume. Please tell me he tied you up." Eva lifted her notebook and pen.

"I'd read that book," David said.

June held a hand up. "Don't even think about collecting this for one of your stories."

"I'm just brainstorming my next Scottish historical erotic novel."

"No, you're scheming."

"I'm using my imagination. There's nothing wrong with that."

"She 'waxes desperate with imagination,'" David added.

Eva took a few notes. June tried to see what she had written, but Eva blocked her view.

"No fair," June said. "If you're going to write about me, I should know the plot."

"Don't worry. I'll make sure you shag the living daylights out of him . . . a few times."

"Eva!" June whispered. "Don't say that."

"Why not? You're an adult. Lennox is an adult. It's not like it's your first time . . . it's not, right?"

"No," June said.

"Are you physically incapacitated?" David asked.

"Struggling with an STD?" Eva chimed in.

"Gay?" David was intrigued.

"No," June said, exasperated.

"Then what is it?" Eva queried.

June glanced at Lennox and had to physically restrain herself from staring. "I just know it's not going to happen. He's not interested."

"You don't know that," Eva said. "You just *think* that's true."

David nodded. "It's a classic rom-com scenario. Guy meets girl. Guy and girl hate each other. Then guy secretly falls for girl. Girl falls for guy. Throw in a makeover or a bet gone wrong, a steamy snog in the rain, a Norah Jones song, and you've got yourself a blockbuster."

June wished things with Lennox were that prescribed. After four nights on his couch, she wasn't sure about anything anymore. They were either hot or cold, fighting or laughing, and at times it seemed that Lennox avoided June altogether. She felt like she was in a game of Chutes and Ladders—the instant they moved closer together, she'd slide all the way back to the bottom of the game board. Lennox refused to talk about his past or his parents, and as for the mysterious Isobel, June was no closer to finding out who she was. Their relationship had been so much easier when she simply hated his guts.

"You even had a good meet-cute," David said.

"What's a meet-cute?" June asked.

"It's an utterly charming first encounter of two potential lovers in a movie."

"I almost died from eating a peanut. There's nothing cute about that."

"It's adorable," Eva said. "I couldn't have written it better myself."

June was even more exasperated. "Fine. Let's say you're right. Let's say that, *hypothetically*, I'm living in a rom-com. What happens next? Hypothetically, of course. From your artist's perspective."

Eva and David glanced at each other and said, simultaneously, "A sex scene."

June's face heated up.

Eva added, "And then I'd probably make it blow up in your face. Come up with a plot twist you weren't expecting."

"Oh, I like that," David said.

June was aghast. "Like what?"

"Depends. Something you and the reader have forgotten about," Eva said. "But I promise the shagging scene would be really juicy. Totally worth what comes after. I highly recommend doing it."

June threw her hands up. "You just told me that if I do, everything will blow up."

"Happily ever after only comes at the end," David said.

"But the sex scenes . . ." Eva smiled. "Those come at the most unexpected times."

"How can I have sex, knowing there's a plot twist coming?"

Eva grabbed June by the shoulders. "Life is full of plot twists you can't control, June. Which is all the more reason to shag like mad when the opportunity presents itself."

June had had enough of plot twists. There would be no more discussion of sleeping with Lennox. No more prying into his life. No more deep stares and electric touches. No more complications. It was best for June just to leave it all alone.

"We better crack on," Eva said, returning her notebook to her purse. "I told Amelia we'd meet her at the hall by now."

June, David, and Eva were scheduled to serve drinks and food at one of the local after-parties. June examined the schedule of events Lennox had written out for her just yesterday. "Can I meet you? There's music down by the water in an hour, and I want to take pictures."

"Ah, the plot thickens." Eva wiggled her eyebrows.

"Meaning?"

David explained. "Happily ever after never happens when people do what they're supposed to do, love. It's when they deviate that the plot really gets interesting."

~

People filled the waterfront in droves for the music. Squad members dressed as Smurfs and Oompa Loompas, small children on their parents' shoulders, different languages threading through the crowd. It was as if, in one day, sleepy Knockmoral had become an international hot spot, more alive than anything June had ever seen, including football Saturdays at Ohio State.

June completed a roll of film and stopped to change it out for another. She was in the zone, not just observing, but *seeing* the day in images. A group of Smurfs congregated in front of the band. June moved around the scene to get the perfect shot of men, kilts, bagpipes, and three-apple-high cartoon costumes. It was equally ridiculous and beautiful, which she was learning was the Scottish way—life was never to be taken too seriously. As she angled the lens to catch the streams of sunlight breaking through the few clouds that had gathered, she felt something sharp in her back.

"Put your weapon down, Peanut, or I'll be forced to give you another wet willy."

June turned. Lennox was in his full Viking costume, minus the helmet that had covered his face this morning. Sunbeams streaked across him, making him look almost holy. His entire face came into stunning focus.

"Don't move." June angled the camera up to his sharp jawline, more anxious than she had ever been to capture an image. The sun reflected off Lennox's armor and made his dark hair glow auburn. Yes, he looked beautiful through the camera. Maybe the most beautiful image June had caught yet, but the gravity of the shot was in the faint crinkle lines around his eyes, his cocky half smile, the lift of one eyebrow.

June captured the image: a brave, gorgeous, and chiseled Viking, but also a boy yearning to let go and have fun.

She lowered the camera. Lennox was like a Van Gogh painting. He was a distinct, concrete image, complete and whole, but on closer examination, June saw all the individual brush strokes, a vast palette, each conveying a feeling that made him much more complex. And it only made her want him more.

She turned away and resumed taking pictures of the band, attempting to calm her racing heart. Lennox stood directly behind her, his body faintly touching hers, bringing with it heat.

"Then you like it?" His breath warmed her ear.

God, June was about to lose herself. Between the Viking costume, bagpipes, and idyllic sunny weather, Eva's Scottish erotic novel wasn't far off. June gathered herself before she did something she'd regret, like rip off her bodice and make him satisfy her burning loins. "I don't know what you're talking about. I don't even like you."

Lennox stepped back. "I meant the camera, Peanut."

His voice was cool, a smack to her face. June pivoted, thoroughly embarrassed. "I love the camera. It's the nicest thing anyone has ever given me." She wanted to say more—that with a simple gift Lennox had brought out a forgotten desire in her, changed her in a way she wasn't even aware she needed.

But she never got the chance. Lennox was due back with the Jarl squad for an afternoon of visits to the local schools before the big event that night.

"How about one more?" June raised the camera to her eye, but Lennox gently lowered it.

"Don't waste your film on me," he said. "Save it for the things you like."

SIXTEEN

The burning of the Knockmoral galley was like nothing June had ever seen in her twenty years. Over a thousand men marched through the streets, dressed in costumes ranging from Smurfs to astronauts to *Saturday Night Fever* disco outfits, complete with multicolored wigs, all following the Jarl squad at the front of the procession. The Guizer Jarl himself stood on the bow of the ship as it was paraded to the waterfront, the dark night lit with torches carried by the men as they chanted and sang the Up Helly Aa song.

Since the general public was not allowed at the burning site, Amelia took Eva, David, and June to a spot where she knew they would be out of the way but still able to view the men throwing their torches into the galley.

Surrounded by thick rings of people, the burning finally began. Torches were thrown into the ship. June had never seen so much fire in her life. She was humbled by how quickly the galley was engulfed in flame. As the longship burned, the men sang "The Norseman's Home" in unison, a slow and haunting song June had never heard.

Fireworks lit the sky in a vivid display as the ceremony came to its end. They made their way to the hall, where all forty squads were expected to visit throughout the night. They would arrive in a parade, each squad with its offering of an entertaining act or dance. More music and drinking and dancing would follow.

Amelia, Eva, and June had dressed up for the evening. Amelia wore a tight green dress that accentuated her auburn hair and long, thin limbs. Eva opted for her usual all black—in fitted pants and a V-neck shirt that teased just enough of her neckline—but with a pair of red heels that made her look almost of average height.

June had dug deep in her dresser drawers for the only somewhat-festive outfit she had happened to pack, an off-the-shoulder black sweater and shimmery purple pants. June had last worn the outfit on New Year's Eve, when she and Matt had attended a party at Janie Langdon's house with their high school friends, all home from college. She had put particular effort into her appearance that night, wanting to look extremely put together so no one from Sunningdale would see the mess she really was. In truth, June had felt as if she had been living in the world's tiniest closet since Josh's death. Each person who gave their condolences, each person who came by with food, each person who called to chitchat—they entered the closet, took more of June's air, made it harder to breathe.

She had not felt like going to a party, but two and a half years of sorority training had served her well. Her hair had hung in loose waves down her back. Her makeup was precise, not too much but not too little. The statement piece—purple retro pants, tight at the waist, butt, and thighs and descending into wide bells at the bottom—had been found in a small boutique in Nashville when June and her roommate, Allison, had gone shopping one Saturday that fall. Allison had called them "fuck-me pants." June had laughed and spent the money, but until New Year's Eve, she hadn't had the guts to wear them. That night June had slipped into the pants, hoping Allison's declaration was true—that someone would pull June from her claustrophobic life, even if only for a few minutes, and numb the anger and sadness with kisses and sex.

June had walked around the New Year's Eve party, shimmering ass on display, hoping someone would take her. One simple pull in the direction of a bedroom and she would have gone. But Matt had stayed with her all night: next to her in the kitchen, next to her on the couch in the living room, next to her outside when June accepted a cigarette from Jerrit Rautenbach.

"You hate smoking," June had said when Matt took one between his fingers.

He merely shrugged. "Who the fuck am I to say smoking is a disgusting habit that only leads to bad breath, yellow teeth, wrinkles, and eventual emphysema and cancer . . . if I've never even tried it? I'm too judgmental. I need to change, June. So what if tomorrow morning I smell like rotten asshole?"

June held her unlit cigarette. "Rotten asshole?"

"Yeah, like moldy, never-been-washed, crusted asshole." June wasn't sure if she was going to barf or laugh. "Smoking is sexy, June. And I love sex. It's like my favorite thing in the world."

Matt leaned back against the house, lit cigarette in hand, and took a drag. In another lifetime he could have been one of those brooding Hollywood actors she'd grown up crushing on, with hair perpetually falling in his pained eyes and a constant look of serious contemplation. Matt had a beautiful mystique that felt untouchable and yet irresistible. But unlike all those actors June dreamed about, Matt *was* hers. She knew what he looked like in the morning, pajama pants hanging loosely from his hips, coffee in hand. She knew how he lounged on the couch, always propping one arm behind his head as a pillow. She knew if she poked him in the side, he'd curl up and convulse in laughter. She knew his smell, coffee grounds and library books.

June swatted the cigarette from his hand. "You're not judgmental. You just don't tolerate bullshit." She knew what Matt was doing. If June was going to be reckless with her life, Matt would join her. He wouldn't let her drown on her own. He would hold her hand until the end. She handed her unlit cigarette back to Jerrit.

After that, June had said she wanted to leave, and they walked the two miles back home, Matt leaving her side only when they had arrived at their neighboring houses.

"Do you want me to come tomorrow?" he had asked. The Merriweathers were planning to scatter Josh's ashes in a small family ceremony at the park down the street, where Josh had played countless hours of football. When June shook her head, Matt grabbed her hand. "I'll be here when you get back. Just come over."

And June knew he would indeed be there.

"Happy New Year, June." Matt pulled her into a hug. She was engulfed in his smell, but the cigarette was there along the edges, too. That was when she knew—if June remained at Matt's side, she would irrevocably hurt him. He would stand as a shield to protect her, take any beating himself so she didn't have to. Matt had always stood carefully outside the claustrophobic closet, but he suddenly stepped inside, cigarette and all, and June was choking on him. The safest person in her life was suffocating her.

Later, in her pajamas, lying in bed, eyes wide open, the smell of cigarette still lingered in her nose. She couldn't stay. She hadn't found escape with another body at the party, but that wasn't the only way to disappear. There were other, grander options. Options that didn't involve ruining Matt. Options that saved him from June. She packed her bag, stole the urn, and called a cab in the middle of the night, bound for Cincinnati International Airport.

June had left with the best intentions, and yet she had found that, from thousands of miles away, she was still able to hurt her best friend. She had left to preserve what they had, and then, inadvertently, June had changed in Scotland.

But tonight the festival kept Matt from June's thoughts. Squad after squad entered the hall to raucous explosions of cheering. People sat or stood, cupping drinks and eating food. June laughed and danced and breathed freely, the claustrophobia at bay at least for the time being.

A squad dressed like Wham! in fluorescent short-shorts filed out of the hall. It was three in the morning, and the Jarl squad had yet to visit. June was beginning to fear they never would. She felt like a fool for overreacting with Lennox and wouldn't be surprised if he wanted nothing to do with her after Up Helly Aa.

The drunken revelry began to die down. People slouched in chairs. Coffee and tea were set out next to whisky and beer. June yawned in her seat, as Eva plopped next to her with a fresh glass of whisky, her words slightly slurred. "So . . . have you decided?"

"Decided what?"

"If you're going to shag the living daylights out of Lennox tonight."

June hushed Eva and took the drink from her hands. "You can't say that." She took a sip.

"And why not? It's just a question about a completely natural occurrence between two people . . . sometimes three."

"I'm not sleeping with Lennox."

Eva blew air through her lips, fluttering them exaggeratedly. "Stop being such an American prude."

"I am *so not* an American prude."

"Yes, you bloody well are. You've been in Scotland for more than a month and all you do is work, work, work, and run. You're the most American . . . American I've ever met. Obsessed with money and exercise. You need to lighten up and take some risks. Have some fun."

"I have fun," June stated firmly. Just three days earlier, she had hung out of Lennox's car window in a snowstorm. "And I take risks."

"You've barely left Knockmoral since you got here."

"I can't help it if I have to work."

"Oh, bullocks," Eva said. "You know Hamish would give you as many days off as you want, but you don't ask. Because you're hiding, June Merriweather. It's high time you throw in a plot twist or two."

"My life isn't one of your novels, you know."

"No, because if all my character did was work and run, I'd have a fucking boring book on my hands."

"I'm not boring."

"No, you are *not* boring. In fact, I suspect there is a very interesting person hiding out in that body of yours, if you would just let down your guard and reveal her." Eva took one of June's hands. "Avoidance builds tension, but at some point, to satisfy the reader, a character must make a choice and deal with the consequences." Eva took the whisky back from June and sipped.

"A choice about what?" June asked.

Eva glanced over June's shoulder toward the door. "Him."

The Jarl squad funneled through the door, still in their Viking costumes. Most people were slowly sagging, getting sloppier throughout the night, but Lennox had managed to get even hotter. The crowd cheered for the squad as June grabbed Eva's drink and shot back the remainder in one gulp.

"He's not a plot twist most women can say no to," Eva whispered in June's ear.

Even if June had tried, which she didn't, she wouldn't have been able to pull her eyes from Lennox. It was as if she had been adrift all night but was now suddenly anchored and awake. The crowd took their seats, ready for the main act. June stayed in the back as the men set up for their performance.

With fifty men in the squad and a hundred more people still in the hall, the heat began to rise. June's cheeks flushed hot. She felt every single body in the room, and yet it felt nowhere near as suffocating as her life had been in Sunningdale. She exhaled deeply.

"Lads and lasses," the Guizer Jarl began, "we have a sad tale to tell on this most important night. A cautionary tale. Of heartbreak. Of longing unrequited. Pay attention and heed our warning, so that you may not make the same mistake."

June's lip found its way between her teeth as she watched Lennox produce his guitar and take a seat next to the Jarl, who stood at the front of the squad. Another player sat beside Lennox, violin in hand. The squad's faces were stoic behind their leader, Hamish included. There had yet to be a somber act, and a silence fell on the hall that June had not experienced all night.

Lennox and the violinist began to play a haunting tune. Lennox was protective around the guitar, focused and serious. June felt as though she was observing a private moment, Lennox lost in himself. She couldn't tear her eyes from him. The sight of Lennox playing guitar was . . . *erotic*. The way his body moved to the beat. The way he closed his eyes and bit his lip, as if obsessed with the music, hypnotized by it, aching for it. If this simple song could possess Lennox, June wondered, what could a human being do? And what could Lennox do with another human being?

Lost in her infatuation, June almost missed the instant the crowd shifted. The melancholy tune suddenly became recognizable. June sat at attention. The crowd began to look at each other. How did June know this song?

And just as the Jarl sang the lyric and June suddenly realized what was coming, she caught Lennox's eye. And he winked.

Hamish stepped forward, ripped off his helmet to reveal Amelia's long blond wig, and shouted, "Hit me baby one more time!"

Capes and helmets came off. The squad tore free of their Viking costumes to reveal kilts underneath. The crowd was on its feet as the speakers began to blare Britney Spears's iconic pop hit.

In a matter of seconds, fifty Vikings had transformed into kilt-clad Britney Spears look-alikes. If that wasn't shocking enough, the entire squad began doing the exact choreography for the song, which June knew from hours of MTV.

Lennox fumbled along to the beat, attempting to keep up. He looked ridiculous, like a giant on a trapeze, and utterly gorgeous. More importantly, he looked as if he was having fun. June had never seen anything more comical and magical in her life.

The room became a raucous carnival, with squad and townspeople all on their feet, dancing and singing. When Britney Spears hit her last note, the crowd exploded in boisterous cheers. The squad took a collective bow as people applauded and begged for more.

June pushed through the crowd, trying to get to Lennox as fast as she could, but the room was crammed with bodies and stuffy with heat. He smiled at her the way he had during the song; God, she actually quivered. But right before she could get to Lennox, a large Viking stepped in front of her, now back in his regal costume, his long salt-and-pepper beard dangling.

The Jarl held two glasses of whisky in his hands. "It's tradition that I dance with a lass and have a wee dram at every hall. Would you care to join me?" He held a glass out to June.

Just over the Jarl's shoulder, Lennox was in conversation with an older woman. He glanced at June with a taunting grin. She took the whisky from the Jarl and choked it down in one gulp. With a laugh, the Jarl did the same. And for the next few minutes, June was flung around the dance floor, held tightly by the Jarl. The moment seemed completely hysterical to her. The whole day had been something of a bizarre dream, but she didn't want it to end.

The Jarl spun June in a circle and pulled her back in by the waist. She laughed as she tripped over his boots.

"Let's try that again, lassie." He flung June wide, twirling her, making her head spin. At arm's length, June lost his grip. She snatched at the air, looking for fingers or palm or anything, but the Jarl had stumbled back in a boom of laughter.

Someone caught June, barely, before she tumbled to the ground.

"Once again, here I am saving your life." Lennox placed June back on her feet.

She brushed her hair from her face. "That was your fault. You made him dance with me."

"I merely suggested that you had a penchant for drinking too much and waking up in a stranger's bed." June gasped and slapped Lennox's arm. He laughed. "I'm just taking the piss!"

June shoved him again. "You're an ass."

Lennox grabbed June's hand and pulled her toward him. "Don't be mad, Peanut."

She tried to remain steady, even with her heart in her throat. Shivers raced down her body. He was close enough that June could rest her head on his chest, and she resisted, but she felt it physically impossible to back away. Lennox's hands drifted down her back, then he grabbed her hips and held her to him. His fingers edged the top of her pants, touching the sliver of June's exposed skin.

She had no notion of whether the music was fast or slow, or whether people were staring at them. All she felt and smelled and heard was Lennox, the rise and fall of his chest, his fingertips on her skin. She tried to reach her arms around his neck, but her lack of height made the attempt almost comical.

"Shall I get you a stool, Peanut?"

June smiled up at him. "I've never danced with a man in a skirt before."

"Kilt."

"Call it what you want. You're still wearing a skirt."

"Your American fraternity boys—"

"I don't have any American fraternity boys. And if I did, they couldn't pull off a skirt. They don't have your legs."

"You've been looking at my legs?"

June rolled her eyes. "I bet girls have been admiring your legs since you put on your first pair of rugby shorts."

Lennox feigned shock. "I feel violated. Do you think I'm that shallow?"

"I think . . ." June examined his rugged face. "You could have any girl in this room. And you know it."

"Not any," Lennox said. "At least one lass has made it perfectly clear she doesn't like me."

June didn't know what to say. She was in a catch-22—speak the truth and risk embarrassment or, worse, rejection or lie and spare herself the attachment and inevitable sadness when she had to say goodbye and live with an aching heart. "Maybe that lass was too quick to judge. Maybe she didn't know you that well."

"And now?" Lennox asked.

Just a week ago, June would have said Lennox was a mystery to her. And on so many levels, that was still the truth—his family and his past unknown to her. But the man who held her was no stranger. June was intimately acquainted with his smell, that he took his tea with honey and milk, how he organized his CDs by release date, oldest to newest, rather than in alphabetical order. He loved Max like an appendage. Lennox was quiet, but June could see his mind constantly moving. He was protective of the people he cared about, like Amelia and Hamish, but he loved them softly.

"Maybe"—June shrugged—"she knows you a little."

Lennox brought a hand to June's shoulder, grazing his fingers along her exposed collarbone. "Maybe it isn't all her fault. Maybe she'd be better off if she kept her distance."

June stepped closer. "Maybe she doesn't take orders that well."

Lennox chuckled. "I've noticed."

But anything he may have said after that was cut off by the Jarl's booming voice thanking everyone at the hall and announcing that it was time for the squad to move on. Lennox and June parted, their connection deteriorating with the interruption. It was nearing four in the morning, and until that point, June had seemed to forget to be exhausted. She had been up early and had spent the day photographing all over town. She must have walked ten miles. Coupled with whisky and beer, and without Lennox to hold her up, June nearly fell over as she yawned.

"Go home, Peanut. You're pure done in."

June stood up straighter, fighting the fatigue. "No way. I'm not leaving. The party's not over." Lennox shook his head with a dark chuckle. "What's so funny?"

"I've never met anyone like you. You're just so . . ."

"So *what?*" A thousand responses swarmed her head.

Lennox leaned down to her, his breath on her skin, the smell of the night's festivities on his clothes. If he tilted closer, June decided, she would kiss him right there on the dance floor.

"Stubborn," Lennox replied.

June crossed her arms over her chest. "You're an arse."

"I know. You already told me that." He grabbed his helmet off a table. "I'll see you at home, Peanut."

"Don't be so sure. I might run away with a Viking tonight."

"You won't."

"And why not?"

In a flash, Lennox had June by the hips again, pulling her close. "Because I warned them that if anyone touched you, I'd rip his head off with my bare hands." He released her. June could barely steady herself in her shock. "Night-night, Peanut."

SEVENTEEN

J une couldn't sleep. She lay on the couch, staring at the ceiling. It was seven in the morning. She had done what she said she would do, staying until the end of the party, then Amelia had dropped her at Lennox's house in the still dark of morning. Eva and David had disappeared sometime around six. Angus was nowhere to be seen after five.

June wondered where Lennox was. His bed was empty. Her last sight of him was when he left the hall hours ago. A lot could happen in a few hours, June knew well, and her mind ran rampant with possibilities. As tired as she was, she knew she wouldn't fall asleep until he was home.

June rolled onto her side and squeezed her eyes closed, willing herself into slumber. The back door creaked. She knew the sound well, from all the afternoons she had entered through the same door to pick up Max for a run. June held still, her eyes closed, pretending to be asleep.

Lennox didn't go up to his room. June sensed every step he took toward her. Soon she felt him near, standing in the doorway of the living room. She steadied her breath, even as Lennox knelt beside the couch.

"Peanut, are you awake?" he whispered. June pretended to be groggy as she peeled her eyes open. "You can't stay here anymore."

June propped herself up on her elbows, worried. "What?" Her voice was raspy and tired.

"I can't let you stay on the couch one more hour. It isn't right." Without asking for approval, Lennox took June in his arms and carried her up to his room. She didn't fight, too preoccupied with being pressed against him.

He laid her on the bed and tucked her in. She hadn't realized just how stiff the couch was making her feel. She curled into a ball and smelled him on the sheets. "What about you?"

"I'll take the couch."

"Don't be ridiculous. Barely half of you fits on that thing."

"Then I'll sleep on the floor."

"Am I so repulsive you'd rather sleep on the hardwood floor?" June rolled over onto her other side. "Whatever. Night-night, Lennox."

This time she really was going to sleep. She had spent too much energy thinking about him. June cursed Eva for putting ridiculous sex ideas in her brain. This evening she would go back to the inn and resume the distance between herself and Lennox. It was better that way. Less . . . infuriating.

But then Lennox climbed into the bed. June opened her eyes at the weight of his body next to hers. Even in a large bed, he felt overwhelming.

"I didn't say you're repulsive." He was shirtless, fatigue in his eyes.

"I believe 'stubborn' was the word."

"Aye." He yawned. "The most stubborn lass I know."

"Don't worry," June said. "I'll stay on my side of the bed."

"If that's what you want, Peanut."

They were facing each other, their bodies inches apart. June could feel the sheets rise and fall with his breath. Lennox lay with his head propped on his bent arm; the tally-mark tattoo on his forearm was visible even in the dimly lit room. June wanted to touch it, to touch him.

Anything to be closer to the man. She tried to close her eyes, but staring at him felt so much better. "It's late, we should sleep."

"It's not late, Peanut," Lennox said. "It's early."

"Why do you always have to correct me?"

He yawned. "Why do you always have to push my buttons?"

"Well, this evening I'll be gone, and you'll be free of me."

Lennox tucked June's hair behind her ear, his eyes half-closed, the weight of sleep seconds away. June's pulse quickened, but Lennox was fading fast into sleep.

She inched closer to him, to the heat of his body. What was she thinking? This was a terrible idea. Crossing this line could only be disastrous. Lennox stoked too much passion in her. Too much fire. When Lennox was near, she ached for him so badly it scared her. She felt out of control, always flying off the handle, speaking before thinking, anger constantly fighting with lust. Lennox had a hold on June like no one else in her life, and deep down, June knew they would implode and destroy themselves at each other's hands. And yet the idea of letting him go . . .

Eva was right. Enough with avoidance. June needed to make a choice. Her foot touched Lennox's leg under the covers.

He opened one eye. "I thought you said you would stay on your side of the bed, Peanut."

"Right," she whispered and pulled her foot away. This was a bad idea. Madness even. No one walked into fire. That would be crazy, and that was exactly what June was doing. She rolled away, biting her lip at her stupidity.

"I meant what I said, Peanut. You're better off staying away from me."

June rolled back to face him. "Is that supposed to be a warning or something?" She began to scramble out of the bed. "Fine. I'll leave."

But Lennox grabbed her and pulled her back onto the bed. In a breath, he was on top of her, June pinned beneath the weight of his body. Her breath hitched; her throat suddenly was dry.

"Not a warning, June," he said. "A reality. I'm not a good man."

Being pinned beneath Lennox was the best she'd felt in days, maybe all her life. Whatever had happened to make Lennox believe he was undeserving didn't matter to June. She didn't care about anything other than him, all of him, right now, together with her. "I don't believe you," she said.

Lennox's head fell into the nook of June's neck. She waited, frozen, as Lennox rested his face in her hair. "That's what scares me."

For a second, she thought he might fall asleep right on top of her. But then a slow shift began. Lennox tilted his head. Or did June move first? It could have been both of them. It could have been an accident or fate or a natural disaster, like plates fluctuating within the earth, not of their own accord but because of their nature. Whatever the reason or cause or whether it was destiny, when June's mouth found Lennox's, warm and wet, the ache she felt for him grew uncontrollably. A frenzy began in her, from the weight of him, the taste, his hands on her hips, his mouth hot on her neck.

Their clothes were soon scattered on the bedroom floor, and being naked in front of Lennox was the least self-conscious June had ever felt. All she wanted was his skin on hers. She grabbed at Lennox, needing more contact, and he clung to her as if she might disappear—as if he wanted her as much as she needed him. His mouth ran down her neck, her collarbones, teasing its way to her shoulder, her breasts, her stomach.

Her breath hitched again as he ran a hand up her leg, teasing the sensitive skin of her inner thigh. She pressed her hips into his, knowing just how much he wanted her. When Lennox reached for a condom, June clawed at him, pulling him back.

"Be sure, Peanut," Lennox whispered in her ear.

June wondered at the nickname, how something she was never meant to have had brought her to this moment, led her to Lennox.

Lennox had taken her kryptonite and made it insatiable, irresistible. She begged him to say her name again and again.

And she realized that there was no choice to be made. If June didn't take Lennox now, her desire would consume her. Her body shook, her breath labored with need. She pulled Lennox to her, grasping at his hips, unwilling to let go until they were both satisfied. When he finally entered her, June gasped with relief.

There wasn't time to wonder at how they had gotten themselves here. No past and no future. Only this between them. No questions. No worries. Just skin on skin. Lips and tongues and heat and a crescendo of craving. How much they could taste, feel, discover, consume of each other. Consequences were far from June's mind. For now there was only herself and Lennox, with no thought or room for anyone else.

EIGHTEEN

I t was near four in the afternoon, sundown already, when June awoke in Lennox's bed. The smell of coffee filtered up the stairs. June felt for Lennox but only found emptiness. She sat up, wondering if she had imagined the morning, but the ache between her legs suggested otherwise. Her skin hummed. Her lips felt swollen and sore in the most magnificent way. She couldn't help but smile at how delicious it all had been.

"I bet I can guess why you're smiling." Lennox stood in the doorway, holding a steaming mug.

"You know me that well?"

"I know you've got a birthmark on your right thigh. Would you consider that knowing you well?"

June felt suddenly bashful and hugged the blankets close. She was wearing a flannel shirt picked up off the floor sometime that morning before exhaustion had finally claimed them both.

Lennox handed her the mug. She took a sip, the coffee how she liked it, with just a splash of milk, she thought, giddiness coursing through her as if she were a schoolgirl. Was there any feeling better than this?

June set down the coffee and pulled her knees to her chest, resting her chin there, her face aching from smiling. She hoped she didn't look too desperate for more of Lennox, but June just couldn't help herself. She could stay in his bed forever and be completely content.

"Amelia called. Good news." Lennox collected June's scattered clothes and set them in a neat pile on the bed. "The guests have left. You can move back into your room tonight."

June sat up straighter. As the amorous fog clouding her mind lifted, she began to take in the scene before her differently. Lennox was showered and dressed. She could smell the soap on him. While June was a disheveled post-sex mess, he had already washed himself clean of her. June was hoping she could stay in bed for days and forget the outside world, but Lennox had already opened the door.

June now saw the coffee, which she had first thought was an intimate gesture, for what it really was. Lennox was telling her to leave. It wasn't so much that June had expected to move in. That would be ridiculous. But she hadn't expected him to press her to go so quickly.

Lennox tucked June's hair behind her ear. "Are you alright, Peanut?"

June flinched at his touch and stood from the bed, pulling the flannel down to cover her legs. "Fine," she said. "I'll start packing." Her mind spun as she collected her clothes.

But Lennox stopped June before she could escape downstairs. He ran a hand through his messy hair—hair that June now knew the feel of, every strand, every curl. She literally craved touching it. She waited for him to say something, silently begging him to pull her back down onto the bed. Forget words. One kiss, and all of June's worries would disappear.

"I just need to step out for a bit, but I'll be back shortly." Lennox took his exit.

June sat back down on the bed in the room, now feeling cold. She grabbed the coffee off the nightstand and slammed it down in a few hot gulps. She needed clarity. Focus. How had this happened? How could Lennox do this to her? She must be overreacting, oversensitive, overreading the situation. Lennox was a good man. He would never kick her out and so quickly. Or would he? He had told June, just last night, that he was a bad man, but she had refused to believe him—had insisted he was wrong. Lennox had warned her, and she had turned a blind eye, out of lust.

June grabbed her clothes and raced downstairs. She changed into a fresh outfit and repacked her belongings, stuffing items into the bag quickly. In the living room, she stacked the blankets and pillow she'd used for the past five days, then wheeled her bag into the kitchen, fully prepared to leave before Lennox returned. Max stood at the door, blocking her way, a tennis ball in his mouth. June felt nauseous.

Max dropped the ball and nudged it toward her with his nose. "I can't, Max. I have to go." But his puppy-dog face broke her heart. June picked up the slobbery ball. "Fine. Just for a minute."

She rolled the ball down the hallway, and Max bounded after it, returning it to her like a trusty companion. "At least one of you is predictable," she sighed.

Just then, the door opened, and Lennox came back in, hair misted with rain, mobile phone in hand. "You're leaving already?" He seemed surprised, but then again, June couldn't trust her judgment. Lennox picked up the tennis ball and tossed it down the hallway for Max. "Can I make you some food? The menu is limited, but I make a brilliant breakfast."

"I'm sure you're anxious to have your house to yourself again."

"Aye, you've been quite a burden. My arms are tired from constantly putting the toilet seat down. And the dishes. How many cups does a person need in a day?"

June forced a laugh while her heart sank. "Well, it's important to stay hydrated."

An awkward silence fell between them then, neither making a move. Max had not gone after the tennis ball and was now intently looking out the storm door. He barked.

"Damn birds always taunting him," Lennox said.

June extended the handle on her roller bag. It was time to go. Lennox took the suitcase from her hands.

"You don't have to do that," she said. "I can make it back to the inn myself."

"With your track record, Peanut, I wouldn't be surprised if a sinkhole opened in the driveway and swallowed you alive. I'd rather be there just in case." Max barked again, and then again. "What the hell, Max? Calm down. They're just birds."

The dog sat still at the storm door, attention on the cab in the driveway of the inn that was picking up travelers to take to the bus station. Twilight had fallen. June felt lost in time. Had the festival only been yesterday?

Max barked again, and Lennox scratched behind his ears. "It's just a guest, Max. You see them all the damn time."

"Speaking of guests . . . I should probably go." June went to leave. She needed to keep moving.

"Wait, Peanut." Lennox stopped her. His fingers traveled down her arm, teasing her one last time.

June couldn't take it. She stepped back from his touch and used her last ounce of energy to act casual. "Don't worry. I won't tell anyone about your VHS collection of *Little House on the Prairie* episodes."

Lennox chuckled. "Appreciated. And I won't tell anyone you sleep with your eyes half-open."

June gaped. "I do not."

"You do too. Trust me. I've spent a good while watching you sleep."

Why did Lennox have to say things like that, only to confuse her? Was this a part of some twisted game? She needed to get out of the house, but when she attempted to leave again, Max blocked her way. He scratched at the storm door, whining to get out.

"Jesus, Max," Lennox said. "What's gotten into you? Do you know that person?"

As it turned out, the cab parked at the inn was not collecting guests, but rather depositing one. As June watched him get out of the car, sling his messenger bag over his shoulder, and examine a piece of paper, June was struck by how familiar it all looked.

"I didn't think Amelia had any new guests checking in." Lennox held Max back by his collar.

"It can't be," June whispered.

"Can't be what?"

It had to be a figment of June's imagination. There was no way what she was seeing was real. June pushed through the doorway, Max on her tail, and took off at full speed toward the inn. It wasn't until she barreled into a real, live human being that June actually believed what was happening. She clung to him, pressing her nose into his scarf, breathing in the scent of coffee and books. June would have disappeared into him, melted into him until she dissolved, if she could.

"June," he said.

Somehow, some way, Matt Tierney had arrived in Scotland.

NINETEEN

June hadn't realized she was crying until Matt wiped the tears from her cheeks. She grabbed at him, still not believing her eyes. His hair was tousled and messy, and small bags hung under his eyes.

"How are you here?" June begged.

"Three flights, two busses, and one very incoherent cab driver." Matt was functioning on thirty minutes of sleep, he explained to June, plus five gin and tonics and a meal that was supposed to be chicken but he was pretty sure was breaded rubber, then eight hours of watching *Sweet Home Alabama* on repeat on the world's smallest screen, all while sitting in the world's smallest chair.

"I can't believe you found me."

Matt cupped June's face gently. "I'll always find you, June."

Whatever anger had passed between them dissipated and disappeared. June felt only relief. Until now, she hadn't fully comprehended just how much she had missed Matt. She held him as if grasping at treasure. As if, with one breath, he might evaporate, and she would feel lonely again.

Max barked insistently at the two of them, running back and forth in the driveway.

"Calm down, Max," June complained. "He's not going to hurt you."

"You know this rabid animal?"

Lennox emerged from next door, leash in hand. "Shut the hell up and get your bleeding arse over here, Max!" The dog obeyed.

June stepped back from Matt as Lennox connected Max's leash.

"Your wild animal might need some more training," Matt offered. "Can't be good for guests."

"He normally doesn't act like this," Lennox said, his jaw tight. "Only when he's suspicious of someone. But thanks for the suggestion." There was no appreciation in Lennox's voice. June was still so dumbstruck by the turn of events, her mouth hung open, but no words came out. "No sinkhole," Lennox said to June, without humor.

The interaction seemed to thoroughly confuse Matt, who was running on empty. "What the fuck am I missing?" he asked.

Max barked again. "Shut up, Max!" Lennox and June said in unison.

Matt squeezed his eyes and then looked at Lennox. "I'm sorry. Who are you?"

As June was about to explain, the inn door opened and Eva emerged, haloed by light from inside.

"What in God's name is going on out here?" she asked.

"Let's go, Max." Lennox pulled the dog toward the house. "We're done here." He didn't spare a glance for June as he retreated.

"Is that how all new guests are greeted?" Matt asked June. "Or am I the only one lucky enough to get the infamous Scottish Attack Dog welcome?"

"Max is harmless," June said.

"And his owner?"

June should have run after Lennox, done the polite thing and immediately introduced him to Matt. But she didn't, because it didn't matter, when it came down to it. *We're done here.* Lennox's words. As if June needed more proof. She didn't think she could feel worse, so instead of clearing the air, she let the bitter taste that Lennox planted in her mouth fester.

"Excuse me?" Eva asked. "What did I just miss?"

Matt held out his hand to Eva, which she took hesitantly. "I'm Matt."

"Eva. Another American?" She glanced sideways at June, who was still occupied with Lennox's retreat.

Matt nodded with a smile. "I'll try to keep my innate obnoxious behavior to a minimum."

"Grand. I assume he belongs to you."

But June was deep in thought. *Remember this,* she told herself. Lennox had walked away like June was of no concern to him. God, she wanted to throttle him, but what did it matter? She certainly didn't owe him any explanations now.

"Yes," Matt answered. "I'm hers."

"And will he be staying in your room, *June?*" At her name, June came back to the present moment. Eva wanted answers June couldn't give.

"It's not like we haven't slept together before," Matt said with a laugh. "Please tell me you're not going to force me on the couch."

"I would never do that." June took Matt's hand. It felt so different from Lennox's. Matt was familiar. June knew the length of his fingers, the softness of his palm, the coolness of his skin, whereas every time Lennox touched her, it was a surprise, a jolt. Her whole body had to recalibrate. She hated that she instantly compared the two men. Was this how her mind would work from now on, every male touch weighed against Lennox's in some masochistic form of torture?

June stuffed her cravings behind a rigid, protective wall. She wouldn't go back there. It was done. If she had to fight the urge every damn day, she would.

"Where were you coming from, anyway?" Matt asked.

June fumbled, not wanting to explain. Something told her Matt would not find any of it amusing—Lennox, in particular.

"She was actually helping me." Eva stepped in. "I was busy, so I asked June if she'd grab something for me at Lennox's house. I left my . . . book there. And I'm at such a good part. Massive plot twist. I just *need* to know what's going to happen. But now that you're here . . ." Eva gestured toward Lennox's house. "I'll just grab it myself. It was nice to meet you, Matt. I'm sure I'll be seeing you around."

Eva headed toward Lennox's. June pulled Matt inside the inn and up the staircase.

"Who is that Lennox guy, anyway?" Matt asked.

"He's just a misanthrope who lives next door."

Matt stopped June on the landing. "Remember Butt-Crack Jim from across the street? He was a total misanthrope. We were convinced he was hiding kids in his basement."

June pointed at him. "I blame you for that. You made us watch *The 'Burbs* like one hundred times. After that, I swear I could hear kids crying at night."

"Turned out, his mom had just died, and it was him crying."

"Don't remind me." June pulled Matt up the rest of the stairs and down the hallway toward her room. "I still feel bad about calling the cops."

"Well, it was criminal to show that much butt crack when doing yard work."

"How did he not feel it? His pants were like halfway down his ass."

Matt shrugged. "We ignore what we don't want to change." June opened her bedroom door. Matt walked in, set down his messenger bag and a duffel bag, and sat on the neatly made bed. "So, this is where June Merriweather has been hiding out . . ."

June hesitated at the door. It still felt surreal that Matt was here.

"Come here." Matt patted the bed next to him, and June joined him, resting her head on his shoulder. "Please tell me you're happy to see me."

June sat at attention. She had rarely, if ever, seen insecurity in Matt. "Why would I not be?"

"After what happened . . ."

"Let's not talk about it, Matty."

He placed a hand on June's. "Agreed. For the next three days, I won't bring up what a dick I was, or how fucking sorry I am, or how much I've missed you."

"Only three days?"

"I have a huge exam next week. I can't miss it."

"Right. College." June nudged Matt lovingly. "Did you really miss me that much?"

"Turns out, I need you, June Merriweather." Matt took June in his arms. His familiar warmth eased down her spine like a trickle of water. But was she happy? That wasn't the right word. She was relieved and confused and surprised. And something told her Matt's appearance held only more surprises.

"Hey"—Matt leaned back to look at her—"are you OK?"

"I just can't believe you're here."

He pulled her closer, and they lay down, bodies curled toward each other like two halves of an oyster. He took her hand and placed it on his heart. "I'm here," he said. "Flesh and bone. Right next to you. For the next three days."

Matt's chest rose and fell steadily under June's hand. Soon he fell asleep, his clothes still on. June took in his serene, familiar face, his long eyelashes, his perfectly arched lips. His lean body spread the length of the bed.

June heard a quiet knock on her door and rose from the bed. Outside her room were her roller bag and backpack. She dragged her belongings into her room and began to unpack again, rehanging clothes in the closet and placing clothes in her dresser drawers. She hid Josh's urn at the back of the closet again, feeling the weight of it even more than before.

Then she pulled on the Ohio State hoodie, brushed her teeth, and climbed into the bed next to Matt. She snuggled in close, hoping maybe, just maybe, his smell would return to the hoodie again.

But the longer she lay there, the less sleepy June became. Staring at the ceiling, she felt the weight of her best friend beside her. He had come for good reasons. He had come for *her*. But Matt's appearance in Scotland instantly changed things, and she had neither expected nor prepared for it. Now her lies, which had been thousands of miles away, were asleep in bed with her.

TWENTY

Waking next to Matt was as jarring as waking next to Lennox, but for different reasons. For a moment, June forgot where she was and who was next to her. She reached across the bed and felt the body under the covers in a wave of anticipation, expecting to find muscle and mass, instead finding the lean figure of her best friend.

He was reading a book. "Jet lag is a fucking bitch. I've been up since four."

June yawned. "Well, you fell asleep almost as soon as you got here. What do you expect?" She pushed herself off the pillow and sat up.

Matt closed the book and set it down. "What are we doing today? I'm starving."

June checked the clock. It was seven thirty in the morning. "I have to work in an hour and a half."

"What? But I'm only here for three days."

"If I had known you were coming, I would have asked for time off, but you just showed up."

"No, I get it." Matt took a deep breath. "But it's good I showed up, right? You and me together, that's a good thing."

The question was wholly unlike Matt, so unsure, and it was her fault.

"Yes," June said quickly. "God, yes. A good thing."

"Good." Matt stood up from the bed and opened his duffel bag. "Now you can have your presents."

"Presents?" June bounced up onto her knees. "I love presents."

"I know. Now hold out your hands." He placed a Resch's Bakery box in June's hands.

She knew what was inside just by the package. She gaped at him. "You didn't."

"Drove my ass all the way there. You owe me a kidney."

June opened the box, squealing as she took out one of the chocolate chip cookies and popped a piece into her mouth. She fell back on the bed dramatically. "Oh. My. God. I think I'm having an orgasm."

"And that's not even the climax."

"There's more?" She was upright again, like a kid waiting for Santa, as Matt rummaged around in his bag. "Did you bring me a puppy, too?"

"Don't be ridiculous. You know I don't do animals."

"A car with a big red bow?" June clapped in anticipation. "Is Jared Leto in your bag?"

"Oh my God. Fucking Jared Leto. I forgot about your obsession with him."

"It wasn't an obsession, Matty. It was true love."

"You made us drive all the way to Cleveland so we could wait in line at some shit-ass mall for eight hours, just to see his greasy hair and smell his patchouli BO in person for five seconds. You owe me both kidneys and a liver."

"I was convinced if he just saw me, he'd fall in love with me."

"You've always been ridiculous."

"I prefer the word 'spirited.' People do crazy things when they're in love."

"Don't I know it."

An intense look came over Matt's face, making June feel suddenly bashful. She wiped at her mouth. "What? Do I have chocolate on my face?"

"No." He took her hand.

June's stomach fell to her knees. The energy between them had shifted. "What is it then?"

"I just missed you . . . this . . . *us*. God, I feel better when I'm around you."

June didn't know what to say. The way Matt looked at her, like he was consuming every inch of June with his eyes, made her uncomfortable. Of course, it felt good to have him next to her. Matt was a pair of perfectly worn-in tennis shoes. A familiar bed at the end of a long day. Chicken noodle soup and ginger ale. Security and ease. And she had missed him. Every day. But she was also frustrated that he was here without her permission, that he felt ownership over June, so much so that he hadn't told her he was coming. And now he was looking at her in a way she hadn't consented to either.

They still held hands. "Matty . . ."

"Confession time," he said. June tensed, fearing what he might say or, God forbid, do. "Remember when you found that stack of Sweet Valley High books in my room, and I said they were my cousin Sarah's? They were mine." He let go of June's hand, the flash in his eyes gone, the space between them light and airy again. "I've always had a twin fantasy. Those books were as good as porn for me."

June grabbed a pillow and smacked him in the head with it. He laughed, his dirty blond hair mussed from the impact.

June hugged the pillow to her chest. She was overreacting and over-emoting and taking it out on Matt, who had showed up out of the kindness of his heart to see her, to be with her. Lennox didn't give June that reverence, and she'd be damned if she took out her frustration on Matt.

"Are you going to give me my present or what?" she asked.

Matt produced a can of Skyline Original Chili, hot dogs, buns, shredded cheese, an onion, and mustard. "I was worried the hot dogs might go bad on the flight, but then I realized they have an expiration date of fucking never, so we're probably safe."

Matt had brought not only cookies from her favorite bakery but the complete ingredients for a Skyline Chili Coney dog, her all-time favorite food. The gesture was so thoughtful. So *her*. The cookies and Coneys and Jared Leto and Butt-Crack Jim—being with Matt was like being with an encyclopedia of her life. He was the ultimate reference on all things June Merriweather.

Almost all things . . .

She was being ridiculous and overly sensitive to think something had passed between them moments earlier, and it wasn't fair to Matt. None of what June had done for the past few years was fair to Matt, and yet she saw no other way if she wanted to preserve their relationship. And she did, with all her heart.

June wiped a tear from her eye and grabbed Matt in a ferocious hug. He had flown across the Atlantic Ocean with groceries in his bag, all to make June happy.

"I missed you, Matty," she whispered into his ear.

When they separated, Matt said, "I have one last thing." He pulled a red sweatshirt from his bag and held it up. Across the front, in capital letters, it read *SOMEBODY IN CINCINNATI LOVES ME*. A large white heart sat below the words. "I saw it at the airport and thought it was fucking tacky as hell . . . perfect for you."

June laughed and took the sweatshirt. "I love it."

"Well, the words couldn't be truer. There are a lot of people in Cincinnati who love you. Just in case you need reminding." He ran a hand through his disheveled hair.

Inspiration struck June. "Don't move. Leave your hand exactly where it is." She grabbed her camera and quickly snapped a picture of Matt looking like a teen heartthrob. "Now all you need is a leather jacket and a chain wallet."

"Don't forget a Rage Against the Machine T-shirt." Matt inspected the camera. "Where the hell did you get that?"

"Someone in town was giving it away and offered it to me." She popped another piece of cookie into her mouth and put the camera away.

Matt smiled, clearly satisfied with himself. "Don't eat those too quickly. I only brought six."

June put the sweatshirt and bakery box in the top drawer of her dresser and grabbed a towel.

"What are you doing?" Matt lounged back in bed, arm behind his head, yawning.

"I need to shower before work."

"Work . . . right. My body has no idea what time it is."

"Take a nap."

"No. I need coffee. I'm coming with you."

"You'll be bored out of your mind."

"I have a book. I'll just hide in a corner and read."

June smiled. "That's so something Jared Leto would do. Seriously, you should see some of Scotland while you're here. Take a walk or hike or something."

"I don't need exercise. A library card works just as well to pick up girls."

"I thought your dancing career was taking off."

"That's not exercise. That's foreplay. And I didn't come here to see Scotland. I came to see you. Plus, I've got research to do." He dug through his messenger bag and pulled out another book. "I figured we could start planning. I earmarked a few places already."

June inspected Matt's guidebook to Paris. "Do these places sell key chains and snow globes?"

"Good to see you're still as tacky as ever. I was worried you'd changed on me."

June registered the offhand comment, but she let it slide, flipping to an earmarked page. "Paris catacombs. Sounds creepy."

Matt got out of bed and stood next to June, reading the book over her shoulder. "There are bones of over six million people down there, and they have tours that run at night. I thought we could get all banged up on wine and bring your old Ouija board. Commune with the ghost of Jean Valjean."

"Who?"

"Jesus, June. Read a fucking book."

She whacked Matt in the arm with the guidebook and then turned to another page. "Sacré-Coeur. I like this one. Sounds less scary."

"It's got one of the best views of Paris. When the weather's nice, people watch the sunset from the steps."

June noticed the book's worn binding. "You've thought a lot about this."

"Well, I've had a lot of time to think lately." Matt took the guidebook back, his fingers connecting with June's. In fifteen years of friendship, they had touched millions of times, but it had never felt intentional like this. Like a message. But Matt stuffed the book back into his messenger bag as if nothing had happened.

"Just promise me that when you're done working, we'll do something fun," Matt said.

"Promise."

On her way to the bathroom, Matt stopped her again, grabbing her sweatshirt from the drawer and tossing it to June. "Don't forget to wear this." As June caught it deftly, he added, "One more confession."

Too much had occurred in too small a time. June was unbalanced, irrational, and confused, on the verge of doing something stupid. She hugged her towel to her chest like a shield and said, "Let me guess. You never *really* tutored Angela House in trig."

A pregnant pause sat between them before Matt threw his hands up in the air. "You got me. How'd you know?"

"It was during your hickey phase. Angela wore turtlenecks for a month straight."

"I loved my hickey phase. I should bring it back." He climbed back on the bed and lay down, one arm behind his head. "OK. Now it's your turn. Tell me something good. You owe me."

June's confessional list was long, and none were stories she wanted to tell Matt. "I'm giving you a kidney," she said. "That's payment enough."

~

Matt sat reading without complaint at a corner table in the Thistle Stop Café. June couldn't help noticing how out of place he looked with his navy-blue wool peacoat, worn leather messenger bag, and gray scarf. In Knockmoral, Matt was a wing-tip oxford among muddy Wellington boots. June had always considered herself as Matt's match—gold and pink, green and royal blue, purple and coral—but seeing him among the customers at the café, how their gaze lingered on Matt, eyeing the out-of-place stranger, the scene felt dissonant. Floral print with polka dots. Leopard pattern and plaid. Black pants and a brown sweater. She no longer felt the deep fusion with Matt that she always had before, which should have made her sad. June loved being linked to Matt, loved being constantly at his side when so many other girls came and went, loved being thought of as a pair—Matt and June, June and Matt—but she couldn't conjure sadness now. All she felt was wonder. Almost a sense of pride at her independence. She had never considered her interconnectedness to Matt as a hindrance, but maybe it was camouflage. Distance had made it impossible for June to hide, and now she wondered if she could ever go back to matching him so fiercely. Had June changed too much? Did she even want to go back?

She kept Matt's coffee cup full and a plate of biscuits within arm's reach. She had just delivered him a hamburger and sat down at his table with her own salmon sandwich when Amelia blew into the café in a frenzy.

"I was hoping I'd find you." She plopped down in the seat next to June, sweat on her brow. June had never seen Amelia move faster than a stroll. Amelia introduced herself to Matt, then turned to June and said, "Max is missing. He got out this morning, and we can't find him anywhere. I've been driving around for hours, but there's no sign of him."

"Max?" Matt said. "The feral animal?"

Amelia ignored him. "I need your help, June. I'm worried something's happened to him."

"Of course." June stood from the table.

"June can't." Matt placed his hand on top of June's. "She's working."

Amelia eyed their physical contact. "I'm sure my uncle won't mind."

June pulled her hand free as Hamish came out of the kitchen wiping his hands on his apron, a red bandana holding back his hair. "What won't I mind?"

"We have a problem, Uncle." Amelia explained the lost-dog situation.

"Course June can go," Hamish said. "This place is as dead as a doornail after the festival. I'll be fine. Might even close early. Go on. Get out of here."

"I still don't understand why June needs to find this rabid dog," Matt said to Amelia.

June didn't want to get into the specifics. She was already grabbing her rain jacket and Wellingtons. "He knows me, Matty."

"Fine. Then I'll come, too." Matt started to collect his items from the table.

Amelia stopped him. "You don't want to spend your time searching for a *rabid dog* in the rain."

"I don't mind—"

"No, she's right," June said as she slipped out of her running shoes and into her rubber boots. Matt wasn't dressed for the weather. His shoes were leather and his coat, while warm and wool, was not waterproof.

Amelia picked up the book Matt had been reading. "There's a brilliant used bookstore a few towns over. One of the best in Scotland. I'll take you there while June looks for Max. I promise it'll be more enjoyable than traipsing around a soggy bog for hours."

At the mention of the bookstore, Matt softened. June played it to her advantage. "I bet they have a copy of Eliot's *Four Quartets*," she said. It was the one book Matt collected multiple copies of, including his prized edition from East Village Books in New York City. "You *need* one from Scotland."

Matt whispered to June, "Are you sure?"

June felt relieved at being able to answer honestly. "Yes. Very sure."

"Grand!" Amelia took Matt by the arm, linked her own arm through his, and pulled him toward her with a wide smile. Matt seemed pleased with the turn of events, being held so close by a gorgeous woman. "We'll meet at the pub tonight," Amelia said, pulling Matt to the door. "Don't worry, June. I'll take good care of him."

And then they were gone. June hated to admit that she was relieved.

"Do you know where to look?" Hamish asked.

June pulled up her hood. "I have an idea." But she knew exactly where to go.

TWENTY-ONE

The path along the waterfront where Max and June often ran was empty this afternoon. Puddles of snowmelt and rain gathered on the pavement. June jogged as best she could in her Wellingtons, yelling for Max. So far, she had seen no sign of him.

She was following their usual route, thinking Max would go somewhere familiar, but the longer she followed the path with no success, the more June worried. She loved that dog. The hours they had spent running together were some of her best in Scotland. He felt more like a friend than an animal, almost as if he were June's dog, too. She was used to the familiar jangle of Max's collar and tags, the trotting sound of his paws on the concrete, the way he'd look up at her, tongue hanging out of the side of his mouth, a huge smile on his face, as if running six miles was nothing for him. Always content, Max made life feel simple. With him at her side while she ran, June's mind would calm. Seeing his serene face, her problems felt far off—pointless almost.

June picked up her pace. She needed to find Max before it got dark, which was quickly approaching. A quarter mile ahead, the path rounded a bend and headed into acres of farmland sectioned off by a stone wall. Maybe Max was frolicking in the open fields, scaring birds and digging holes, just as he liked. As June approached the bend, she heard the footsteps. Maybe another runner had seen Max and could point June in the right direction. But as she rounded the bend, June came face to face with a panting Lennox. She halted, as did he. They stood on the path staring at each other, out of breath and wet from rain and sweat.

"What are you doing here, Peanut?" Lennox's tone was accusatory.

"What do you think I'm doing here? Looking for Max."

"Go home. Get warm. It'll be dark soon. I don't need another problem on my hands."

"No."

"I'm not in the mood for your stubbornness." Lennox brushed past June and walked further down the path, yelling Max's name. A leash dangled from his back pocket.

June followed. "Well, I'm not in the mood for your bossiness."

Lennox rounded on June and growled. "Just turn your bloody arse around and go home, goddammit!"

"You're not the only one who cares about Max!" June yelled in his face.

At that, Lennox physically deflated, his usual commanding presence wilting before June's eyes. His shoulders slumped, but it was Lennox's helpless eyes that gutted June. She felt as if someone had punched her in the stomach, stolen her air.

"I'm sorry for yelling, Peanut," Lennox said softly. "It's just . . ."

June felt his hesitation, knew the feeling intimately. "It's OK. You can tell me."

"After my parents died . . ." Lennox looked down at his empty hands. "A friend recommended that I volunteer at the animal shelter. She thought it might be helpful for me to walk dogs and play with the bloody cats. I told her I hate cats. Still do." He glanced at June with a half-hearted smile. She wanted to touch him, hold his brokenhearted face between her hands and wipe clean the pain from his body. "I was terrified my first day."

"You, terrified?"

Lennox began to regain his stature, the heaviness lessening as he talked. "I could barely get through a day back then without wanting to rip someone's head off. I was so angry and miserable. I thought for sure I wouldn't make it an hour before they fired me. But that's the thing about dogs. They don't care about your past. They don't judge you when you've had a bad day or month or bloody year. They still love you even when you're a complete shitbag."

"You're not a shitbag."

"I promise you. I was." Lennox ran a hand through his damp hair. The rain had stopped. He walked over to the stone wall and leaned against it. June followed hesitantly, carefully, desperate for more but not wanting to press him. "I still remember the day Max showed up at the shelter. He was thin, his ear and neck were badly cut, and he didn't want anyone to touch him. He just crouched in the corner, shaking, ready to pounce on anyone who got too close. And I thought . . . I know how this dog feels. I went to the shelter every damn day after that. I just had to see him. I had to make sure he was OK. Slowly he got used to seeing me. And then one day, I walked through the door and he ran right up to me. Practically jumped into my arms. I swear that damn animal smiled for the first time in his life, and I almost cried."

"You almost cried?"

"I thought I could never be trusted to care for anything or anyone again, Peanut." Lennox took a breath. "There was no way I was letting anyone else have him. I needed to make sure he was protected. That no one would ever hurt him again. So I adopted him." Lennox bowed his head, curls falling over his forehead. "He's the reason I joined Fire and Rescue. He made me believe I was a better person than I actually am. That I could be different if I tried hard enough. I never want to let him down. Damn it, I can't lose him now."

"Look at me." June risked touching his face, lifting his chin with her fingers, feeling the stubble there. "We are *not* losing him. We'll find him. I promise."

Lennox took June's hand and placed it on his thigh, palm up. He ran his fingers gently down hers, like a feather dusting the surface. "He lets me play with his paws. He'll just lie there, so calm, so different from the dog I first met. It's amazing what love does to us." Lennox's touch was hypnotic. Stroke after stroke June felt herself more lost in him, in the mossy, damp smell around them, the thick air between their bodies that seemed to hold them encased in a protective, intoxicating bubble.

Lennox brushed his fingertip along the inside of June's wrist until he found her pulse. The past twenty-four hours dissolved. All June's anger, all her frustration, all her embarrassment at being tossed aside disappeared, and it was just Lennox and June, sitting in the misty Scottish countryside at dusk, inches apart. She wanted to close the gap, surrender herself to him, forget the past and make love right there, unguarded, like they'd never hurt again.

Lennox's eyes floated up from June's hand, slowly, as if he were taking her in inch by inch. She knew they would kiss. It would be physically impossible not to. Static crackled between them as she waited, impatiently, achingly. She wanted to feel Lennox's wet tongue on hers. She wanted his breath on her lips, his hands on her breasts. She wanted Lennox to take her by the hips and pull her close, relieve her of the tension she couldn't shake.

But his eyes stopped. Hot static turned to angry friction.

June's coat had fallen open, revealing the sweatshirt Matt had given her: *SOMEBODY IN CINCINNATI LOVES ME.*

She closed the coat, but it was too late. Lennox stood, paced. He pulled the leash from his pocket and wound it tight around his hands. Just as June was about to explain the stupid sweatshirt, they heard the distant sound of paws on pavement.

"Max?" Lennox looked around frantically. "Where in bloody hell are you?"

And then Max came bounding down the path, tongue dangling from the side of his mouth, as if he'd had the best day of his life. The dog was as happy as June had ever seen him; he ran right up to Lennox and sat at his feet. Lennox knelt, frantically petting and nuzzling Max while chastising him for running away. Max licked Lennox on the cheek repeatedly, and Lennox's anger melted away.

Then Max lumbered over to June, expecting more love. June obliged. "You're not supposed to go running without me, buddy." She scratched behind his ears. "You know that."

"Come on, Peanut. I'll take you home." Lennox hooked the leash onto Max. "I'm parked just down the road."

June then realized how odd it was that she and Lennox had run into each other. Of all the places in Knockmoral, why did he come to that path? She asked him.

Without a glance at June, Lennox said, "I thought he might be looking for you."

~

After a hot shower, a change of clothes, and some much-needed food, June had walked to the pub with Angus, David, and Eva. Lennox was nowhere to be seen. June doubted he'd come after their awkward, silent car ride home and brisk goodbye.

It didn't matter, anyway. June had given herself a pep talk in the shower. For the next few days, her priority was Matt. He deserved that. Her emotions had been clouded by Max's temporary disappearance, but nothing had changed. Lennox had still kicked her out of his bed the moment he was done with her. She may not have heeded his warning then, but she wouldn't forget it now.

June had deserted Matt for reasons she felt guilty about. Even if his sudden presence would have landed awkwardly at the best of times, and even if her mind was preoccupied with Lennox, it was unfair to avoid Matt. Her feelings and problems could not infringe on his visit. He had traveled so far and brought June nothing but love and gifts.

Anderson's Pub was bustling when Matt and Amelia walked in, shopping bags in hand. Eva waved at them as June gathered her confidence. Matt sat down next to her, and Amelia took her own seat.

"Nice to see you again, Matt," Eva said. "I see you did some shopping."

Matt set his bags at the foot of his chair with a thud. "I have no fucking control in a used bookstore." He slipped out of his coat and scarf and draped them on the chair.

"We stopped at a few other stores as well," Amelia said. "I also thought it necessary he go home with plenty of souvenirs." She pulled a blue, green, and red tartan balmoral cap from one of the bags and fitted it to Matt's head, the pom-pom slightly askew. "Doesn't he look brilliant?"

Matt whispered to June, "I thought you'd appreciate the tackiness."

"I do." June honked the pom-pom.

"He looks like a fucking wanker if you ask me," Angus said curtly, elbows on the table, his sleeves rolled halfway up his arms, exposing the Celtic cross tattoo on his muscled forearm.

"Ignore Angus," Amelia said. "He's just jealous. He's never actually seen the inside of a bookstore."

Amelia passed Matt a pint, but Angus intercepted the beer and gulped down most of it. He passed the last few sips to Matt, who did not pick it up. "So, Yank, what do you do in America?"

"I'm in college. English lit major."

"Are you a poof?" Angus asked.

"*Angus.*" Amelia jabbed him in the side, hard.

"Don't mind our obtuse friend," David said. "His vocabulary is as limited as his brain cells."

"What? No point in beating around the bush." Angus raised his hands in apology. "Not saying there's anything wrong if you are."

"No, I'm not gay," Matt said flatly. "I actually plan to go into civil rights law so I can sue small-minded, imperceptive pricks who think they can throw around derogatory terms like fucking confetti at a gay-pride parade and get away with it." Matt took June's half-drunk beer and downed it in a single gulp. Eva choked on hers. Matt removed the balmoral and put it back in the bag. "Looks like we need more drinks. I'll buy."

"I'll come with you." Amelia stood from the table, glaring at Angus, who watched heatedly as the two retreated to the bar. Angus grabbed the edge of the table, the muscles in his arms taut, his attention never leaving Amelia and Matt.

The whole scene surprised June. She had been accepted so easily when she arrived. But Angus was clearly on edge, Amelia was being overly attentive to Matt, Eva was enjoying a creative feast for her novel, and all June wanted was to hold her life together until Matt was safely on his plane home.

When Matt and Amelia came back with pints for everyone, June was quick to offer a suggestion, in hopes of salvaging the conversation. "Let's play a game, Never Have I Ever. Everyone knows how to play that. We each state an experience or action we've potentially never done, and those of us who have done it, drink."

"Are you sure that's a good idea?" Angus asked. "Your Yank might be hiding something."

"I'm a goddamn open book," Matt said. "June knows that."

"Let's start with an easy one," June said with forced enthusiasm. "Never have I ever had a one-night stand." Everyone at the table drank. June took an extra-long gulp to calm her nerves.

Eva went next. "Never have I ever had sex in a public place."

Angus, Eva, and Matt all drank. Stories followed of the hazards of sex on the beach, and Eva told a naughty story about a backstage rendezvous at the Glastonbury Festival three years ago.

The table fell into a bantering cadence of "never have I ever" statements and accompanying stories. Pints quickly diminished. The tension eased. With each sip of beer, June relaxed. Angus and Matt even laughed a few times. June just needed to keep the night on track.

"Never have I ever skinny-dipped," Eva said.

Everyone drank. Matt eyed June, intrigued, as she sipped and shrugged. "Last year. Phi Gamma Delta date party."

"I knew I didn't trust those fuckers," Matt said.

June rolled her eyes. "Might I remind you of Sasha Trager and the bathtub, sophomore year?"

"That was different," he said.

"How?"

Matt smiled. "You're supposed to be naked in a bathtub."

Amelia held up her beer. "I've got one. I've got one. Never have I ever . . . kissed someone of the same sex."

Angus crossed his arms over his chest exaggeratedly, smiling at Matt, who also, pointedly, did not take a drink. June, David, and Eva did.

"Who?" Matt begged June.

"Freshman year. A girl in my dorm. I just wanted to see what it was like."

"And . . ." Angus enquired, leaning forward.

"All I really remember is that she tasted like a raspberry Slurpee."

"Is that why you get one every time we're at 7-Eleven?" Matt said.

June shrugged. "Maybe."

"I can't believe you never told me that."

"Maybe you don't know your lass as well as you think you do," Angus offered loudly.

"Maybe you should shut the—"

Under the table, June squeezed Matt's thigh as hard as she could.

"OK. Who's next?" Amelia asked.

Angus said, "Peanut, you're up."

"Who's Peanut?" Matt asked.

A surly smile grew on Angus's face. "Have you not heard that story either?"

June could have strangled him. Why couldn't he just leave Matt alone? What was he trying to pull? She would rail at Angus later; right now, June needed a distraction. She pulled out her camera. "Picture time. Everyone squeeze together."

She snapped a picture.

Matt took the camera, handed it to Amelia, and requested a shot of just him and June. He pulled June toward him aggressively. "We need to document our first international trip."

But when Amelia said "smile," somewhat unenthusiastically, June was unable to. *Our* first international trip? Scotland was hers and hers alone. Matt had interrupted that, without her permission, and now he was trying to take over her experience as his own.

Or . . .

Was Matt just being a best friend, documenting a significant moment in their lives together? June's oversensitivity was rearing its ugly head again.

"What a cute couple," Angus said, clearly not meaning it.

June chuckled. "Couple? That would never happen."

"It wouldn't?" Amelia asked, surprised.

"No way."

"Why not?" Matt asked.

"For starters, you haven't been faithful to a single girlfriend. Ever."

Matt spoke quietly. "That's because they didn't mean anything to me."

"And that's supposed to make it better?" June asked.

Matt leaned so close to June, she could smell the hoppy beer on his breath. "I would never cheat on you."

Like he and June had potential to be a couple? It was laughable. Impossible. This whole situation felt that way to her. Matt in Knockmoral, the gifts, the whispers, the clinging, the awkward pulse between them when he touched her. None of it made sense. How had her life turned upside down so quickly?

The air in the pub was stifling and thick. Too many people in too little a space. June stood up, feeling choked by the stagnant air. "I need to go to the bathroom." She raced toward the door, aching for fresh night air. If she could just breathe and wipe the cloudiness brought on by beer and hypersensitivity, then maybe she could see things clearly. Feel clearly.

But just as she reached the door, it opened, and Lennox stepped into the pub, throwing June further off balance. Her head spun, her ears buzzed, and as she took a step back, her knees threatened to give way. She was going to faint, right there, onto the grimy pub floor, and then she would have to explain why.

Lennox grabbed her around the waist. "Jesus, Peanut, you're white as a ghost."

His words barely came through the fuzz clouding June's head. With Lennox's grasp on her, images from their night together rushed back to her. His hands between her thighs. His mouth on hers. The weight of his body above her as he rocked. The burn of desire for more of him, and the ecstasy of release.

"June, what the hell is going on?" Matt's voice broke the spell, and too quickly, Lennox let June go.

The two men stood facing each other.

"She doesn't look well," Lennox said flatly.

"What the hell, June? Are you alright?" Matt pulled her close, away from Lennox. He touched her cheek.

The change was disorienting—two bodies, wholly different. June felt her clammy forehead. "It's just stuffy in here."

Lennox made his way further into the pub.

"Wait. Did you find your animal?" Matt called to him, still holding June.

"Aye." Lennox made no mention of June's presence that afternoon.

"I'm glad. June was worried." Matt's grip tightened. "I've got her from here." He ushered June over to an empty barstool, set her down, and touched her forehead like a parent checking on a fever, regularly glancing over his shoulder at Lennox.

"I'm fine, Matty."

"You did me a favor, June. I was about to commit first-degree murder. Angus is a fucking asshole."

"He's not an asshole."

"He's a one-dimensional blunt object from a small town, who thinks he's better than everyone. He hates that I'm here with you."

"Angus hates that you spent the day with Amelia. He's madly in love with her."

"Then he can back the fuck off. She's hot, for sure, and in the past, I definitely would have indulged in a horizontal refreshment with her, but not now. Can we just sit here, away from that fucker? Just you and me."

Matt ordered two more pints, and for the next hour, he and June sat at the bar. June tried to focus on him. She kept eye contact as best she could. She responded and nodded and hmm-ed at the appropriate times, and she thought she had done a good job of acting engaged, until Matt touched her leg.

Her attention had drifted to Lennox, who sat at the table with her housemates, the seat next to him empty.

"June. Are you OK?" Matt asked.

"I'm fine." She took a long sip of beer, wishing it wasn't lukewarm.

"How well do you know Lennox?" Matt's voice was flat and unemotional.

"Why?"

"Never mind." Matt put his hand on June's, again asserting a touch that felt anything but genuine. "We should take a trip to New York City this summer."

"What?"

"It's the perfect time. Before we graduate and all hell breaks loose. We've always wanted to go together."

Had they? June didn't remember that. Angus ambled over to them then, empty pint glass in hand. He put it down on the bar, right between Matt and June. "Are you two done yammering? Come back to the table. We've got more games to play."

"We'll stay here," Matt said. "But thanks."

"Is he holding you hostage?" Angus asked June. "Do you need me to save you?"

Matt stood up. "She doesn't need saving, especially from me."

Angus grew two inches instantly. "I'll let the lass answer that question."

The men were too close, too postured for June's liking. Lennox had gotten up and was now approaching slowly.

"You don't need to worry about me, Angus," June stated.

"I'm just looking out for you, Peanut."

"Jesus, fuck off," Matt said. "She doesn't need you to look out for her."

"What did you say?" Angus was tense and cold.

"Matt." June pulled on his arm. "Let's just go."

Matt shrugged out of June's grasp. "Fuck. Off. Was that slow enough for your dull-witted brain to follow?"

What happened next transpired in slow motion. Angus pulled his arm back, fist clenched, and aimed at Matt's face. June saw taut muscles, the bulge of the tattoo cross on Angus's forearm, the veins running down his arms like vines. None of this was supposed to happen. If June hadn't left Matt with Amelia, Angus wouldn't be jealous. If she had been honest with Matt years ago, she wouldn't be in Scotland right now. The list of June's transgressions was growing. In a moment, a pub fight would further swell the list. She needed to control the situation.

June threw herself between Matt and Angus before the whole scene could unravel. What she didn't take into account was that a man intent on punching another human being can rarely stop himself. Physics and ego prevail.

June had never been punched before. In fact, she had never been hit, not even slapped, though she had seen the desire in her brother's face more than a few times. Angus's fist was inches away from knocking June square on the cheek when, at the last minute, his body turned, held back by Lennox. Angus spun, narrowly avoiding contact, but he lost his balance, and his shoulder collided into June with the force of a boulder. She flew forward and fell, her head hitting the wood floor.

"Jesus Christ, Peanut!" Lennox was at her side, though June had no idea how he got there. She was shaking, and her head hurt. She touched the tender spot on her forehead to check for blood. Thank God, there was none.

"June, look at me." Matt knelt beside her. She bit back tears. He snapped at Angus. "What the fuck is wrong with you?"

"Me? You think I did this on purpose?"

"You're a fucking thug. I wouldn't put it past you."

"It was your face I was aiming for, Yank. I would never hurt her."

"Angus, stop," Lennox said through tight teeth.

Angus knelt over June, regret boldly written across his face. "You know that, Peanut. You know I would never hurt you."

"Why do you keep calling her Peanut?" Matt exploded.

Lennox lashed out, shoving Matt so hard that he fell onto his ass with a thud. Lennox was over him instantly, holding a startled Matt by the shirt, his free hand balled into a fist. "Get the fuck away—" Lennox growled, pulling Matt closer, but Amelia stopped her brother.

"It's alright, Len," she said calmly. "Let him go."

Lennox released Matt's shirt. The pub had gone quiet, a crowd gathered around the scene. Lennox stepped back from Matt and forced open his clenched fist.

Rebekah Crane

Angus stepped to Matt, who was still on the floor, shocked. "The only reason your girlfriend is alive, Yank, is because we saved her goddamn life when she almost died from eating a peanut."

Matt climbed to his feet, brushing his pants off. June was still in shock. "You never told me that."

"Sounds like there's a lot she doesn't tell you, mate." Angus slapped Matt on the back, too hard, and Matt had to catch himself on a chair.

June could barely feel her body, let alone find the words to explain.

Matt took money from his pocket and placed it on the bar. "Fuck this. I'm out of here." And he stormed off.

June tried to rise, but the pain in her head wouldn't allow it. She finally fumbled to her feet and grabbed at her swimming head.

"Peanut." Lennox took her arm to steady her.

She shoved him away. "Don't." She thought she might puke. "Why did you do that?"

"I just . . ." But Lennox fell short of words.

"What is wrong with you? He didn't do anything."

June needed to find Matt, and quickly. She needed out of the pub and away from all the eyes. She needed aspirin. She needed to lie down. But as she tried to leave, Lennox stopped her.

"I need to look at your head, Peanut. You might have a concussion."

June pulled away. "How many times do I have to tell you—leave me alone."

She burst through the pub door into the cold night air, where Matt was pacing the sidewalk, eyes downcast, focused. When she called his name, he stopped.

"I'm sorry I didn't tell you about the peanut but—"

Matt grabbed her. He picked her off the ground and held her tightly to him. Warmth returned, calm followed, and June's heavy head fell to his shoulder.

"I can't believe I almost lost you," Matt said. June clung to him as if he were a buoy in the middle of the ocean, something steady in the chaos. "Were you scared?" Matt whispered into her neck.

"Terrified."

He set her down and took her face in his hands. They were just inches apart, so close she could feel his heat even in the cold night.

"Fuck, June . . ." He rubbed his thumb over her cheek. She couldn't calibrate where she was or what had happened. Panic, pain, and confusion muddled her mind.

"You forgot your—"

Matt and June turned, his hand falling from her face, to find David carrying their coats and bags, and June's camera.

"I'm sorry," David stammered. "I'll just—" He motioned toward the pub.

"No. Thank you." June collected the items from David.

"Are you sure Lennox shouldn't . . ." David trailed off.

"No." June turned to Matt. "I'm fine. Let's just go."

"Then I bid you both *adieu*." David bowed and added, "'This is the very ecstasy of love, whose violent property foredoes itself and leads the will to desperate undertakings.'"

June and Matt left David outside the pub and walked back to the inn. After two Advil tablets and a lot of water, June began to feel better. She and Matt climbed into bed, facing each other, and fell asleep. Two sides of a single clam shell. But June awoke multiple times that night, her head aching. She tossed and turned, trying to find a position to make the pain go away, but nothing worked.

June replayed the night over and over, like a bad movie, until one thing became abundantly clear. Matt Tierney may be lying in her bed, but he was not the same Matt she had left in the States. He wanted something from June. What exactly, she wasn't sure, but whatever it was, it terrified her.

TWENTY-TWO

Matt stood in front of the unicorn statue in Falcon Square in Inverness. June snapped a picture of him. The day was cool but sunny, which meant that every person in the Highlands was outside. People crowded the square, clutching shopping bags or sitting on restaurant patios, bundled in down jackets and hats, but basking in the sun.

"Between this unicorn, fairies, and skirts, I'm rethinking my stereotype of the Scots," Matt commented.

"People who call them skirts usually end up kilt." June took a picture of two children running around the square.

"Very punny."

"You have to admit, it's beautiful here."

Matt nodded. "It's nice."

Nice? Matt was never so simple with his opinions. Future lawyers never were. If you asked what he thought of the falafel he ate for lunch, you'd get a diatribe about the gaseous nature of the chickpea. "But . . ." June begged.

"But nothing," he said. "It's great."

"It's great," she mocked. "You must have more to say than that."

"I'm just taking it all in."

At June's request, Hamish had given her the past two days off, and in that time, she and Matt had spent every second together, drama-free. No arguments. No contrasting opinions. No snarky commentary about the Brits' bad teeth, or their propensity for monochromatic food, or how the men wore too-tight jeans. Matt couldn't walk down the street in Columbus without remarking on the cracks in the pavement, but for two days, he hadn't said a critical word. And while that, and the quickly healing bump on her head, should have made June happy, it only made her more anxious. Matt may not have been sharing his opinions, but he had them. He was hiding them for a reason, and June feared the moment they would overflow.

"Well, I for one find carpet in pubs rather charming, don't you?" June said. Matt agreed too quickly. "And the tartan curtains. The Scots have really embraced the decorating diversity of flannel. Oh, and the coffee. Maybe the best I've ever had."

Finally, Matt broke. "First of all, flannel should have died in the nineties with Kurt Cobain. Second of all, carpet in pubs is definitely a health-code violation. And third of all, lukewarm brown water isn't fucking coffee. It's sewer water. I'd rather drink tea. And I hate tea."

Finally, a glimpse of raw honesty, the first June had seen from Matt in two days. She linked arms with him as they walked toward the train station. "Just because I like it here, doesn't mean you have to."

"I'm just surprised you like it as much as you do."

"Why?"

"You hate rain."

"I don't hate rain."

"In high school when it rained, you made me drop you off at the front door of the school so your hair wouldn't get all messed up."

"That was a teen insecurity issue, not the weather."

"And the clothes."

"What about them?"

"Forget about the fucking tartan obsession. Track suits and soccer jerseys?"

"Football jerseys."

"Look." Matt took both of June's hands. "I get the charm of this place. It's very Tolkien Shire-like."

"You're such a nerd."

"It's true," Matt said. "Everyone wants to live in the Shire because it's quaint and charming and there are small people smoking weed and drinking beer and they all look so happy. And then you realize the reason they drink and smoke weed is because they're bored. And they're bored because they're so far removed from the rest of the world and all anyone really wants is to be Frodo or Sam and get the fuck out of the Shire. Not to mention the inbred nature that makes them small, with disproportionately hairy feet. You really want that for your children?"

"You're ridiculous." June laughed.

"I just think you like it so much because you don't know any better. When we see Paris, you'll feel differently."

June swallowed her response, not wanting another fight, but Matt's condescension was clear, and it grated on her. "Let's head this way." She pulled him toward a row of shops.

"You're so predictable." Matt smiled. "You just can't resist a tacky souvenir shop, can you?"

"You need tartan underwear to match your balmoral cap."

Matt wrapped his arm around June's shoulders as they walked. "I wonder if they have tartan thongs."

And with that, she forcefully held her frustration at bay. She found the tackiest shop on Academy Street, its exterior draped in plaid and Scottish flags, displaying postcards of sheep and men with flipped kilts mooning the camera. Inside, the store smelled like cheap plastic and cigarettes. June scanned shelf after shelf of spoons, plates, snow globes, calendars, stuffed animals, and fluorescent T-shirts individually wrapped in plastic. There were three more racks of postcards. June spun the circular stand, examining the images.

Matt picked up a figurine of Mel Gibson as William Wallace, its face painted blue.

"Even that's too tacky for me," June said. She pulled a red-and-blue-patterned scarf from a rack and wrapped it around Matt's neck.

"But is it tacky enough?"

"You're too hot for tacky. You can't pull it off."

Matt took the scarf from his neck and wrapped it around June's waist, pulling her into him. "You think I'm hot?"

Their hips touched. June shoved him away before she got uncomfortable. "As if you need another girl telling you that. I've smelled your morning breath. It's the great equalizer."

Matt cupped his hand in front of his mouth and checked his breath. "Smells fine to me."

June moved to another part of the store. She breathed. Moments like that threw her off most. The touching. The flirting.

She picked up a stuffed Nessie, the Loch Ness monster. "Found mine."

She made her way to the cashier, but Matt intercepted her. "Are you going to get the scarf?" He took Nessie out of her hands and placed it on a shelf. "I have a better idea." He dragged June out of the store.

June almost tripped keeping up. "What are we doing?"

Matt came to a stop a few storefronts down. "This is the souvenir we should get."

A sign welcomed walk-ins and tourists: THISTLE DO NICELY TATTOO AND PIERCINGS. Displayed in the window were illustrations of Chinese symbols, dragons, fairies, and, of course, thistles.

"You can't be serious, Matty."

"Dead serious."

"But you don't even like tattoos."

"That's not true," he said. "I don't like *some* tattoos. Barbed wire. Angel's wings. Tributes to dead grandparents. And recently, Celtic crosses. But we wouldn't do that." June watched the man inside working on a client. She heard the buzzing of the needle. "It's a souvenir we can't lose or break. Every time we look at our tattoos, we remember our first trip abroad together."

So much of that sat sourly with June. For starters, the word "trip." It meant a stumble, a break, a gap in real life. Spring break in Cancun. Florida to vacation with her grandparents. Scotland may have begun that way, but it wasn't just a mere gap anymore. And why did Matt seem hell-bent on claiming it? He was a visitor, not a traveling companion. "Why would you want a permanent reminder of Scotland? You don't even like it here."

"I want a permanent reminder of *you*."

June backed away from the tattoo parlor. "We should head to the bus station. If we miss the last bus, we'll be stuck here for the night."

"And that would be such a bad thing?"

"I want to drop this film at the store before it closes."

The setting sun painted the Scottish Highlands in orange and pink during the ride back to Knockmoral. June didn't care what Matt said. This place wasn't the small Shire he depicted. It may not be a big city, but it offered just as much. The fact that Matt didn't see that annoyed June. The more time she spent with him, the more she dreamed of getting away from him. For over a month, she'd longed for Matt to be physically close, and now that he was, June wanted distance. She counted down the hours to Matt's departure.

Twilight had descended when the bus finally pulled into the depot. Matt and June walked to the convenience store on the high street so that June could drop off film and pick up her developed pictures. Ivan, the man behind the counter, set his newspaper down when June and Matt walked in the door. She knew him from the café: egg salad sandwich and tea with milk and honey.

"I was worried you left town," Ivan said. "Haven't seen you at the café the past few days."

"Jesus," Matt grumbled. "You take a shit in this town and everyone knows."

June bit her tongue and approached the counter. "I just took a few days off, but I'll be back next week." She gave him three rolls of film to develop.

Ivan handed June three packs of pictures. "My wife was wondering if you do weddings? Our daughter, Isla, is getting married this summer. We'll be needing a photographer."

Matt sidled up to the counter with Kit Kats and Smarties, Cadbury chocolate bars, and two tubes of Pringles. "Do you have Miller Lite?"

"No," Ivan said. "I'm sorry, I don't."

"Bud Light?" Matt pressed. Ivan shook his head. "Coors Light? Corona? Icehouse? PBR? Anything that comes chilled in a bottle or can?"

"Do you like Tennent's?" Ivan smiled. "Or Stella, maybe?"

"That one." Matt pointed. "Finally."

Ivan offered to retrieve the twelve pack. Matt leaned on the counter, annoyed.

"Why are you being so rude to Ivan?" June asked.

"I'm not."

"Yes, you are."

Matt gestured to the items on the counter. "I just thought it would be fun to get all our favorite things for our last night. And I know how much you like Miller Lite. That's all."

Ivan returned with the beer and bagged everything. June paid and thanked him. "I'll be back at work on Monday. Egg salad and tea waiting for you."

"And think about the—"

"Cheers, mate." Matt wrapped his arm around June and pulled her toward the door. She stopped him on the street outside, her own annoyance bubbling. "What?" Matt asked.

June didn't know how to articulate her frustration without causing another fight.

"Look. I'm sorry I didn't want to hang around chitchatting with the fucking cashier," Matt said, "but it's our last night and I want you all to myself. Is that so bad?"

It wasn't an unreasonable request. It was totally rational. Understandable.

"Not bad at all," June conceded.

"Good." Matt grabbed her by the arms and pulled her close. His thumbs pressed into her, like an imprint in concrete. "Because I want to eat Coneys and drink crappy beer, and when we're nice and drunk, I want to gorge on candy and eat an entire tube of Pringles. Just like high school."

June ignored Matt's grip on her. "Only if I get the sour cream and onion."

"Fine, but only because I love you."

Back at the inn, June dropped Matt at her room with their goodies before checking to make sure that the kitchen was clear of Angus. She then knocked on Eva's door. Eva answered, her blond hair pulled into a high ponytail, thick black glasses perched on her nose.

"Hiya," Eva said.

June didn't know what she was doing. She just knew she needed a break from Matt.

"Do you want to come in?" Eva asked.

"I don't want to interrupt."

"You're only interrupting a bad case of writer's block." Eva opened her door wider. A scented candle burned on her desk, filling the room with the smell of lavender.

"Smells good in here."

Eva blew out the candle. "It's supposed to calm me down when I write."

"I think I need one." June went directly to the window. Not a single light was on at Lennox's house.

"He's not home," Eva said.

June tried to act like she hadn't kept a constant eye on the house, like she wasn't consumed with thoughts and worries that proliferated and kept her up at night. She had been so angry and frazzled at the pub that she had aimed her pain and frustration at Lennox, but did he deserve it? June didn't know up from down lately. But every time Lennox's car was gone, she wondered where he was. Every time a light was on, she wondered what he might be doing. It was driving her mad.

"I thought maybe after Up Helly Aa . . ." Eva said.

"You thought wrong." June looked at the wall of stories. It had grown by two. "You still haven't found the right story?"

Eva shook her head. June pulled the most recent page from the wall. The prose was fresh and interesting. Even from the small amount she could read, June liked what it said. Eva was talented, and yet all of it was going to waste if she couldn't finish a story.

"Why not this one?"

"Because it's not right."

"But why not? It's beautiful so far."

"Who cares, if there isn't depth to back it up? Messy stories are more interesting than beautiful ones."

"But doesn't it drive you crazy? Couldn't you just force yourself to finish one? So what if it's not the right one, at least you'd have written a whole story."

"No, I would have wasted my time."

"And this isn't wasted time?" June gestured to all the papers on the wall.

"There's as much value in the word 'no' as there is in the word 'yes.' Maybe even more, because we, as women, so rarely say no."

June handed the paper back to Eva. "I better go before Matt finds Angus and World War III breaks out." She made her way to the door.

"So you made your choice?"

"I wasn't aware I had a choice to make."

"Darling," Eva said kindly, "anytime a 'yes' needs to be spoken, a 'no' comes before it."

June didn't want that burden. Her only goal was to get through one more night with Matt and see him safely away. But back in her room, Matt stood by June's bed, where her pictures were spread out in a collage. At the sound of June's entrance, Matt turned, a storm already brewing in his eyes.

"What are you doing?" June went to the bed, suddenly protective of her collection. She gathered the images into a pile, but it was too late. Lennox was the subject of too many for Matt not to notice.

"June," he said. "Enough is enough. Come home with me."

"Is that why you're here? To get me to leave with you?"

"Would that be so bad?"

How had June been so stupid? The gifts, his agreeable nature, even the flirting, it was all a part of a very calculated ruse. "Did my parents put you up to this?"

"No. They have no idea I'm here. But I'm sure they'd agree with me. It's time to go home, June."

"You don't know what my parents want."

"Maybe not, but I can guess. You abandoned them, just like you abandoned me."

June was flabbergasted. "What?"

"You abandoned me, June."

"So, this is all about you? That's not fair."

"No, June. What you're doing isn't fucking fair. You left me with no explanation. And I'm just supposed to let you go without a fight? Fuck that."

June bit the inside of her cheek, stopping a waterfall of confessions. She didn't want to argue with Matt, hadn't wanted any of this to happen in the first place—a dead brother, or the lies, or her guilt. And right now, she didn't want to see Matt Tierney. She had stuffed down her annoyance, stuffed down her frustration, played the part of a best friend, and Matt had been lying the entire time.

June felt the walls caving in on her. "I need to get out of here."

Matt blocked her path to the door, taking her by the arms. "After everything we've been through, you're willing to throw it all away? I thought we meant more to each other." Matt's eyes brewed with an intense, angry passion June had never seen before. She pulled away. She couldn't handle the heat, didn't want to know what that meant. But Matt refused to release her.

"Let me go." But as she backed away, he only moved closer. "I mean it, Matt. Let me go!"

"I can't, June. When you left, it practically killed me. I won't do it again."

A tiny voice in the back of her mind knew she could have fought more, pushed back, made Matt release her. He hadn't been that forceful. But she didn't. Maybe it was the intrigue, the years of wondering what it would be like, the small seeds of jealousy planted every time Matt spoke about another girl or shared intimate secrets about his sexual conquests, teasing June to speculate as to what it would feel like to kiss him. Maybe she was tired of holding herself together and wanted to give herself to someone else, let go of the burden, have him carry the pieces. Maybe she simply wanted to be wanted, devoured, instead of cast aside.

The way Matt Tierney kissed June was anything but trite. It wasn't playful or hesitant or gentle. It was thirst and hunger in one. It was deep. It was a message in action. A telling. A stake thrust in the ground. Matt's hands knotted around June's shirt, fists clenched as if he were fighting an invisible enemy. June was lost in it—in the taste of his tongue, the feel of his lips, the press of his body into hers. He beckoned her closer with his hips. June clung to the violent bliss of being discon-nected from the world, allowing herself to drown in it. She had wanted a way out of the emotions of the past few days, and it was happening.

The room grew quiet. Tension melted from them both. Her mind went delightfully blank, and her body took over, reacting instinctually.

Matt pulled June toward the bed. She felt how much he wanted her. How desperate he was for her. Finally, she could give him what he wanted. After months of letting him down, years of lying, June could be everything Matt wanted right now. But what about after, when they put on their flippantly discarded clothes and left the bedroom and found themselves in the world again? What happened then? Who did June want to be *then*? Was being wanted worth the price when the fever calmed? Panic weaseled its way into her system.

She pushed Matt away, catching her breath, her mouth hot and wet. "What is it?" he begged.

"We can't do this."

"Why not?"

June tried to formulate her very logical reasons for why kissing Matt was a terrible idea.

He gestured to the pile of photos on the bed. "Is it about him?" June had been too startled by Matt's kiss even to contemplate Lennox, but in the very recesses of her mind, he had always been there. "I knew something was going on. I hate everything about that fucking guy."

"Did you just kiss me because you're jealous?" she said.

"No." Matt was on her again, grabbing her hips, holding her to him, but June refused to crumble. She couldn't lose herself in him again. It was too hard to think with him this close. "Listen to me, whatever's happened here is done. All I care about is taking you home."

She pushed him to arm's length. "I can't, Matty."

He ran a hand through his hair, frustration replacing desire. "Fuck, June! This is crazy! Why not? What could possibly be the reason?"

"I just can't!" Panic grew like a monster in June, slowly eating her insides. She shook out her hands at her sides, feeling the edgy tingles that told her to run at any cost.

"What does that even mean, you can't?" Matt asked, exasperated. "Look around you, June! You think you actually belong in this small fucking town? You think these people know you?"

June squeezed her eyes closed, her breath labored, and wished herself anywhere else. The closed bedroom door felt like a concrete wall. The air felt heavy, poisoned, unbreathable. She felt as if she might explode if she didn't escape, so she broke for the door again, but Matt wouldn't let her go. He held her in place, hands on her arms, squeezing, torturously rooting her still.

"You can't give me a reason because there isn't one. This place isn't you. Lennox doesn't know you like I know you, June." Matt's body was so close that June felt the weight of it, the burden. "You know I'm right. Just stop running from me and say yes!"

"I lied to you!" June screamed.

Silence invaded the room.

June took in a gulp of air. "Is that what you want to hear? Fine! I lied to you. I'm lying to *everyone*, Matty."

Matt backed away. June felt the distance grow, like a tide moving out from the shore. It would only increase from that moment on. He had pushed this on himself. This was his fault. If he would have just stayed away like he was supposed to, none of this would be happening. He had come to her rescue without asking whether she wanted that. June had to let him go. He had left her no other choice.

"Lying about what?" Matt asked.

June looked at him, tears collecting in her eyes. "Everything."

TWENTY-THREE

J osh Merriweather, found in a small apartment in Marion, Ohio, had been pronounced dead at the scene. Cause of death: heroin overdose.

Phil had insisted that the officer was wrong. He had sworn, demanded to speak with a supervisor. How dare the officer assume the cause of death without an autopsy? Nancy had taken the phone from her husband's shaking hands and asked the officer to repeat what he'd said. June had pulled on the drawstrings of her hooded sweatshirt and wished then and there to disappear. To run. To hide. To get away, as fast as she could.

It was the third overdose the officer had seen that week. The Merriweathers could request an autopsy if they wanted, but he knew what an overdose looked like, he had said. And there were drugs in the apartment.

An ocean away from Marion, June shook as she confessed the story to Matt, her hands balled into fists at her sides. Her skin crawled, and she wished she could zip out of her own body as if it were a one-piece jumper.

"How long?" Matt asked. "How long was Josh . . ."

On heroin. June knew why Matt trailed off. It was one thing to drink and smoke weed. Hell, at Stratford it wasn't odd to see the occasional line of cocaine. But heroin? Heroin was a dirty word, a drug done by dirty people, who deserved to die in a dirty way. June had felt the same, three years ago when she had found Josh's stash hidden underneath the loose cabinet floorboard in their shared bathroom, buried there like a bomb. Filth had infiltrated their clean house, right under their noses. June had been disgusted, but more than that, she had been embarrassed and ashamed. How could her brother have been so weak? How could he have brought that into her life? What would people in Sunningdale think? Did he know he threatened the reputation of their family?

Three years later, he was dead.

After Josh's death, June saw everything differently. Her family's denial was a plague. Josh had had a problem, but they were all sick, maybe June most of all.

"A while," she answered Matt.

"A while like months, or a while like years?"

June couldn't meet his eye. "Years."

"Jesus Christ, June."

She scrambled to soften the blow. "But it's not like he woke up one morning, gave me a call, and said, 'Hey, June! I'm a heroin addict! Spread the word!'"

"But you knew something was wrong," Matt pressed.

June nodded. "He never recovered after his second surgery. He was in so much pain, and the pills made him all loopy and tired. He couldn't handle his classes, so he quit. He was supposed to go to rehab, get off the pills, and go back to school in the fall. He promised he would. But he never did."

Matt looked as though he was retracing the past few years in his mind. "So for *years* you've been lying to me. Every time I asked about him. Every time he didn't come home for holidays or school breaks and I wondered where he was. Every fucking time I said his name, you lied."

"My family never talked about it! My parents refused to! They didn't want anyone to find out. Can you imagine the rumors, the gossip?

Sunningdale's golden boy, a heroin addict. It was better just to pretend he was busy at school. We all just kept hoping he would change. Get better."

"Jesus Christ, the funeral . . . the supposed heart condition . . . all of it bullshit."

"I hated that funeral, but my parents—"

"Fuck your parents. Don't blame them for this."

"How was I supposed to tell you, Matty?"

"Do you think my dad wanted me to spill my guts to you when he got caught fucking some twenty-something on his desk? But I did."

"It's not that simple," June pleaded.

"But it *is* that fucking simple. I thought you trusted me."

"I do trust you."

Matt paced the room, collecting his toiletries and clothes. "You know the saddest part of all, June? I would have supported you. I would never have told anyone. I would have done whatever you wanted, because that's how much I fucking love you. But you didn't give me the chance. You robbed me of it."

"Matty, please." June followed him around the room, frantic to explain. "It's why I left. I was so tired of pretending. His funeral made me sick. To sit there as if Josh had been someone different, someone else. To see all those people crying over a complete stranger. It was all so *gross*. I was done lying to you, to everyone. It was eating me alive. And I knew if I stayed, you'd do anything to help me, even to your own detriment. Because you're *that* amazing. But I don't deserve your help. I couldn't let you sacrifice for me, so I left. I ran away. It felt like the only answer."

"Bullshit!" Matt finally stopped moving. The darkness in his eyes made her step back. "That's always your answer, June. You run. Because you're weak! I'll tell you the worst part. It isn't the lies. It isn't the lack of trust. It's that I was expendable to you. You purposefully pushed me away. I'd seen you do it before to other people, but never to me."

"You're not expendable! Leaving you was the hardest thing I've ever done."

Matt got right in June's face and spoke slowly. "But it should have been *impossible*, June." He slung his messenger bag over his shoulder. "Stay in Scotland. I don't care." He made his way toward the door.

June tried to stop him. "Wait. Don't go."

"For fuck's sake, be honest for once," Matt said. "You don't want me here. You haven't this entire time."

June fought to respond, truth and lies choking her together.

"You broke us, June," Matt said. "Remember that."

TWENTY-FOUR

To: j_merriweather42@hotmail.com
From: tobin@wcsunningdale.org
Subject: Thank-you cards

Dear June,

The 115 thank-you cards you owe to us are past due. Please know that showing our appreciation to donors and members benefits *you* most. Your scholarship comes directly from these funds.

As was stated clearly in your scholarship agreement, you are required to fulfill certain duties in order to maintain your funding. Without the completion of these tasks, the WCS board can review and revoke your scholarship at any time.

I do not want to see this happen over thank-you cards. We at WCS are sensitive to this difficult time, but we cannot continue to make exceptions for you. It wouldn't be fair to the other scholarship recipients.

Best,
Mary Tobin

To: j_merriweather42@hotmail.com
From: nanmerriweather@aol.com
Subject: News

Thank you for the pictures, June. Scotland looks beautiful. I hope someday Dad and I can see it in person. You have quite the eye when it comes to photography. I had forgotten that talent of yours. I'm glad you've revived it.

In other news, I got a job! Your old mom is the newest sales associate at Macy's. I know what you're thinking. Macy's? Well, you know me. I love to talk. And the house feels too lonely most days. I don't like being here by myself while Dad is at work, so I go to the mall. I met a woman named Hortense, who works in the shoe department. She lost her daughter, Veronica, to cancer six years ago. I pretended to try on shoes for three hours just so we could keep chatting. She said the worst part was wondering if her daughter was scared when she died. As a mother, you never want your kids to be afraid. I've worried about the same thing with Josh. Did he know what was happening? Did he panic and wish he could change his mind? Or did he just close his eyes and drift away?

Hortense keeps the porch light on for Veronica every night. She said she wants her daughter to know she can always come home for a visit. Isn't that lovely? I started doing the same. For Josh and for you. Please know, June, that no matter what you do, you can always come home. I know I made mistakes with your brother. Regret is the hardest part about death. Some days I worry it might eat me alive, but it's nice to have Hortense to talk to about it. I hope you've found someone in Scotland who listens.

Anyway, the job is part-time, the pay is so-so, and I'm pretty sure they hired me out of pity, but I love it. Who would have thought retail would be my *thing*?

The light is on when you want to come home.

Mom

June flipped through her pictures as she sat on the end of her bed. She had barely moved in twenty-four hours. She was paralyzed and manic at the same time, wanting out of her room but feeling unable to leave.

June Merriweather was at an impasse.

Matt was gone. She had let him leave. After she herself had left the States to *preserve* her friendship with Matt, his arrival in Scotland began to dissolve the very thing she had tried to save. Yesterday evening, when Matt walked out of June's life, he had closed the door to her future, taking with him any reason for June to go home. She had left to protect him, but in the end, it didn't matter. Everything had gone so utterly wrong.

And yet her life in Scotland was on loan. Her job, her room, even the camera wasn't really hers. Hell, she was borrowing the whole damn country. It was all one giant distraction—an illusion. June had made a comfortable life in purgatory for the past six weeks to avoid facing reality. But reality had showed up. In the end, that avoidance had crushed the only life she really had.

Matt was right. June was a runner, and she had successfully extracted herself from her own life. She couldn't move because there was nowhere to move to. Last night, after Matt had stormed out of her room, June had done what she had always done—packed up her bags and prepared to leave. And then it hit her. She had nowhere to go. Who cared if the whole wide world was available when she had no purpose in it?

June's bags sat packed on the floor by her door, when it suddenly opened.

Eva barged in, laptop in hand. "I have something to show you. And don't be pissed at me. Before you tell me you don't want to, just know that it's a truth, universally acknowledged, that every artist is scared shitless to put their work out in public. But you're good, and people deserve to see it."

June barely felt the pictures in her hands. What had Eva said? She wiped a tear from her face. "Now's not the best time."

"Bloody hell." Eva examined the packed bags, the made bed. "Are you leaving?"

June shrugged.

Eva set her laptop on the dresser and sat beside June on the bed. "This is about the Yank. What happened?"

June's face was swollen from crying, her stomach hollow. How could she possibly convey to Eva the depth of what had taken place in her bedroom the night before? The heat. The anger. The kiss. "I said no, and now he hates me."

June's empty stomach turned sour as the memory came back to her. Matt had gripped her as if she might disappear, his mouth and hands hungry for her. It had been a violation of their friendship. And yet . . . June had let it happen. She had leaned into the moment like a child touching fire, mesmerized by the flame. For as angry as June had been at Matt for making the first move, for breaking that unspoken barrier between them, in some way-back space of her heart, she had wanted it. She had *always* wanted Matt Tierney to kiss her like that—like she was breath and he was near drowning—because it was forbidden and dangerous for their friendship.

And now she could have none of him. Matt was no longer June's.

"Turns out, saying no sucks," she said to Eva.

"That's why so many people won't say it. They'd rather spare themselves the pain than walk through it to something better."

Eva wrapped her arm around June, but June shrugged her off. She didn't deserve sympathy or care. This was all June's doing. She had broken everything.

"Problem is . . . I have no idea where to walk to," June admitted and started sobbing again. She was beyond lost. She was floating in space, a speck in an infinite universe. She hadn't considered what came after "no."

Eva patted June's leg. "I think I can help with that. Close your eyes."

"Why?"

"Just trust me."

"I can't take any more plot twists, Eva."

"Don't worry," Eva said. "I do this with characters all the time, when they're not working right in a story."

"But I'm not one of your characters."

"Don't be naive. We're all characters, June. If something's not working, it's time to reimagine yourself. Now close your bloody eyes." June did as instructed. "Pretend your brain is a room. Something is hiding in there, and you need to find it."

June opened her eyes. "I don't even know what to look for."

"That's the point," Eva said. "If you knew what you were looking for, we wouldn't be doing this. Sometimes, we get so stuck in who we think we are, we forget to take in our lives from another view. You aren't a reflection, June, like a flat mirror. You are a three-dimensional person. You've just gotten used to seeing only one side of yourself."

"Maybe you're wrong," June protested. "Maybe this is just who I am."

"That's complete bloody bullshit and you know it. Now close your damn eyes." June did, if only to disappear into the darkness. "Imagine your mind is an infinite room, and hidden in that room is something you need to find. There are drawers filled with memories and bins everywhere, with any item you can dream of."

"How will I know when I've found it?"

"Because you'll say yes."

June settled back on the bed and let the darkness slowly morph into a concrete image, a room lined with endless drawers and overflowing bins, just as Eva had described. June noticed familiar objects: her CD collection, her running shoes, her great-grandmother's broach, the baby blanket from the day she was born, her high school yearbooks, medals from swim team, cross country, and honor roll.

June paused on the headshot of Jared Leto. She didn't want to open memories of Matt, but there they were: summer nights sleeping in a tent in his backyard, the bike streamers he gave her for her eighth birthday, his worn copies of T. S. Eliot's *Four Quartets*, hangover breakfasts at Mitchell's Diner, the local greasy spoon where June always ordered blueberry pancakes and Matt insisted on a burger and fries. Matt's pet peeve about "that" versus "who." June's obsession with sock puppets and scrunchies.

"How's the search going?" Eva asked.

"I'm a mess," June sighed. "Potentially dead inside. Definitely in need of a therapist."

"Sounds like you're human. Keep looking."

But June didn't want to look. What was the point? She already knew these things about herself. Every item, she recognized. Every memory. Nothing was different.

And yet there was an edge of discomfort in her body, like wearing shoes a size too small or a too-tight headband. Sure, she could place every item in the timeline of her life. Sure, she knew the feel of them in her hands, where they were located in her bedroom, how much they weighed, and who had given them to her.

Same with her memories. She knew the little girl who once stopped her bike using her feet and ended up in the hospital, missing a toenail. The girl who raced home from the pool every summer day to watch Stone and Robin's love story on *General Hospital*, who once got so mad at Josh that she dumped a glass of milk on his head.

As June lay there, eyes closed and completely exhausted, a scent crept up from the blanket underneath her.

Cedarwood.

Lennox crept into her mind without her permission.

I hate when you do that, she said to him. *You're so distracting.*

Right now, the problem isn't me. It's you. Lennox's voice was a perfect replica in her mind, his rolling *r*'s and deep tenor, the end of his sentences lifting slightly.

Even in my imagination, she said, *you're exasperating.*

Aye, but you like it.

Shut up, I'm looking for something. June dug through the imaginary bins, pulling items out quickly and tossing them to the side.

Why don't you let me help you? Lennox asked.

I don't need your help. June abandoned the memory bins and went to the drawers, pulling one after another free. Memories blurred.

You're not looking in the right place, Peanut.

What do you know?

I could help if you'd just stop for a second and listen.

No.

Lennox grabbed hold of June and forced her to look at him. *Would you stop being so damn stubborn for once?*

No! No! No! You pushed me away! You made me leave.

This isn't about me. This is about you. Just say it, June.

No. She whimpered even in her head. *My answer is no.*

But you're tired. Lennox came so close that June practically felt his chest pressed to hers. *You won't find what you're looking for in these bins and drawers, because one thing is missing.*

What's that? June snapped.

You, Lennox said. *You don't belong here anymore.*

June looked at the mess of her life around her—the strewn items, the memories. *They* weren't off. June was.

Am I right? Lennox asked.

Yes, June finally said. *But if this isn't me anymore, where do I belong?*

"Find anything interesting?" Eva asked, dissolving June's imaginary conversation.

She looked around the room, but it had disappeared, too. She was alone, in darkness.

Alone.

For an instant she saw her brother, lying on the cold bathroom floor, dead for days.

Alone.

Alone.

Alone.

June didn't want to live like that.

June didn't want to die like that.

She opened her eyes, frantic. "I have to go."

Eva smiled knowingly. "*Yes.* You do."

June tore open the door and stepped outside her room for the first time since Matt had left. She paused, looking back at Eva on the bed, surrounded by pictures. "You called me an artist, Eva. No one has ever said that before."

"Welcome to the club," Eva said with a knowing smile. "The pay is shit, you'll have to work until you die, you'll battle self-doubt like a bad case of acne, but you'll be happy . . . most days."

June regarded her friend. "Thanks."

"*June, Reimagined,*" Eva said, "that's what I'm going to call your story."

"Just tell me it has a happy ending."

"That, darling, is entirely up to you."

TWENTY-FIVE

To: j_merriweather42@hotmail.com
From: hotgirl14@hotmail.com
Subject: don't be mad

okkkkkaaayyyyyy, don't be mad . . . i kind of gave all ur stuff to goodwill. but it wasn't my fault! it was a total accident! i didn't have enough room in my closet for all my clothes and since u r gone, i figured u wouldn't mind if i used ur closet, so i boxed up all ur stuff and put it in the basement with all the rush shit and old date party t-shirts and junk we never use and then marcy told the pledges they had to clean out that entire room and donate the stuff for their community service proj-ect. i went to goodwill (which smells like ass by the way) and tried to find all ur clothes but either they were gone (a total compliment if u ask me) or they were so pathetically homeless-looking i didn't recognize them among the pit-stained t-shirts and polyester pants (and u shouldn't want that stuff back anyway).

please say u forgive me, sister!

—Al

June stood at Lennox's front door, out of breath. She knocked and waited. She knocked again. No answer.

She crept around to the back of the house and peered in the kitchen window. Max was lying on the floor, but Lennox was nowhere in sight. She tapped on the glass. Max lifted his head. She tried to open the back door, but it was locked. Max barked.

Lennox was probably at work, but June needed him. All the energy storming around her body for the past day was finally moving. And it felt right. She couldn't go back to her claustrophobic room. If left to marinate, she might find a reason not to tell Lennox how she felt, what a fool she'd been, how she had pushed him away to protect herself, because being alone meant not getting hurt and, more importantly, not hurting others. But that was all she had done since her brother died, when she pulled the drawstrings down on her hooded sweatshirt and tried to disappear from life.

June had made a complete mess of everything, but she was determined to fix it. She went back to the inn and grabbed her key to Lennox's house. Max was waiting patiently at the door when June walked inside.

"Hi, buddy." She scratched behind the dog's ears. "I've missed you."

God, she loved the smell of Lennox's house. She loved his tea-stained mugs, the rubber boots at the back door, the dog bowls and dishes stacked neatly in the drying rack next to the sink. She loved the mismatched towels in the bathroom and the clothesline hanging in the backyard.

She even loved his flannel shirts. June had grown an affection for the plaid that hung so deliciously on Lennox's body. It held scents well, and June knew that if she went up to Lennox's bedroom, she would open his closet and be greeted by cedar and mint.

Max looked at her. "Don't say a word, Max."

June crept upstairs. Lennox's bed was neatly made. God, how she loved his bed, how her body felt in it, the smell of his sheets, the space Lennox inhabited, his feet dangling off the end. She was tempted to crawl into it now but resisted. Instead, she went to the closet and flung open the door. She stepped in and pressed her nose into a shirt. A tiny moan escaped her lips. She slipped the shirt off the hanger and put it on, hugging it around herself.

June knelt down and sat on the closet floor, tired from all that had happened with Matt, tired of resisting how much she felt for Lennox. She pulled her knees to her chest and rested her chin there, more relaxed than she had felt in days, rooted to the floor, grounded.

There were few shoes in the closet: old hiking boots, sneakers, a pair of black dress shoes that appeared new. June picked up the boots and put them on, giggling at their sheer size. Then she noticed a box, tucked in the back of the closet. She reached for it. Opened it.

She was surprised to find pictures. Tons and tons of pictures. At the very top of the stack was a photo of the family—Amelia, Lennox, and their parents—standing in front of the Nestled Inn, the building in better shape back then. Lennox was young, maybe ten or eleven, and dressed in a kilt that matched his father's. Amelia, all legs even as a child, had short hair. Mother and daughter wore floral dresses and hats. The men had serious faces, but it was as if Lennox and his father were forcing their seriousness, pressing their lips when they really wanted to bust up laughing. June flipped the photo over: *7/15/88 Hamish's Wedding Day.*

June began frantically flipping through the photos. Lennox playing rugby, and Amelia in a school uniform, looking disgruntled as ever; their parents kissing while the kids looked on, horrified. Family vacations to the beach; Christmases in matching pajamas. Lennox and his dad fishing, hiking, and skiing, the father's arm lovingly wrapped around his son in each. Amelia up to her elbows in flour, baking with her mother; the two of them at a Madonna concert dressed like the singer, in lace and leather. The whole family at a soccer game, decked head to toe in Scotland gear. Lennox's father asleep on the couch, with his newborn son resting on his chest. Their mother pushing Amelia in a stroller, with Lennox alongside on a bike. Both kids hanging off their father as if he were a jungle gym. Baby pictures. It was a reel of the Gordons' life together. So many beautiful shots, so many beautiful memories, all tucked in the back of a closet, like they had never existed.

A noise downstairs startled June from her snooping. She dropped the pictures into the box and shoved it back into the shadows of the closet. Then she stood, listening to footsteps downstairs.

Two people. June crept out of the closet and edged her way toward the bedroom door. The voices were muffled, but as she got closer to the doorway, she recognized Lennox's and Angus's deep voices.

"Are you sure you want to do this?" Angus asked.

"Aye," Lennox responded. "I fucked up. I can't do it again."

"You're too damn hard on yourself. Any man would have done the same. It's impossible to resist in the heat of the moment. Trust me, I know."

"Well, I should have," Lennox said. "I know better. Nothing good comes of it, but I got caught up seeing her like that. Lost bloody control of myself."

June held her breath and pressed herself against the wall.

"Aye," Angus said. "It's hard to resist when the lass is on her back in need of you."

"Makes me cringe just thinking about it. It was a goddamn mistake I wish I could erase, but I can't."

A gasp almost escaped June's lips, but she clamped her mouth shut with her hand and bit the inside of her cheek. Was Lennox actually calling their night together a "goddamn mistake"?

"So, you're going to Isobel?" Angus asked.

"Aye. She's good for me. Best damn woman I've ever met. I need her. I've got to let go and move on. She's the best person for that."

Angus chuckled. "Took you long enough to figure that one out, mate. I'm glad you're finally doing it. Isobel'll be happy you're making the commitment."

"That woman's been waiting five bloody years for this. 'Bout damn time I made her happy."

"How long will you be gone?"

"Don't know." June heard the familiar sound of Lennox filling the tea kettle. "I know I can't change the past, Angus. God knows I would have if I could. But I don't have to repeat it."

"What do you want me to say if . . ." Angus trailed off.

"Nothing," Lennox said. "Just make sure the lass doesn't burn down the inn while I'm away."

"She might be gone when you get back," Angus said. "Have you thought of that?"

"That sure would save me an awkward conversation, wouldn't it?"

Angus chuckled again. "Aye." The kettle started to whistle. Lennox offered tea, but Angus said he was needed at the inn to help Amelia paint the living room, which had recently been emptied of its old furniture and now sat empty.

"She's changing a damn lot," Lennox said.

"It's about time, don't you think?" Angus said.

"Aye," Lennox groaned. "Aren't we all."

Angus left. June tried to steady her breathing, but her heart was pounding. She hadn't considered that, while, in her mind, she had said yes to Lennox, he might just say no. Worse, he might want someone else. June grabbed at her aching heart, then panicked. She was stuck in Lennox's bedroom, wearing his clothes, like a raging lunatic. As if Lennox needed another reason to consider her a mistake.

She listened as he shuffled around the kitchen. Tea bags in a jar next to the stove. Milk in the fridge. He liked honey, to cut the bitterness of black tea. June had teased him, saying he took his tea like a teenage girl takes her coffee, light and sweet. To which he had replied, in a gravelly tone, "That's the only thing light and sweet about me."

June had laughed and wanted him more. She had never considered it a warning. How stupid.

Honey was in the cabinet to the right of the sink. The fact that she knew his house so well only made June's heart ache more.

Lennox licked his lips when he drank tea, grabbing every bit of sweetness. He had a small dimple on his right cheek. He slung his arm over the back of the couch when he sat. He ran his hand down the strings of his guitar like he was making love to it.

June already felt the loss of him. But this was no time to crumble. She heard Lennox leave the kitchen. Soon his guitar sounded from the living room. This was her chance.

She flung off Lennox's boots and hung up the flannel shirt. Objects she had conveniently avoided in Lennox's room came into focus: The bed perfectly made, the room too neat. A packed duffel bag. And on top of it, a small velvet jewelry box.

June stood staring at it. Did she dare open it to see what was inside?

She stepped closer, reached for it, picked it up. The surface was soft. June cracked the box, just the tiniest bit, then dropped it back on the bed like a hot coal.

One very large problem remained. June was still upstairs. Lennox was downstairs. She crept on tiptoes to the staircase. Max was at the bottom. When he saw June, he picked up his head and barked.

"Wheesht, Max," Lennox hollered from the living room.

This was June's opportunity. She stepped cautiously down the first few steps and paused. Then a few more, to hear better. She steadied herself, her back pressed to the wall. She put her finger to her mouth to hush Max, then counted ten more steps. A right turn, four long steps to the door, and she would be free. Lennox would never know she had been in the house.

June bolted, as fast as she could, but near the bottom of the staircase, her foot caught on the crooked lip of a step. She stumbled and grabbed for the railing, only to realize there was no railing. Her ankle hit the bottom step and twisted. She yelped in pain as her knees gave out, and with a gigantic thud, she landed in a heap on the floor.

Max barked at her side. Lennox burst into the kitchen, where June was grabbing at her ankle, wincing at the pain.

"What the hell are you doing on my floor, Peanut?"

"Falling down your stairs," June said, trying to be casual and funny when she really wanted to cry from both pain and embarrassment.

Lennox gently picked her up. "Are you hurt?"

"I'm fine." June stood, without putting any pressure on her foot.

"No, you're not. What in bloody hell were you doing upstairs?"

June forced nonchalance, but the longer he held her, the more unnerved she became. "I just came over to take Max for a run." She shook out of Lennox's grasp.

"I didn't hear the door open."

"You were playing guitar. I didn't want to disturb you, but I couldn't find the leash. I thought it might be upstairs." The lie came out smoothly, and June thought she had gotten away with it, until Lennox pointed to the leash hanging by the back door.

"That one?"

"I swear that wasn't there. And if you must know, Scotland has a huge staircase problem. I don't think I've seen a flight of stairs that's ADA compliant. And your lack of wheelchair ramps is criminal."

"Is that right?"

June pointed at the stairs. "These steps are horribly small and crooked. And no railing. There is no way they're up to code."

Lennox crossed his arms. "And what code is that?"

"The . . . Homeowners . . . Care . . . and Decency . . . House . . . Code." She pressed on. "You know, for someone who's constantly worried about other people's safety—to a problematic level that probably needs medical attention and a good therapist—I'm surprised you'd allow a staircase like this in your house."

"I'll take your remodeling suggestions into consideration, Peanut."

"You know, I could sue you," June said. "For a lot of money. You're lucky I just twisted my ankle and didn't break my neck, or you might have a big lawsuit on your hands, mister."

"You're quite threatening for a wee lass who's breaking and entering."

June held up her house key. "I didn't break into anything."

"Would you just sit your bloody arse down and let me look at your ankle?" Lennox forced June into a chair and pulled off her sock. When his skin touched hers, she shivered. "Does that hurt?"

The ache in her ankle was nothing compared to the ache in her chest. June wanted to fling herself on Lennox. She wanted to apologize for being an idiot. She wanted all of him to cover all of her. But then she saw, on Lennox's forearm, right below the bend in his elbow, the tally-mark tattoo. She had wondered about it so many times. Five tallies. Angus said Isobel had waited five years for Lennox. A coincidence? Or had Lennox permanently marked his body for another woman?

June pulled her foot out of his grasp. "Like I said, it's fine."

Lennox got a first-aid kit from his cabinet and wrapped a bandage around June's foot and ankle. "Ice it and wear this tight 'round your ankle for a few days." When he was done, he put on June's sock and shoe, the laces loose to allow room for the bandage and her swollen ankle. He stood in front of her.

June needed to leave, but suddenly she couldn't force herself. Shouldn't she fight for Lennox? Beg him to stay, to pick her? But what did that matter? She would only humiliate herself further. He clearly wanted to forget her. Erase her.

June stood from the chair, gritting her teeth against the pain throbbing up her leg.

"I'll help you home." Lennox moved to wrap his arm around June's waist.

But she couldn't handle him so close. A hollowed heartbreak had settled in her bones, and she backed away. "I'll manage."

Lennox didn't insist. He let her walk out the door, alone. It took everything June had not to limp, not to look weak. To keep her head up and her back straight, even in the midst of pain.

On her way to her room, June ran into Eva.

"Back already? In need of more condoms?" Eva joked.

In the hallway, she could smell the lavender candle burning in Eva's room, but June was anything but calm. She pushed past Eva.

"Wait, June." Eva gently touched her arm. "I thought . . ."

"You were wrong," June said. What she meant to say was *I was wrong*, but she was so hurt, her mind so cloudy and angry, that she needed a victim, anyone but herself. "Stop trying to make my life into one of your stories. Just stay out of it."

TWENTY-SIX

To: j_merriweather42@hotmail.com
From: shs@sunningdaleboosters.org
Subject: Your RSVP is needed!

Are you attending the Josh Merriweather Invitational Golf Tournament and Gala sponsored by the Sunningdale Boosters?

WHERE: Sunningdale Country Club

WHEN: May 31, tournament starts at 7am, evening gala to follow.

This event is almost sold out. All proceeds benefit the Josh Merriweather Athletic Scholarship Fund. Please RSVP by clicking the link below.

We hope to see you there!

The noise of three children was louder than any concert June had ever attended. When one's snotty nose was wiped, the next one spilled milk. When one wanted to watch television, another pulled an entire shelf of board games to the ground. And no matter the situation, one was crying.

Hamish's wife, Sophie, had left a detailed schedule for June. It was already seven thirty, and June was two hours behind. She was meant to have the two bigger kids fed and on their way to the bath by now. While the two were bathing, June was supposed to feed little Ian a bottle, burp him, change him, and put him to bed with at least two songs to soothe his sensitive tummy, *while* keeping an eye on the older girls in the bath.

June needed two bodies. She wiped a hand across her forehead and leaned back on the kitchen counter, Ian on her hip. The messy house had been made worse when the older girls had pulled the cushions off the couch to use as crash pads for jumping off the furniture. June was sure one of them would break a bone, the cherry on top of an absolutely awful evening.

The Stone Roses, Hamish and Sophie's favorite band, were playing a concert in Edinburgh, one night only. June had forgotten about her promise to babysit in exchange for days off when Matt had been in town. Just another ripple effect from Matt's visit that kept knocking June on her ass. But when Hamish said it would be their first night away from the kids in years, June couldn't say no, even if it petrified her to be alone with three children overnight.

A pot of noodles boiled on the stove. June had no idea how to transfer the noodles to the colander in the sink with baby Ian in her arms. Every time she set him down, he started to cry. She couldn't screw this up and let Hamish down. She had yet to tell him that she would be leaving Knockmoral soon, before her sixty-day deadline with Stratford College. Every time she tried, Hamish cut her off, asked how her work visa was coming along, insisted that he couldn't wait to pay her a real salary once everything was official or that he couldn't have gotten through the past couple months without her.

June wasn't anxious to get back to her life in the States, but she couldn't stay in Scotland either. At least at home she had her scholarship at a good college. Scotland was a dead end. She had run long enough on a road that wasn't meant to go on forever. Now she just needed to stay a little longer and make enough money for a plane ticket. Asking her parents to fund the flight would have been unfair. She had put them through enough. Between her tip money and her new income selling her photos at the café, she was nearly there.

June had set up a display of Up Helly Aa images and sold the lot within a week. Ivan bought five. People came in asking for more. The town, June suspected, took pity on her, like passing the collection plate at church, their good deed done, probably hiding away the pictures in a drawer once they got home.

Hamish's middle child, Sorcha, interrupted June's self-criticism. "When are Mummy and Daddy going to be home?" she asked, tears welling in her eyes.

"Not until tomorrow, honey."

One round tear rolled down a rosy cheek. "I miss Mummy. She's better at this. She makes me laugh. You're no fun at all."

June wanted to sink into the ground and disappear. How could she be fun when all three kids were on the verge of death at all times? Every second it was something. June had caught herself holding her breath, numerous times, amid the chaos. How did Sophie survive this?

The water started boiling over the top of the pot.

"Shit." June turned down the burner.

"You said a naughty word," Sorcha chided.

"No, I didn't."

"Yes, you did. I heard you. You have a potty mouth."

"No, I don't."

"Yes, you do. Mummy says you shouldn't lie. It's bad for your breath. She says the more lies you tell the worse your breath stinks and no one wants to be around you because you smell so bad. You won't have any friends. Your breath must be really bad because you said a potty word *and* you lied."

June leaned back on the counter. This four-year-old was so much smarter than her.

It had been three weeks since Matt had left Scotland. She had written and deleted at least fifty emails to him. Nothing she said was sufficient. "Sorry" felt trite. And was June really sorry? Yes, it was wrong to keep the truth about Josh from Matt for so long. She should have trusted him, but he had also been wrong in coming to Scotland under the guise of wanting to see her, when it was all a ploy to get her to go home. And the kiss . . . time had not made it less confusing. In the end, June decided silence was best, but detached from her best friend, a part of her felt unanchored.

And then there was Lennox's empty house, which sat, lights off, day after day. Part of June wished she'd never overheard his conversation with Angus, and part of her was glad she had. Amid all her uncertainty, one thing was true: Lennox didn't want her.

Innis, Hamish's oldest child at six, came into the kitchen. "I'm hungry. Is dinner almost ready?"

"The noodles are almost done."

"I don't want noodles," Innis whined. "I want shepherd's pie."

"Well, I don't know how to make shepherd's pie."

"Are you married?"

"No."

"Do you have a boyfriend?"

"Not that it's any of your business, but no."

"Is there something wrong with you?"

"Why would you say that?" June balked.

"Do you want to have kids?" Innis pressed.

"What does that have to do with anything?"

"Well, you shouldn't. You'd be a terrible mum. I'll make the shepherd's pie myself." Innis went to the cabinet and began rummaging around. June saw disaster unraveling before her eyes, but right then Ian grabbed her hair and pulled as hard as he could. June yelped and began trying to detangle his sticky fingers from her hair when an entire jar of tomato sauce broke on the floor, splattering glass and liquid everywhere.

"Shit!" June yelled.

"You said another naughty word!" Sorcha began to chant. "June stinks! She has no friends! June stinks! She has no friends!"

"That's why you don't have a boyfriend," Innis added with a laugh. "Because you stink!"

June held back tears. Along with the completely deconstructed living room, now the kitchen was a disaster. How was she supposed to feed the girls, put Ian to bed, and clean up shattered glass without anyone getting hurt, never mind while getting bullied by children who weren't entirely wrong about her!

And how was she going to become a teacher? If she couldn't handle three kids, how on earth could she manage a classroom of thirty?

June tiptoed to the phone and rang the inn. When Amelia answered, June pleaded with her to come to her uncle's, just for a bit, so she could get Ian to bed. After that, with a baby off her hip, June was sure she could manage the two girls. A movie and some popcorn and the girls might not tell their parents what a dumpster fire the night had been.

Amelia promised that help was on the way. June relaxed and stared at the tomato sauce covering the ground. Glass was everywhere, but so far no one had gotten cut. It would have to wait until Amelia arrived.

"OK. We're gonna play a game," June said.

"What kind of game?" Sorcha asked.

"I don't want to play," Innis whined. "I want to eat. My stomach hurts I'm so hungry."

June ignored her. "It's called Freeze. You have to stay right where you are, perfectly still. First person to move loses."

"What do we get if we win?" Sorcha asked.

June hadn't thought of that. "You get to choose what movie we watch. The game starts—"

"Can we blink?" Sorcha asked.

"Yes."

"Can we breathe?"

"Yes, please breathe."

"What about my toes?" Sorcha pressed. "Can I wiggle my toes?"

"Toes are fine, but you can't talk." June eyed the girls. Innis still looked skeptical, but she hadn't moved. "The game starts now."

For ten blissful minutes, there was silence in Hamish Gordon's house. No one moved, other than baby Ian, which disqualified June almost immediately.

Sorcha and Innis were in a dead heat when the front door opened. At the sound, a flood of relief washed over June.

"Thank God, Amelia," June hollered. "I thought you'd never get here."

"Sorry I'm late."

June froze, her stomach dropping to her toes.

Sorcha moved first, breaking her pose to throw herself at her cousin. "Lenny! You've come to save us!"

"Ha!" Innis said, shaking out her arms and legs. "I win."

Lennox carried a bag of groceries. He took in the mess, the tomato sauce and broken glass, the now soggy noodles. Ian began to cry.

"At least you're consistent, Peanut," Lennox said. "Disaster loves you."

"June said a naughty word, Lenny," Sorcha said. "Twice. And she lied. Her breath stinks."

Lennox went to the sink and grabbed a rag. June wanted to explain, but nothing came out of her mouth.

"I don't know, Sorch . . . she smells pretty damn good to me."

At his smile, June scowled. How dare he be charming at a time like this.

And he looked good. Better than good. June didn't think it was possible for Lennox to be any more gorgeous, but she had been wrong. He looked well rested, but it was more than just that. He was buoyant, an addicting, intoxicating lightness in his eyes that June had never seen. She wanted to swim in the liquid peace of those hazel eyes, hold his hand to check whether it felt lighter, too.

Being away had been good for him, and that sat painfully sharp in June's heart.

Lennox clapped his hands. "How does breakfast for dinner sound?" The girls cheered, happier than they'd been all night. Lennox pointed toward the bathroom. "Start the bath while I clean this up."

They marched out of the kitchen like soldiers under orders.

"That's not fair," June pouted. "Why do they do that for you and not for me?"

"Because I'm more fun," Lennox said.

"I'm *way* more fun than you."

"But you lack something important." He pulled coins out of his pocket. "They know if they behave, I'll leave money under their pillows."

"Cheater!"

"It's called collective bargaining." Lennox took Ian from June. "Now, why don't you go change into something of Sophie's? We can put your clothes in the washer. They'll be dry by morning. I'll clean the kitchen while you watch the girls in the bath."

"Why are you here?" June asked. It was one thing to fail in front of kids, but another for Lennox to witness her incompetence. "I called Amelia."

"And she called me," Lennox said. "Sorry to disappoint you, Peanut."

The problem was that June wasn't disappointed. Not in the least. In fact, she felt better than she had in weeks, as if the sun had just come out in Scotland. She hated that Lennox had that kind of power over her. It made June feel all the more pathetic. She held nothing over him.

"Whatever," she said curtly. "Just make the girls dinner and go."

~

When the girls emerged from the bath, the kitchen was clean and two plates of eggs, rashers, sliced tomato, and toast sat on the counter waiting for them. June had changed into a T-shirt and a pair of sweatpants from Sophie's drawer, and while the pants were a bit long, the waist was just about right. Even so, June felt like a child in adult clothes.

"I put Ian to bed," Lennox said as he set the plates on the table.

"May I please have some milk, Lenny?" Sorcha asked.

"I'll get it," June said. "Do you want some as well, Innis?"

With a mouth full of food, the six-year-old nodded.

"Are you hungry?" Lennox asked June. "I brought plenty."

She felt hollow with hunger, but June shook her head. "You can go."

"Don't, Lenny," Sorcha said quickly. "Stay and watch the movie with us."

"It's a wee bit late for a movie, don't you think?" Lennox said.

"You're right," June said with a pat on Lennox's arm. "It *is* late. Past your bedtime. Better run along home."

"But June *promised*," Innis whined. "And I won the game, so I get to pick."

Lennox leaned back on the counter, crossing his arms. "Well now . . . I don't know. A movie sounds quite nice."

"You better pick a good one," Sorcha warned. "I don't want Lenny to leave."

Innis thought long and hard. "*Mary Poppins*."

Lennox threw up his hands. "How did you know Julie Andrews is my favorite actress?"

"We can have popcorn, too!" Innis said. "Right, Lenny?"

Lennox gestured to June. "The lass is in charge, not me."

If June forced Lennox out, she'd disappoint Innis and Sorcha, even more than she already had. "You can have popcorn," she conceded. "But you have to brush your teeth before bed."

June excused herself to check on Ian. By the time she returned with popcorn, Lennox, Innis, and Sorcha were gathered on the couch. The girls huddled into their older cousin like bear cubs, their hair of the same red tint as Hamish's, their faces favoring Sophie's softer, rounder features. Like Lennox, both girls were tall. June had no doubt they would tower over her once they hit puberty.

"It's about to start," Innis said. "Sit by us, June."

"That's OK. Looks a little crowded."

"There's plenty of room, Peanut." Lennox patted the empty space next to him. "I don't bite . . . except by request." He winked at her, all sexy and endearing. What kind of game was he playing?

"Tempting," June deadpanned. "But I'll sit here." She plopped into a chair on the other side of the room. Lennox's teasing made her feel weak and pathetic. How dare he call her a mistake, something to erase, and then entice her with kindness and flirting?

"June?" Innis asked. "Will you watch us again?"

"*Please*," Sorcha begged.

The night had exhausted June. Settled into a comfortable seat, she struggled to keep her eyes open. She didn't have the heart to tell the girls that tonight was almost goodbye. "We'll see," she said.

Innis and Sorcha smiled and looked at Lennox. In the morning, June would wonder if she had dreamed of Lennox giving both girls shiny coins just before she fell asleep.

~

The television was off when June jolted awake. A blanket had been placed over her. She sat up in the chair, alarmed.

Lennox was on the couch. "Don't worry. I put the girls to bed an hour ago. And I made them brush their teeth, as instructed."

Embarrassed, June stood. "Look, I know you don't owe me anything, considering you saved my ass tonight." She paused and hugged the blanket to her chest, her eyes diverted from Lennox. "But please don't tell Hamish and Sophie what a terrible job I did. I just wanted to do something nice for them. They've been so good to me, and if they know what a disaster tonight was, it'll ruin it. I know Hamish. He'll blame himself for wanting a night off instead of actually blaming the person responsible."

Lennox came to stand in front of June. "Your secret's safe with me, Peanut."

June had a hard time taking a full breath with him so near. She stepped back and placed the blanket over the arm of the chair. "Thanks." She noticed the time, almost eleven. "Go. I've got it from here."

"You didn't eat."

"I'm not hungry."

"Really?" he countered. "When was the last time you ate?"

"That's none of your business."

"You need to eat something."

"Excuse me, but if you haven't noticed, I'm an adult. I'll eat when I want to eat." She was, in truth, famished, but her first priority was getting Lennox to leave.

He walked into the kitchen and started pulling ingredients from the pantry and fridge.

"What are you doing?" June challenged him.

"Making you breakfast."

"It's not morning."

"Well, it's the only thing I make."

Why wouldn't he just leave? She had given him every out. "I'm capable of taking care of myself. I don't need a babysitter."

"I'm not looking to be your nanny, Peanut. Though I will admit, I have wanted to spank you a few times."

June gasped. Lennox seemed pleased with himself.

"Stop trying to control me," she seethed.

"Like anyone could do that. You're a bloody rainstorm." Lennox set the eggs on the counter and a skillet on the stove.

June marched over to him. "Leave."

Lennox leaned down, his face inches from hers. "No." He straightened, then lit the burner.

June wanted to tear her hair out. Being in the same room with Lennox was delectable, euphoric, maybe the best feeling June had ever known. She physically ached with her craving for him. But over the past few weeks, she had detoxed from Lennox. Kind of. As best she could. He was with another woman. June had seen the ring box, heard the words come out of his mouth. And now Lennox wanted to waltz back into June's life as if everything hadn't already changed between them?

She grabbed a spoon and held it up to Lennox's face like she might swat him. "Put the ingredients down, Lennox."

"Are you threatening me? I'm twice your size."

"Try me." June raised onto her tiptoes, still short next to Lennox.

Lennox ignored the warning and reached for the eggs. June whacked his hand. "Damn it, Peanut! That hurt."

"I warned you."

Lennox relaxed against the counter and threw his hands up. He turned off the burner. "Fine. I won't make you breakfast."

June stepped back and gestured with the spoon toward the door. "Thank you. Now go." A fistful of flour hit her shirt and exploded in a powdery cloud. She gaped at the mess on her chest.

"That was for my hand. If you're going to spank me, Peanut, I prefer you swat at my arse," Lennox said with a shit-eating grin.

June grabbed an egg from the carton and smashed it on his chest. Yolk and shell dripped down his T-shirt in a goopy mess. Her hand flew to her mouth to stifle a laugh.

Lennox shook his head. "After all that I've done for you tonight . . ."

"You should have left when I told you to."

"Fine." He held out his hand. "Truce?"

June paused. The word held deeper meaning, resonated beyond just this moment. A truce meant moving on, amicably releasing what had happened. She slid her hand into his, wanting to believe she could let go, but fearing she would never be rid of Lennox Gordon.

The heat of his touch was a delightful passing distraction, allowing just enough time for Lennox to pull June to his chest and whisper, "I had my fingers crossed behind my back." Then he dumped a cup of cold water on June's head.

She blinked as it fell into her eyes and onto her shoulders. "You're such an arsehole!"

Lennox laughed harder than June had ever seen him laugh before. His whole demeanor changed from heavy to light and luminous. He was more intoxicating than ever. *Damn him for that,* June thought. *And damn Isobel. Damn their happiness together.* And damn June's stupid heart for caring.

She bolted to the fridge, grabbed a container of ketchup, opened it, and aimed the bottle at Lennox.

His laughter stopped. "Now, take it easy, Peanut. Don't go doing anything rash."

June stalked him, her hands itching to squirt ketchup all over Lennox's shirt. It was the least he deserved after how he had treated her, after calling their night together a goddamn mistake, after leaving for another woman and just moseying in tonight, all happy and effervescent, rubbing it in June's face. She lifted the bottle and pointed it at his nose.

"Come on now, Peanut," he pleaded. "Think of all I've done for you. I saved your life, for God's sake. A few times. Do I really deserve this?"

The question gave June pause. Did he deserve her anger? He had made no promises and even warned her of his wicked ways. He was under no obligation to choose June. What future did they have, anyway? Her life was in America, and his in Scotland. And he *had* saved her, on more than one occasion.

Facts swirled in technicolor in her mind, illuminating the truth that Lennox wasn't the bad guy. His only offense was not wanting her the way she wanted him. And that wasn't a punishable crime, even if it did break June's heart.

She lowered the bottle, defeated. Lennox knocked it from her hands, grabbed June, and spun her around, pinning her back to him.

"Damn it!" June wiggled, trying to break free. "For a second, I actually felt bad for you!"

"Now, I didn't want to have to do this, Peanut, but it looks like I'm gonna have to force-feed you." Lennox dragged June over to the fridge as she protested and squirmed in his arms. He opened the fridge and perused his options.

June could feel his breath on her neck, his cheek on her cheek as he held her. All felt divine. Outwardly, she protested, but inwardly, she swam in the familiarity of Lennox. She knew his body well, like a map she had studied over and over again: His wide shoulders that narrowed into his waist, his hips, and his strong, long legs. The lines and angles and muscles of his body. His hands that gripped her—the creases and tendons and calluses. She hated that she knew them so well. Hated that she was desperate for Lennox even now, even knowing he didn't feel the same. How pathetic, and yet she couldn't stop herself. She had told him to leave, but she was frantic for him to stay.

"Mustard? Mayonnaise? Orange juice?" Lennox asked. "What are you in the mood for? Maybe a wee bit of all three?"

"You wouldn't."

Lennox retrieved a pressurized can of whipped cream. He popped off the top, June wiggling against him. "Oh, I would, Peanut. And I'd enjoy it. Now open wide."

He held her closely, inching the can closer and closer to her tightly closed lips. She needed to get away from him, or she might do something she'd regret, something foolish, like kissing him.

"Fine!" June blurted out. "You can make me breakfast!"

Lennox eased his grip enough for June to shake out of his embrace and catch her breath. Casually, Lennox tipped the can of whipped cream and gloatingly ate a mouthful.

"Barbarian," June groaned.

"Come on, Peanut." He lifted the can to her. "You know you want some."

June backed away. "I'm not falling for that."

"You don't trust me?" Lennox grabbed June's arm and pulled her close to him again. Then he whispered, "I promise I'll be gentle."

God, he was making this more and more torturous. June was losing her resolve. She let him hold her again. Let him tip her face up toward his. Never in her life had she wanted to kiss someone as badly as she did right now.

Lennox ran his thumb along June's lower lip, making her freeze. He looked down at her mouth. If he took her right then and there, June decided, she would let herself be devoured and deal with the consequences later.

"Did you miss me, Peanut?"

June wanted to look away, wanted to tell him that, no, she hadn't missed him. She didn't wake up wishing she were in his house, in his bed. She didn't listen for the familiar sound of Max's paws on the wood floor, or the whistle of the kettle, or Lennox's low, frustrated growl. She didn't dream about his hands, his hips, his mouth.

Tears pooled in June's eyes, against her will. She missed Lennox like a drowning person misses air. And now that he was back, the longing only intensified, the craving now more ravenous. Maybe she had been wrong all this time. Maybe he hadn't chosen Isobel. Maybe Lennox had come back for June. Maybe this was finally their moment. June laid her head on Lennox's chest and felt his beating heart. He was here after all.

"Did you hear that?" Lennox whispered.

June heard wailing from Ian's bedroom. She wasn't sure who moved first, but suddenly there was space between her and Lennox, a gaping hole that grew wider and wider the louder Ian got.

"There's a bottle in the fridge," June said and turned to retrieve it.

"I'll do it."

"You've done enough. I can do it." She looked around at the messy kitchen, ingredients everywhere.

"I'll feed the wee bairn," Lennox said. "You clean the kitchen."

Too tired to fight, June gave Lennox the bottle. He disappeared into Ian's room, and the crying stopped almost immediately. By the time the kitchen was back to its original condition, June's hair was almost dry, and it was nearly one in the morning. She borrowed another one of Sophie's shirts and checked in on Lennox and Ian. Little Ian was fast asleep in his crib, and Lennox was asleep in the rocking chair, empty bottle on the nightstand. June couldn't bring herself to wake him up.

She made up a bed on the couch in the living room, and as she rearranged pillows, Lennox's phone vibrated on the coffee table. At one in the morning, it could only be Amelia with an emergency or one of the people at Fire and Rescue. June flipped the phone open.

"It's me. I know it's late, but I'm just calling to say I love you, and we can do this. Don't be afraid—"

June looked at the caller ID: Isobel. She snapped the phone closed, her breath caught in her throat, and threw it down on the table as if it burned her skin. She curled into a ball on the couch, knees tucked for protection. How could she have been so naive? All of her maybes were just fantasy. Lennox didn't want her. He never would.

June slept, the words *I love you* etched in her dreams.

TWENTY-SEVEN

To: j_merriweather42@hotmail.com
From: Merriweather_Phil@aol.com
Subject: Dues

Hi honey—

I got a bill for your sorority dues. I haven't paid it yet.
Are you planning on staying in Tri Gamma? You know,
in my day at Michigan State, only communists joined
fraternities. But then again, all of us hippies eventually
turned into yuppies and voted for Reagan. I guess we
all change, no matter how much we think we won't.

Anyway, let me know what you want me to do.

We had Mom's new friend, Hortense, over for dinner a
few weeks ago. She said I needed a hobby, so I signed
up for a painting class. I'm not sure the teacher appreciated my technique of throwing paint at the canvas,
but it felt good. I brought my first creation home, and
your mom said it looked like an abstract painting of a

chicken with its butt on fire. She hung it over the fire-place in the living room. Now, every time we walk past *Chicken with Its Butt on Fire*, we laugh.

Yesterday, I snuck out at lunch and went to the art studio for two hours. I went back to the office with paint under my nails. I felt like Clark Kent hiding Superman. But don't tell anyone your stuffy old dad is moonlighting as an art-ist. I kind of like having this secret. Who knows, maybe in ten years, if I keep at it, I'll actually be good.

Love,
Dad

To: j_merriweather42@hotmail.com
From: hotgirl14@hotmail.com
Subject: apartment next year!!!!!!

so . . . i haven't heard from u since "the clothes incident," which i swear was totally an accident and i promise i'll never do it again. and anyway, thrift t-shirts are totally in now, so it's not a complete disaster. we'll laugh about it when we r forty and drink too much chardonnay and r slightly overweight from having kids. (being preg-nant will be so awesome. we can finally eat whatever we want.)

i have good news. u know those houses on court street? well, shannon totally scored a lease for one for next year!!!!!! rachel, nikki, and i are in. there's one bedroom left. ayla wants it, but i'm like no fucking way. i can't put up with that whore all year. i told shannon u get the room. and shannon was like, is june even still alive? and i was like, fuck off, yes she is. i talk to her all the time. and she was like, fine then she needs to put in for the deposit on the place. i was like, CALM DOWN LUNATIC, june will totally send u the money.

so . . . shannon needs $500 from u.

—Al

In mid-March, the return of the sun and unseasonably warm weather brought people in the Highlands out of their winter hibernation, shedding layers of clothing and exposing skin that had not seen the sun since the fall. The hills around Knockmoral shined an iridescent green and brown, the ocean a navy gray that sparkled in patches, the partly cloudy sky peppering the earth with rays of light. People walked the streets with grocery bags and strollers, and couples strolled hand in hand with nowhere to go, soaking up the warmth that had been at bay for months.

The rain stayed away for over a week, and people in Knockmoral whispered about the good weather, as if speaking too loud might provoke storms again. Could winter really be over? Would spring come that easily? People drank in the fine weather like an expensive wine—slowly but indulgently, not sparing a drop for tomorrow, for fear it would turn sour overnight.

June wanted to join the revelry. Her toes, fingers, and nose were all warm, maybe for the first time since arriving in Scotland. Her clothes felt fully dry. For the last week, her tennis shoes hadn't needed the newspaper she stuffed into them. During her runs, there were no puddles to dodge, no rain jacket required, no hot cup of tea to warm her bones when she returned to the inn. One afternoon, she found herself looking up toward the sun, sweat dripping down her cheeks and forehead, not a cloud in the sky, and she thought, *I might need sunscreen.* Sunscreen! She had lived through the cold, dark winter and had made it to the spoils of spring, and yet June couldn't fully enjoy it. There was no upside to the brightness, the sunshine, the warmth, because June was leaving Scotland.

June Merriweather would apologize to the Women's Club of Sunningdale and keep her scholarship. She would finish out her junior year at Stratford College, make up lost time in summer school, and move into the house on Court Street with Allison. In a year, she would graduate with a degree in education, look for a teaching job, get an apartment of her own, and, hopefully, start educating young people. Just as she had planned for the past two and a half years.

Tomorrow, she thought, she would take the bus to Inverness and collect her plane ticket home to Ohio from a travel agent she had spoken to earlier in the week. The purchase would nearly wipe out her bank account. But June needed a proper ending. A period to this run-on sentence.

After she purchased the ticket, she would tell Hamish and the rest of her housemates. As for Lennox, she doubted he cared. Isobel's message—*I love you*—rang in June's ears like a church bell, every hour, reminding her that it was time to go. She had used the message as an incentive to avoid him, not that he was seeking her out. After the babysitting night, Lennox had been just as distant as when he had been gone. Practically invisible. June needed no more proof to solidify that what had happened between them was a blip, a mistake, a memory that would slowly dissolve into a quiet whisper.

Anderson's Pub was crowded as June thought about her departure, the pub humming with unusual energy for a Thursday night. She leaned back in her seat, half a beer in her hands, trying her hardest to enjoy herself, but a rock sat heavy in her belly.

June snapped a picture of the busy pub just as Amelia arrived with a tray of pints and said, "Family meeting. I have an announcement."

"I don't want to be a part of this family," Angus said, leaning back in his chair and crossing his strong arms.

"And why not?" Amelia protested.

"Because I can't shag you if we're family."

"Family meeting it is!" Amelia pronounced, banging her hand on the table. "I have some news, and it involves all of us."

"I'm gonna stop you right there, lass," Angus said. "Won't work. Too many people. Three you can handle, but five . . . there just isn't enough room in the bed."

"Is sex all you ever think about?" Amelia chided.

"No. I think about sex. And I think about you. And I think about the space-time continuum." Angus pounded his chest and burped. "Sometimes all at once."

"Can we kick Gus out of the family?" David asked.

Angus leaned back in his seat. "No one would believe someone as good looking as me was related to a wee bawbag like you, anyway."

"Every family has at least one pervy uncle," Eva said.

"Yeah, David," Angus said.

"That's right, Uncle Angus," David said simultaneously.

"Wheesht," Amelia said. "What I have to say is important." At Amelia's serious tone, the table grew oddly silent. June sat up straighter. Amelia actually looked nervous. No one moved. "We're selling the inn."

A heaviness settled on the group.

"Plot twist," Eva said, but there was no enthusiasm in her voice.

"I've wanted to sell for ages," Amelia explained. "I'm no innkeeper, you lads know that."

"What changed?" June asked.

"Lennox, actually. It was his decision." Amelia wouldn't meet June's eye, as if she were hiding something.

But June knew Lennox's secret. Anything between them was officially over. As if June needed a more definitive ending, her lease was literally up.

"What made him change his mind?" David asked.

Amelia swirled her beer around in its pint glass. "The inn was my parents' dream, not ours. We're both ready to let it go and move on."

"What will you do?" Eva asked.

Amelia's face brightened. "I'm going to Thailand. Lennox bought me the ticket."

"Well, I'm coming with you," Angus announced. He grabbed her hand and pressed it to his chest. "Where you go, I go, Amie."

Amelia yanked her hand away. "Like hell you are."

Eva perked up, eyes alight. "Why don't we all go?" Everyone looked as if Eva had just spoken in tongues. "Come on, lads. We're all about to be homeless anyway. Why not? This is exactly what we need."

"Plot twist," David said and took a swig of his beer.

"It'll be brilliant," Eva said. "The beaches, the temples—"

"The ping-pong shows," Angus added.

"I hear the prisons are quite lovely in Thailand," David said, patting Angus's back. "Do write us when you get there."

"What do you say?" Eva asked, raising her beer.

"I'm in." Angus lifted his drink. "You jump, I jump, Amie. Remember?"

Amelia feigned disgust. "Don't use *Titanic* on me." She slowly raised her glass and shrugged. "But why not? I've put up with you lot this long."

David was next. "'Though this be madness, yet there is method in't.' It's not like I'm performing bloody Shakespeare at the museum. I doubt they'll miss me."

Eva looked at June. "That leaves you, Yank."

The faces of her enthusiastic friends weighed on June. Their raised glasses. How could she tell them that she had already reserved a ticket home?

"How 'bout another round?" June stood quickly and made her way to the bar. She tried not to cry. As if the news about the inn wasn't hard enough, knowing that Lennox was selling it to continue his life with Isobel was gutting. And while Thailand sounded incredible, it was out of the question. June was days away from losing her scholarship, her place at Stratford, her life in the States.

She ordered beers and was waiting for them when Amelia approached the bar. "Please, no more plot twists," she said to Amelia. "I can't take another one tonight."

Amelia raised her hands in surrender. "I just wanted to say I'm sorry."

"For what?"

Amelia nervously fidgeted with her hair. "That things didn't work out . . . in Scotland."

The undertone of the apology was obvious. June didn't want to talk about it. Amelia tucked her hair behind her ear, and a familiar sight caught June's eye.

"Your earrings." She pointed at the hummingbirds.

Amelia lovingly touched her earlobes. "They were my mum's favorite. I thought they were lost, but Lennox found them, miraculously."

No wonder Lennox had been so protective, months ago, when June had found the earring caught in the blanket. And she had been such a petulant child that day.

"He's changed, you know," Amelia said. "Doing things I never thought he'd do. I thought maybe . . ." She grabbed the tray of beers. "I guess we're all moving on, right?"

Amelia made her way back to the table. June lingered at the bar, unsure how she could go back and let her friends down. But she didn't have a choice.

Eva and David approached June.

"We know what you're thinking," Eva professed.

"Not this again," June sighed.

"You've hit the end of your story," David said. "The bad guys are closing in and you're done for."

"But David and I have been discussing this," Eva said before June could explain, "and we think you're wrong. We think this is the inciting incident."

"What does that even mean?" June asked.

"It's a life-changing moment that every character has at the beginning of a story," David said. "Frodo learns he has the One Ring. Luke discovers Princess Leia's message to Obi-Wan Kenobi. Hamlet learns his father was killed by Claudius."

"Romeo meets Juliet," Eva offered.

"The character has to choose," David continued. "Do I return to the status quo, or do I venture on a new path? 'To be or not to be—that is the question.'"

"We know you think this story is almost finished." Eva pulled a piece of paper from her notebook and handed it to June. "But maybe it's just the beginning."

"What is it?" June asked.

"Your inciting incident, perhaps," Eva said. "Should you choose to accept it."

June opened the paper, a printed email.

To: eva.f.oneill@hotmail.com
From: Ronan.Gill@thecornerartist.com
Subject: Art show

Hiya Eva—

Thanks so much for sending me a sample of your mate's work. You're right. It's brilliant. I'd like to offer her a spot in our upcoming summer art show. It runs from June 1 to August 31. The gallery takes a 25% commission on all sales, but it's a good opportunity to showcase her photography and get exposure around Edinburgh. We see a lot of foot traffic during tourist season.

If you would, please share my contact information with June. I look forward to hearing from her.

Cheers!

Ronan Gill
The Corner Artist
Leith, Edinburgh

"I know you told me to stay out of your business, and I know I didn't," Eva said, "but I just had to try."

"How did you . . ." June couldn't find her words.

"I stole some of your negatives when I was in your room a few weeks ago and had them reprinted. I tried to tell you about Ronan then, but you were . . . occupied with other things," Eva said delicately. "Your work is bloody gorgeous, June. And Ronan is really dialed into the Edinburgh arts scene, so who knows what could come of it. The gallery might be small, but it's a start, right?"

Tears stung June's eyes. "Why would you do this for me?"

David wrapped his arm around her. "Because artists survive on the love of other artists."

"We love you, June Merriweather," Eva added. "Now, say you'll join the ranks of the highly sensitive, most introverted, always anxious, best most-fucking-brilliant nobodies you'll ever meet, and come with us to Thailand."

June spoke the only words that came to her. "I don't want to be a teacher."

The declaration released pent-up tension June didn't even know she was carrying. She didn't want to gut out a major she had no interest in. She didn't want to abide by and appease the members of the Women's Club of Sunningdale, in their Talbots outfits and Charlie Red perfume. The only reason she had applied for the scholarship in the first place was to escape Josh and his addiction, but that was moot now. June didn't want to go to Stratford College and live in a house with Allison and three other girls she barely liked. She didn't want to go to fraternity parties every weekend and drink crappy beer and waste her precious life settling for a mediocre future she didn't even want.

June didn't want to go home.

She wanted an inciting incident.

She wanted to be one of the best most-fucking-brilliant nobodies.

"Imagine the pictures you'll take in Thailand." Eva smiled.

Thailand. Temples, long-tail boats, crowded markets. Kelly-green rice terraces, aqua-blue water, saffron-robed monks. June could capture it all.

Just then the pub door burst open, sending a chill through the crowded room. Hamish rushed in, panting like a tired dog. Sweat dripped down his forehead. He ran up to June and grabbed her arms. "Where's Angus? We need help."

"What the hell is going on?" June asked. And then a smell she had grown intimately familiar with followed Hamish into the pub. The scent of a cozy fire after a long run in the Scottish rain.

Eva gasped, her pint slipping from her hands and shattering on the floor. Her face was sheet white. "Bloody hell. I forgot to blow out the candle."

TWENTY-EIGHT

It had been a perfect storm: an unseasonably warm day, a cracked window, a slight breeze. One sheet came loose in a room decorated with paper, fell like a dried leaf, swaying with gravity and grace, and landed on the flame of a lavender candle. As the fire caught, it burned more paper, then clothes and towels and bedsheets, then wood.

June ran from the pub, toward the inn. Unknowingly, she had trained for this moment. Her legs were strong. Her breath was steady. The alcohol buzz dissolved into clarity and focus. June should have been thinking about her pictures or clothes or passport or the stash of pound notes carefully zipped in her backpack that she needed for a plane ticket. But all she saw was the shelf in a dark corner of her closet, the urn hidden in the shadows.

As many times as June had considered lifting the lid and taking out Josh's remains, prying open the plastic bag, and letting her brother go to the wind, she had never followed through. She couldn't let go of Josh until her guilt was absolved. Until then, her burden remained.

June's chest pulled tight, her lungs squeezing the life out of her, as she ran toward the inn, where the Knockmoral Fire and Rescue crew, mostly volunteers, tried to contain the blaze. Extensive damage already scarred one wing of the building. Red, yellow, and orange flames clawed out of Eva's window like the hand of a demon trying to get loose.

June reasoned that she could be in and out within a minute. She mapped her course in her head: up the main staircase, down the hall to the left, four steps into her room. She might even be able to hold her breath. With the fire on the other side of the house, she could make a safe exit. She would crawl if she had to.

She started to run, but someone grabbed her.

"Are you bloody mad, Peanut?" Lennox yelled. "Get away from here!"

"I need to get in there!"

"Like hell you do!"

"You don't understand. Something important is in there and I need it." She struggled in Lennox's grasp, barely breathing in her panic.

"What's so important you'd risk your damn life?"

"My brother!" June yelled.

"What in bloody hell do you mean by that?" Lennox held her, trying to catch her eye.

June's resolve gave way to a gutting sadness that weakened her knees. "I took him, Lennox. I took his urn. When I left the States. And now he's in there, trapped, and I need to get him out." She panted and pushed but with little effort, hampered by the weight in her arms and legs. She pleaded, but even her words felt heavy. "*Please*. I can't leave him now. I can't let him go."

Lennox grabbed June's face. "Where's the urn?"

"In the back of my closet."

"Don't even think about moving until I get back."

Lennox disappeared into the old house. June fell to her knees, giving in to gravity and grief. She hugged herself tightly, trying to hold herself together. What had she been thinking, bringing Josh's urn with her to Scotland? She couldn't lose him. Not again.

Angus ran up to June, his face covered in sweat and ash, and collected her off the ground. "Is he fucking insane? What is he thinking going in there?"

The noise of the sirens echoed in June's head. Hamish and Amelia stood nearby, locked in an embrace, watching their family home burn.

What had June just done?

She had allowed Lennox to go into a burning building. She had let him run toward death to save a dead person. An irrecoverable, incurable, irretrievable person. June could keep Josh's ashes until the day she died, but he would never come back to her. His life had ended, and yet she was still willing to risk others for it, to sacrifice someone she loved just to soothe her own guilt.

If Lennox died, she would never forgive herself.

June tore from Angus's grasp and ran toward the house. She felt him behind her, reaching for her, but June was faster than he was. She was almost to the front door when Lennox emerged, out of breath and carrying both the urn and June's backpack.

"I told you not to move, Peanut!"

He dragged June away from the building, dropped her stuff on the ground, and bent at the waist, trying to catch his breath. June wanted to grab him, hold him, ensure herself that he was real, solid, strong.

"I took . . . what I could," Lennox panted, streaks of ash and sweat on his perfect face. He was still alive, so alive—a solid, breathing body, fire in his eyes. "Now listen to me . . . I can't take care of this with you around . . . I need you to go away." June started to protest, but Lennox silenced her. "For once in your goddamn . . . stubborn life, just do as I say . . . My house . . . Now."

June gritted her teeth, fighting her desire not to let him out of her sight.

Lennox pointed to the house. "I want to see you walk away . . . and don't come back."

June finally did as she was told, looking back over her shoulder, once, and seeing Lennox disappear into smoke and darkness.

TWENTY-NINE

J une sat on the couch in Lennox's living room, Max at her feet. She had no idea of the time. All she knew was that darkness was starting to fade. The sirens had stopped, along with the flashing lights, but time had become muddled in June's mind, and she wasn't sure how long ago that had happened. Lennox still wasn't home.

June couldn't watch the fire from the windows without wanting to run from the house, so she sat in silence, her face still streaked with soot, her clothes smelling of smoke. If Lennox died, she doubted she'd ever move again, unable to leave the night behind. It would consume her.

There was no thought to her future. No contemplation of what would happen after the fire. Everything before Hamish entered the pub felt like a dream. There was only the reality of waiting for Lennox now. Her bones ached from lack of movement, but for the first time in June's life, she stayed with the pain, counting each twinge and burning throb.

When the back door opened, Max startled and picked up his head. There was no guarantee it was Lennox. June knew the disappointment of wishing that a person dead was still alive. How many times had she opened Josh's closed bedroom door to see if his room still smelled of sweat and laundry detergent, to imagine the massive pile of dirty clothes in the middle of his floor, to get angry at the shower running too long, only to smell the wood cleaner her mother used to dust, and no clothes on the floor, and no sound of the shower?

June held her breath. If it wasn't Lennox, she'd hold the breath until she passed out.

But Lennox stood in the doorway, his hair a tangle of curls. June turned away, shame overwhelming her. She didn't deserve to look at him, rooted as she was to the couch, in purgatory, awaiting judgment. To look at him would be to see his beauty, and June had lost that right.

"Sorry I took so long," he said. "Damn paperwork."

Was he actually trying to be funny? And how dare he apologize to her? She was the guilty one. June didn't laugh.

"I'll just be in the shower," Lennox said.

June listened to the water run. Lennox was alive. A floor above her, he breathed and moved, inhabiting tangible space. And yet June still couldn't move. Even when the water stopped. Even when she heard footsteps coming down the stairs. Even when he stood in the doorway again, a pile of blankets and a pillow in his arms.

Lennox approached June, and she was finally able to pick her body up, like ripping roots from the soil. Lennox was too close. His wonderful smell made June weak. She didn't deserve this bliss.

June crossed the room, putting space between them, her eyes fixed on the wall. Lennox needed to leave her. Never see her again. For his own good. The thought ripped at June's heart, but she knew it was true.

"Damn it, Peanut," Lennox said, frustration in his tone. "I'm sorry I bossed you around tonight, but it was for your own good. Don't be mad at me."

No, damn *him* and his kind heart. Didn't he see what June had done to him tonight? She was poison. Unwell. So lost in her own grief and guilt, she'd risked another life for her own need. She couldn't stop herself from crying. The more Lennox talked, the harder she fought the softening inside her. His voice was a tonic, a balm, but he was an obsession she had to break.

Lennox took another step toward June, but she backed away, choking on a sob. "Don't."

The room was still again. June felt frozen. All she wanted was to be near him, but she had earned this punishment.

"Fine," Lennox said. "If that's what you want."

June turned on him, fury in her sadness. "Like it matters what I want. You've made your choice."

"What in bloody hell are you talking about?"

June knew it was wrong to bring up Isobel, to expose her jealousy, her broken heart, after everything Lennox had done for her tonight. "Never mind. I'll leave." She moved toward the door, though she had no idea where she would go.

Lennox caught her arm and growled, "You're not going anywhere, Peanut."

June yanked her arm out of his grasp, hating and loving the nearness of him. "Why do you care where I go?" she barked through her sorrow. "You don't want me."

"What the hell are you talking about?"

June didn't want to rehash everything. She attempted to leave again, but Lennox blocked her way, boiling June's blood. She tried to jostle around him, but he was too quick. She pushed, but he wouldn't move. God, she hated how steady he was. How strong. How protective and brave and kind. How someone else got to have him, and she didn't. She shoved him again, hard, in the chest.

Lennox didn't falter. "I won't let you leave until you tell me!" he yelled.

"Fine!" she shouted, all her strength gone. "I know about Isobel!"

Lennox stepped back. "How the hell do you know about Isobel?"

June hung her head. She was so, so tired. "I overheard you and Angus talking about her. I know you're with her. I know you need her."

"You heard that?" Lennox asked, his question burrowing into her skin.

"Am I wrong?"

Lennox sat on the couch, as if the fight had left him, too. "No. You're not wrong."

That was all June needed to muster the last strength she had to leave. She took a step, but Lennox placed a gentle hand on her hip. The softness, the intimacy of the gesture, startled her still.

"Are you going to let me explain?" he asked quietly.

"You can spare me the details of your love story. I know enough."

Lennox stood. "And what about you?"

"What about me?"

"You and that skinny Leonardo DiCaprio look-alike. He had his fucking hands all over you. God, I could break him in half with one hand. Don't tell me there isn't something there."

"Matt is my best friend," June countered. "And he showed up, without my permission, to take me home, but I stayed. *I stayed.* Not that it mattered. I hope you and Isobel have a great life together. You wanted to erase us, consider it done."

Lennox grabbed June around her waist, pulling her close.

"Let me go." June tried to wiggle out of his grasp.

"I won't," Lennox said. "Not until you hear me out."

"I don't want to hear you out! I want to leave!"

"Would you just stop fighting me, Peanut, and let me talk?"

"I'm sick of talking!"

"Fine! Then you're going to bed!"

Lennox threw June over his shoulder and stomped upstairs. She dangled like a fish and protested, but he carried her all the way to his bed, cast her down, and stood catching his breath, his hands on his hips. Gray bags hung under his eyes. His hands were raw and red. What was she doing fighting with him, after the night he'd had?

"Please," June said, guilt choking her again. "I can't sleep here."

"I'm not putting you back on the couch."

"It's not that."

"Then what the hell is it, Peanut? Is it Isobel? Because—"

June raised her hand to stop him. She couldn't take the sound of Isobel's name coming out of his mouth. But as much as June wished she could blame the woman, June herself was the problem. She was selfish and irrevocably broken, and she didn't deserve any sort of kindness from Lennox.

He stepped back from her. "Is it me?"

If she could just lie, could just say in a convincing voice that she didn't want him, that she cared nothing for him, that from this moment forward she would never think of him again, then June would save Lennox, and this would all be over. She stole a breath, anchored her resolve, and faced him. But seeing his hazel eyes, raw with deep sadness, June faltered.

She gritted her teeth, stealing one last delicious look at the man she desired more than anything else in the world—his unruly hair, the scar below his eyebrow, his wet lips and parted mouth, his broad shoulders and strong arms, the understated tally-mark tattoo that was so intimately *him*.

"Is it me, June?" Lennox begged.

"It can't be you, Lennox." June gestured to the tattoo. "I don't even know you."

She squeezed her eyes closed to stop the tears as she walked away. He didn't stop her as she made her way toward the door. Her fear had finally come to fruition—Lennox had let her go.

And then right as June was about to disappear down the stairs, out the front door, and into the night, Lennox said, "Five years."

June held the door handle, still prepared to leave.

"It's been five years since my last drink." Lennox sat on the bed. "I'm an alcoholic, Peanut." June whirled around to face him, but his attention was on the ground. "I add a mark for every year I've been sober."

June thought back to Up Helly Aa, the nights at the pub. She had never seen Lennox with a drink.

"I didn't want to tell you because I'm not proud of the person I was." Lennox rubbed his thumb into the palm of his hand. "I'm the reason my parents are dead. They were coming to get me out of the drunk tank at the police station in Inverness when a truck hit them head on. The driver had fallen asleep. I was there for eight hours, hung over to hell and pissed that they hadn't shown up, when Hamish came to get me. Amelia wasn't even old enough to drive."

June came to the bed and sat beside Lennox. He immediately moved, opening space between them.

"I wish I could say I got sober right then, but I didn't," Lennox said. "I spent the day of my parents' funeral drunk in a pub in Glasgow. I left Amelia to mourn alone. I disappeared for two months, got as stinking drunk as I could get, and hit as many people as I could hit. I was worthless and pathetic, and I wanted to blame everyone but myself. Then I met Isobel, and she saved my life."

June tried to remain steady. "She must be very special."

"She is, Peanut." Lennox smiled. "She's also fifty-five and married, with three kids."

"What?"

"She's my AA sponsor. And a goddamn saint for putting up with me for five years." Lennox stood and ran a hand through his hair. "I was doing so well, and then you came along. I swear I've never met a more infuriating person in my life. God, I wanted you to go away."

"I get it." June stared down at her hands, ashamed.

"No, you don't." Lennox knelt in front of June, his warm hands lifting her face to meet his eyes. "I only thought I was doing well. I thought I was living my life, but I was just surviving it. I was on a constant loop of guilt and penance. For Christ's sake, I hadn't touched my guitar until that day you made me. I didn't even think I deserved music. I thought if I kept everything as it was when they were alive, then they would be preserved somehow. If I saved as many people as I could, then maybe the guilt wouldn't strangle me so badly. If I told myself I didn't deserve anything or anyone, then no one would be at risk because of me. And then you showed up, and my God, I've never wanted anything more in my life. You drive me crazy, Peanut. And it scares the shit out of me. In five years, I've never come as close to punching someone as I did when I saw you lying on the floor of the pub. I almost strangled that Yank of yours with my bare hands. The thought of him touching you . . ."

Lennox stood and stepped back.

"I swear, Matt's just a friend."

"It doesn't matter who he is, Peanut. It matters how I reacted. Scared the piss out of me. I hadn't felt that kind of anger since my parents died. All that work and pain, and somehow I still reverted back to that drunken idiot with a bad temper and big fists. That's why I went to see Isobel. I needed her help, because you deserve better than that person. I was willing to let you go, too. For your own sake. But I can't. God, you're all I think about. You brought me as close to the brink as I've been in five years, and I still want more of you." Lennox sat back on the bed, so deliciously close to June. "Goddamn it, Peanut, if you tell me you want me, I'll be yours forever. Just say the words."

This was June's moment, to escape, to spare Lennox from her brokenness. All she had to do was say the words—*I don't want you.* But June was so sickeningly full of lies. They ate at a person like a cancer, growing until, one day, June would lose every bit of herself to those lies. What kind of life would that be?

Lennox's head fell to June's lap, bowed and vulnerable. "Just say the words," he pleaded.

"I want you," June whispered. "I want you."

Lennox's lips were on hers in an instant. He grasped her face between his hands, frantically holding her to him. And June let herself be taken. She had no fight left in her, no desire to resist. If Lennox wanted to devour her inch by inch, she would gladly succumb to that intoxicating agony.

His tongue glided along her neck, her collarbones. Soon, June's shirt and bra were off, discarded on the floor. His hand traveled the length of her inner thigh before unbuttoning her pants, fingers teasing the soft fabric of her underwear before traveling further down and making her gasp. His mouth found her breast, his teeth teasing her nipple until she moaned. Her nails dug into his bare back as she tried desperately to hold on, not to unravel. Their heat, their sticky sweat, their rhythmic pulse, inching them closer together.

When Lennox finally entered June, they both gasped. They clung to each other, moving deeper and deeper until she was consumed with him and he with her, staring into each other's eyes, pleading for more, aching for sweet relief.

Lennox braced himself over June. "Stay with me, Peanut," he whispered. "Stay with me."

She clung to his arms, her fingernails digging into his tattoo, and bit her bottom lip, desperate to hold on to the sensation of him. June wanted nothing more in that moment. Just Lennox. Forever. When they both finally gave in, she wailed at the release, unable to contain herself. They collapsed, euphoric and exhausted.

Later, the bedsheets lazily draped across them both, Lennox slept peacefully. June watched his chest rise and fall, the beautiful life in him, the air coming and going in rhythm. The small movements of his body. So beautiful. So strong. So brave.

June eased out of bed carefully, though she doubted he would wake after the night he'd had. She crept downstairs, clothes bundled in her arms, and dressed quickly. Her backpack smelled slightly of smoke, but inside were her passport and wallet, fully intact and without a burn mark on them. Little did Lennox know that the act of saving Josh's urn and June's few possessions now offered her the chance to bestow the same grace to Lennox. She wanted him more than she had wanted anything before. And she was sure now that Lennox wanted her. But in his beautiful admission lay a deeper truth.

June was not good for Lennox. He had saved himself five years ago when he got sober. Every day, June had wished that same fate for Josh. If she could go back, she would have done anything to make it happen. Even if that meant saying goodbye. So she could not become the reason Lennox lost hold of his sobriety. He had saved her life months ago, and now it was June's turn to save his.

Gray clouds hung over Knockmoral as June held Lennox's house phone to her ear, listening for an answer on the other end. When the call connected, she said, "Don't hang up. It's me." The words that came next felt like razor blades, but she needed to put an end to this rash escapade. "You were right. I don't belong here."

Then June walked out of Lennox's house the same way she had entered his life—bag in hand, a traveler in need of absolution.

THIRTY

To: j_merriweather42@hotmail.com
From: tobin@wcsunningdale.org
Subject: Missing funds

Dear June,

It has come to our attention that you have withdrawn all scholarship funds from your account. We have contacted your parents and spoken with Stratford College. Neither seems to have any idea where you are.

As you are aware, using scholarship funds on non-educational purchases puts you in violation of your contract with the Women's Club of Sunningdale and thus revokes your scholarship and all future payments.

I'm sorry it had to end like this.

Best,
Mary Tobin

To: j_merriweather9802@stratfordcollege.edu
From: Admissions@stratfordcollege.edu
Subject: Attendance

Dear Ms. June Merriweather,

We have received notice of unexcused absences in one or more of your classes for a total of 60 days this semester. You have been automatically unenrolled from Stratford College. To address this issue, please contact the Admissions Office.

Regards,

The Admissions Office
52 Court Street
Lyons, TN

To: j_merriweather42@hotmail.com
From: nanmerriweather@aol.com
Subject: I love you

Honey,

What happened in Scotland? What do you mean you made a mistake and needed to leave? Just know that, no matter what happened, we love you and the light is on when you want to come home. Nothing will ever change that.

Mary Tobin called from WCS. I swear that woman gets off on gossip. Don't worry. I told her I had no idea where you are.

I hope Paris is as wonderful in real life as it looks in your pictures. But if I'm being honest, and I'm really trying to do that these days, nothing compares to Scotland.

I love you,
Mom

June sat on the steps of Sacré-Coeur as the sun set over Paris. A beret was perched on her head, and she wore a sweatshirt that said *Paris Is for Cheese Lovers*. The city was mostly cool and rainy in the spring, but the clouds had parted, and rays of light shined down on the City of Lights in shades of red, pink, orange, and yellow.

Around June, the steps of the basilica were lined with people. A small band had gathered to play. People danced and kissed and ate baguettes with cheese and ham and lazily sang along while sipping wine.

For the past seven days, June had come to the church, leaving the confines of her small hotel room in Montparnasse to take the Métro north to the city center, to the Château Rouge stop, walking to the steps of Sacré-Coeur to wait for him. It had become a sort of pilgrimage. When doubt niggled at her, and she thought he might never show, June reminded herself that she had nowhere else to go. She could wait, at least until the money ran out.

But that evening, as June sat like a sentinel on the steps, the band playing "La Vie en Rose," Matt Tierney appeared, holding a bag at his side and wrapped in a wool jacket as if he fit perfectly into the puzzle of Paris, scarf and all.

He pointed at June's beret and sweatshirt. "Please tell me you didn't pay for those."

"An arm and a leg. But high fashion has a cost." June stood and wrapped her arms around Matt, pressing her nose into the familiar nook of his neck, breathing him in. Despite nearly two months of silence between them, June had known that, when she called, he would come to her.

"I'm sorry I wasn't here sooner," Matt said. "Fucking midterms."

June pulled back to look at Matt's jet-lagged, beautiful face. "I almost called Jared Leto."

"So it's over then?"

June nodded. She may have left Scotland, but her old life no longer fit either. Going back to the States felt physically impossible, as foreign to her as France.

"What now?" Matt asked.

"Absolution?" June offered.

Matt looked over his shoulder at the church behind them. "You've come to the right place." He extended a hand to June, and she slid hers along his smooth palm until their fingers intertwined. "Let's go inside."

In the seven days that June had spent at Sacré-Coeur, she had never once gone into the church. Matt now pulled her toward the intimidatingly large entrance, with its beautifully arched travertine stone columns. Once inside, they walked through the nave and then sat in one of the smooth wooden pews. Overhead an angelic Jesus in white, with widespread arms and a radiating heart of gold, looked down on them. June had never been in a more beautifully intimidating space.

"You want absolution," Matt said, pointing up. "I hear he's good at that."

"How do I start?"

"Jesus always liked a good story, though he tended to telegraph the moral, so his endings were fairly predictable."

June smiled. "Only you would critique Jesus."

Matt nudged her. "How about this for a start?" Then he whispered, "Confession time . . ."

June looked at Jesus above her. She took a breath. And started at the beginning.

~

June now saw death for what it was—a living entity. Death was very much alive in a person, planted years before and watered by moments until it grew to full strength. When June looked back on Josh's life, she blamed herself for the planting. She had dug the hole with her bare hands, not knowing the blood she would see on them years later.

The entire town of Sunningdale saw Josh Merriweather's shoulder injury as a tragedy, save one person—the injured. Josh saw it as a blessing. He had lain on the field in agonizing pain and smiled. Most took his silence in the hours and days after the incident as contemplative mourning. In truth, he had spent that precious time envisioning his new life without football. He had always wanted to try acting, but Friday night games interfered with the fall play. And what about a job? Josh was strong and liked to work with his hands. Maybe a landscaping company, or an apprenticeship with a mechanic, or fixing potholes and hanging Christmas lights in the town square on the weekends for the City of Sunningdale.

In a whispered confession one night, when June had been tasked with bringing her brother his dinner and pain medicine and as she set the tray of food on his lap, Josh's right arm strapped to his body, he told her of his plans, of how one moment had allowed him to reimagine his life.

"Every time I walk onto the field, I get nauseous," he had said, poking at his lasagna with his good arm. "I hate the lights. I hate the sound of the crowd. I hate the smell of my own damn uniform. Do you know what my first thought was when I was lying on that field?"

"What?" June asked.

"Thank God, it's finally over. I don't ever have to play this fucking sport again."

June took the fork from Josh and stabbed at the food, taking a bite for herself. At her mom's request, June had been waiting on Josh hand and foot since he'd come home from the hospital. And to make matters even more aggravating, the smell of lilacs was getting to her. One floor below, their house looked like a florist's shop. Nancy didn't have enough vases for all the bouquets that had been delivered. She had started to put them in water glasses, but inevitably, some died from neglect. There were balloons and stuffed animals and trays of food lining the freezer. And just that afternoon, Josh's girlfriend, Siena, had personally delivered her handmade get-well card and a blow job.

"You're such an asshole, Josh," June said as she chewed. "Do you know how many people came to the hospital? If I died tomorrow, fewer people would come to my funeral. The house wouldn't look like this. You have no idea how good you have it. This town loves you. You could be drunk, having sex on a park bench in broad daylight with a girl who isn't your girlfriend, and no one would care. The police would drive by and tell you to have a great game Friday night. Do you think people will do the same when you're collecting their garbage for the city? You're crazy to give up what you have, Josh. Not to mention, it'd be a total dick move to Mom and Dad. And me."

"What the hell does this have to do with you?"

"Do you think I'd be invited to parties if I wasn't your sister? I was the only freshman girl asked to homecoming by a junior."

"So I should keep playing football so you can get drunk and hook up with older dudes?"

"No," June said. "You should keep playing football because you don't know what it's like to lose. If you quit, all of this will be gone. Forget the flowers and the balloons and the hot girlfriend with loose morals and big lips. Do you know what Archie Williams got for being the lead in the fall play? The word 'fag' written on his locker. You only know life as a winner, Josh. Do you honestly think you can handle being a loser? Because that's what you'll be. And then what?"

Josh went silent. He poked at the food on his plate.

"Ugh, I'm not feeding you like a baby," June said.

"I'm not hungry," Josh murmured.

"Well, I'm not taking the tray back downstairs. Mom can get it later." June turned to leave.

"Wait." Josh pushed himself up straighter on the bed. "Hand me my pain pills."

June tossed them onto the bed. "By the way, I hear they're doing *Bye Bye Birdie* for the spring musical, and there's a tap number. You'd look good in tights and a top hat."

"Fuck off."

June pretended to tap dance out the door. The next day Josh was at the physical therapist, determined to get his arm back into working order for his senior year.

In the years to come, when Josh's arm became irrevocably damaged, when June found her brother barely conscious on their living room couch, when he lost weight and grew skittish and pasty and quiet, she would look back at her mistake and see that losing back then might have saved Josh's life.

June told all this to Matt as they sat in the church, shaking her hands at the mute Jesus overhead. "I told him not to quit. I convinced him to keep playing. I handed him the pills. If I had answered him differently, Josh would be alive now. I should have told him to go for it. Fuck what other people think. Do what makes you happy. Be a nobody. But I didn't. Now he's dead, and it's my fault."

Tears dripped down her face. June didn't bother wiping them dry. She waited for a lightning bolt to crack the ceiling, or a priest to drag her out of the church in stocks. She waited through the deafening silence that followed her confession, until Matt whispered, "No."

June looked at him.

"What about the doctors who prescribed the medicine in the first place?" Matt asked. "Or your parents, who put him in football to begin with? Or the cornerback who knocked him over? Or the person who gave him heroin for the first time? Or the college coach, for putting him in the game that ended his career? The list goes on and on, but Josh is the one to blame. He became who he was by his own volition, just like the rest of us. You can carry the burden of his death, June, but it won't change Josh's choices. It will only change you. You can let his death be your undoing, or you can let it go and become who you want to be, because Josh couldn't. Do you think he'd want you to make the same mistake he did and out of penance no less?"

June's eyes were so clouded over with tears that Matt's face was a blur. "But it's not fair that I can decide who I want to be, and he can't."

"It's not fair that I love you and you don't love me the same way," Matt said. June tried to refute him, but he stopped her. "Don't tell me otherwise, I saw it in your eyes in Scotland. I know you, June. Better than you know yourself sometimes. The night I left, I thought I was mad because you had lied to me, but really, I was mad that you don't want me like I want you. That some other fucking guy gets to have you instead. But I'd rather have you any way I can get you than lose you over my fucking pride. Josh would want the same."

"Do you mean that, Matty?" June blubbered.

"I can't believe I'm saying this, but yeah, I mean it."

June threw herself on Matt right there in Sacré-Coeur, with Jesus watching overhead, and she held him until her tears dried.

"Now can we get out of here? I'm fucking exhausted," Matt said. "And Jesus is starting to creep me out. He knows way too much about me."

They stood and walked toward the doors, arm in arm. "Let's go find some snails to eat," she said.

"Only if you promise we can go see the Bouquinistes along the Seine tomorrow."

"I have no idea what that is, but yes." June nodded. "Sounds *très chic*. And we'll buy all the snow globes we can find."

"You're gonna make me wear a beret, aren't you?"

June took the one from her head and put it on him. "Looks good on you."

Matt laughed. "Have I ever told you what a pain in the ass you are?"

"Maybe."

"Well, you're a stain on a white shirt, June Merriweather. A hangnail I can't get rid of. A hole in only one sock." He hugged June closer. "You've been a thorn in my side since the day I met you."

"Consider yourself lucky. I could have been a splinter."

"Splinters." Matt cringed. "How can something so small cause so much pain?" They stopped at the back of the nave and turned to take one last look at the basilica. "Confession time?" Matt said.

"Is this another story about Farty Marty, because you owe that kid an apology."

"I'm saving it for our ten-year high school reunion."

"Are we really going to that?"

"No. Of course not." Matt balked.

"Thank God. You had me nervous for a second," June said. "So then is this about the summer your hair turned bright blond and you told everyone it was natural, when you really used Sun In? Or how you used to go to the tanning salon with Bethany Crandell?"

"That was strictly for foreplay."

"How about the time you faked having diarrhea, so you didn't have to swim in gym class?"

"Everyone did that," Matt said.

"Please tell me the rumors about you and Ms. Bliss weren't true."

"I'll go to my grave with that one." Matt wrapped his arm around June. She felt a seriousness come over him. "Be honest. I need to know for my own sanity. That Lennox guy. You like him."

June couldn't lie anymore, so she nodded.

"Do you love him?" Matt asked. June's refusal to say was answer enough. "You know I will now hate him with a fucking passion for the rest of eternity, right?"

June chuckled. She knew Matt would marry a beautiful girl one day, someone who liked poetry and politics, who preferred the subway to cabs, who's idea of cooking was ordering from the Indian restaurant down the street, who did the Sunday *New York Times* crossword, and who wore a leather jacket she'd bought at a thrift store when she was eighteen. A part of June would despise her. A part of June would want to tell this girl that June was the first person Matt had loved. A tiny part of her might even regret the moment when she turned down romantic love in honor of their friendship.

But more of her would be happy for Matt. More of June would love this woman for what she brought to Matt's life. And June would know that she couldn't have loved Matt like this woman did, and that giving Matt up was the greatest gift she could have bestowed on a best friend.

"It doesn't matter anyway," June said, pulling Matt toward the exit. "It's over. I can't go back there."

"I guess only one question remains then," Matt said. "Where exactly *do* you want to go, June Merriweather?"

THIRTY-ONE

To: j_merriweather42@hotmail.com
From: amie.gordon@yahoo.com
Subject: I should tell you . . .

I let the dog out.

At Perk's Coffee House, a popular High Street café among Ohio State students and professors, June wiped down the table and collected mugs on a tray. The front door of the café—conveniently located near Matt's apartment, so June could walk to work—was propped open, allowing the warm late-May breeze inside. Over the past two months, June had watched the trees lining her running path go from bare to bud to full bloom, and they now brimmed with vibrant green leaves. A few times, she had taken her camera, capturing a caterpillar on a leaf or the wet pavement scattered with pink tulip petals after a spring thunderstorm. Richard, the owner of Perk's Coffee House, had even hired June to take pictures for the new website. She spent an afternoon shooting artfully decorated lattes and handcrafted sandwiches and students huddled around a table, clutching warm drinks and wearing university gear.

Her first few paychecks had gone toward buying the new camera. It had been an adjustment to go digital after using film, but change was necessary, even if June missed the anticipation of getting her pictures developed. Change had been her mantra since returning from Scotland. Instead of running away when her life got uncomfortable, she sat with the uneasiness. Some days had been easier than others.

June had been nervous to see her parents when she and Matt disembarked from their flight from Paris months ago, but Nancy and Phil had immediately showered her with hugs and kisses, happy to see their daughter safely home.

Josh's urn was returned to the Merriweathers' mantel without fanfare, as if it had never left. Discussions on when and how to scatter the ashes were put on hold. With June's unenrollment from Stratford College, and the nullification of her scholarship from the Women's Club of Sunningdale, Nancy and Phil had assumed their daughter would move home, but June and Matt had come up with a different plan.

A week after June's arrival back in the States, she had moved into Matt's apartment in Columbus, occupying his couch. And two days after that, with a reference from the Thistle Stop Café, she had secured a job at Perk's Coffee House. Except for the money spent on the new camera, nearly every dime June earned went toward paying back the scholarship funds. She was determined to detach herself from the Women's Club of Sunningdale, one dollar at a time.

June took the worn-out piece of paper nestled in her pocket and examined the letter, as she did every day since leaving Scotland. The night of the fire, in haste, June had shoved the printed email from Ronan into her pocket. She never did reach out to the gallery in Edinburgh. Once home, she reasoned it was better to cut all ties to Scotland. Emails went unread, and June had left no forwarding number. But she wondered daily how Hamish was doing without her. Had he hired someone else? What of the inn? Did they decide to rebuild? Did

Ivan find a photographer for his daughter's wedding? How badly did Lennox hate her now?

Matt and Lottie McBride walked hand in hand into Perk's. June returned the letter to her pocket.

"You packed?" Matt asked.

"Nearly."

"Let me translate for you," Matt said to Lottie. "June hasn't even fucking started."

June pretended to be offended, but she instantly caved. "I'll be ready in a jiffy. Promise." She took off her apron and hung it on a hook behind the cashier counter.

"You have a dress, right?" Matt asked. "It said formal on the invitation."

"If she doesn't, she can borrow one of mine." Lottie smiled. The dancer was about five inches taller than June and twenty pounds lighter, but June appreciated the offer, as did Matt, who had been spending most of his time at Lottie's house. She would not be his forever, June knew. But she was good for now.

"Thanks, but I have a dress," June said.

"It's not that ugly green thing you wore to homecoming that one year, is it?" Matt asked.

"It was not ugly! I loved that dress. It was crushed velvet."

"It crushed your chances at getting laid, that's for sure."

"Oh, piss off, Matty." June whacked him with a dish rag. She had in fact gone shopping for the coming weekend's festivities, buying a red knee-length dress. If June had to endure the weekend in Sunningdale, listening to people boast about Josh, she might as well look hot.

"Are you bringing a date?" Lottie asked as the three of them walked out of the café.

"Indeed I am." June smiled. "I plan on spending most of the evening with my camera."

~

Matt and Lottie dropped June off at her parents' house at dusk. She walked in the front door and smelled burgers on a charcoal grill, a familiar scent from her childhood. Phil was outside barbecuing with Nancy, who sat sipping a glass of white wine. The evening was warm, with little humidity and no bugs, one of the best Sunningdale could offer.

June let her parents know she had arrived and, having come straight from work and smelling of coffee, went upstairs to shower and change. She passed Phil's masterpiece—*Chicken with Its Butt on Fire*—hanging over the fireplace in the living room, and smiled.

After her shower, June dressed in pajamas. Her bed was freshly made, the carpet vacuumed. Nancy had even set a towel and washcloth on the end of the bed, like she did for all guests. *I'm a guest now,* June thought, and while that was slightly unsettling, it was true. The girl who grew up in the room didn't fit there anymore.

June paused at Josh's open bedroom door. His bed was also made, and the carpet vacuumed, but June noticed that his posters had been taken down. The trophies that had lined the dresser were gone, replaced by a family photo. June went in and opened one of the dresser drawers.

Empty.

The closet. Also empty.

She looked under the bed. Nothing.

"Did you know your brother hid empty vodka bottles under his bed?" Nancy stood at the bedroom door with two glasses of white wine. "I cleaned out five bottles and two empty cases of beer."

"Those were from a party we threw when you and Dad went to Lake Cumberland." June smiled at the memory. "I forgot he hid those there. We were afraid you'd notice them in the garbage."

"And he had a naked poster of Madonna in the back of his closet. Did you know about that?"

June nodded. "With a pack of tube socks, no doubt."

"Men can be so disgusting." She handed June a glass of wine and sat down on Josh's bed.

"I can't believe you got rid of all of his stuff."

"I didn't get rid of it," Nancy said and took a sip of wine. "I passed it on to people who need it more than us. Hortense suggested it, and I thought Josh would have liked that. He wouldn't want his room made into a mausoleum. Hortense said that if we want healing to come into our lives, we have to open ourselves up to it. So I thought, why not open the room up for change? Who knows what might move in here." She stood from the bed. "Which reminds me . . ." Nancy swallowed tears and forced the words out. "You can tell them, June. Tomorrow at the gala. Tell them the truth about how Josh really died. I want my son to be remembered as he was, flaws and all. Being perfect doesn't make a life worth honoring. Being honest does. I'm sorry I ever lied about it in the first place. I was so ashamed, not of Josh, but of myself. What kind of mother lets her child die of a drug overdose? I should have saved him."

June set her wine down and grabbed her mother into a tight hug. "Josh had choices just like the rest of us, and he became what he chose. That's not your fault." She wiped tears from Nancy's face. "Want to play a game?"

June went into her room and got a tennis ball from her desk. She instructed her mom to sit on Josh's bed, positioned herself on her own, and threw the ball at Nancy. It landed on Josh's bed. "Now you throw it back to me," June said.

Wine in hand, Nancy tossed the ball back. "This is surprisingly fun."

"I know. Josh and I used to play for hours."

June settled back on her bed, and for the rest of the night, mother and daughter tossed the ball back and forth across a hallway that once felt like a great divide, but had now become a bridge.

THIRTY-TWO

The large dining room at the Sunningdale Country Club was crowded. Sun had kissed the cheeks of the golfers during the tournament earlier that day. June squirmed in her red dress, offstage, wishing she had picked a more comfortable outfit. She couldn't believe the number of people in attendance. Every table was full. The golf proceeds alone had raised forty thousand dollars. Her parents sat at the front of the room, closest to the stage, at a table with friends.

"You always fidget when you're nervous," Matt said. "Stop it."

"Confession time, Matty. I don't think I can do this. I'm better behind a camera, not in front of one."

"Bullshit. You're fucking gorgeous."

"You have to say that. You're my best friend."

"No, I don't. Remember when you had braces and I told you that you looked like a lightning rod?"

"I still hate you for that. I got worried every time it stormed."

"You were right to be scared," Matt said. "There was a lot of metal in your mouth."

"I might throw up."

"No, you won't."

"Everyone is going to stare at me."

"That's the point," he said. "You're giving a speech."

"I don't want to give a speech anymore."

"Well, it's too late to back out."

"Can't I just thank them for their money and call it a day? They all know I'm a failure, anyway."

Every person in Sunningdale knew about June's scandalous behavior with the Women's Club of Sunningdale and her departure from Stratford College. That was simply the way the town worked. Like a spider web, each Sunningdale family was connected to the next, by design.

"They're judging me," June said. "I can tell."

Matt grabbed June's shoulders. "Fuck what those people think. They have to see failure to protect themselves. If they saw the situation for what it really is, they'd have to examine their own lives. Denial is easier than self-evaluation and vulnerability. Tonight isn't about them. It's about Josh."

"What if I puke on the mic?"

"I'll clean it up."

June threw her arms around Matt. "You're the best."

"Now get out there." Matt smacked June's butt.

"You just wanted to smack my ass."

"What can I say? It looks really good in that dress."

The lights felt like a thousand degrees as June took the stage. What she wouldn't give to be curled up on Matt's couch, drinking wine and watching the latest Reese Witherspoon movie. If June was bad at babysitting, she was dismal at public speaking. She had agreed to do this amid fits of grief and shame, months ago, right after Josh's death. Her parents had said it would be good for her. What was one little speech? But as she stood before the packed room, June realized just how bad the idea had been.

"Hi." The mic squeaked, and she took a step back. Her palms were sweating, her mind blank. June had toiled over what to say after talking with her mom the previous night. Should she do what Nancy requested and speak honestly about her brother? Did she lay her family's secrets on the stage for the whole town to see? "I'm June Merriweather. But you know that already." The crowd laughed, but was it at her or with her? She hadn't meant to be funny. "I, um . . ."

June fidgeted with her dress and looked at Matt. There was a high probability she would puke. The crowd was too quiet, too static. June felt undressed, stripped down, desperate to cover herself. Why were they all so still?

Instinct told June to run away as fast as she could, but then someone moved in the back of the room, catching her eye. He stood in the doorway, haloed in light and leaning against the doorjamb. June thought she was dreaming, or had passed out on the stage and was having an out-of-body experience. Because there was no possible way Lennox Gordon was in Sunningdale. God, she was so nervous she was hallucinating.

Her mom coughed, ever so slightly, drawing June's attention. She snapped back to the moment, assuming her delusion would evaporate. He didn't. Lennox walked into the dining room and stood at the back. He was dressed in a navy-blue suit, a look June had never seen on him, which made the situation all the more odd. If she was imagining this, why would she put Lennox in a suit? She didn't even think he owned a suit.

The crowd sat expectantly.

"One second," June excused herself. She ran offstage, directly to Matt.

"What are you doing?" he asked.

"What the hell is going on, Matty?"

"You're giving a speech. Did you forget?"

"Not the speech." There was only one reason Lennox Gordon would be in Sunningdale, one person who knew of her attachment, one person who knew where to find him.

Matt looked downright pleased with himself. "Confession time," he said. "Do you honestly want to live on my couch?"

"I like your couch."

Matt grabbed June by the shoulders. "You deserve so much better than my fucking couch."

Tears welled in June's eyes. "I can't believe you did this, Matty."

"Just so we're clear," he said, "I still hate the guy." Then he spun June back toward the stage and shoved her toward it.

June collected herself and walked back to the mic. For two months, she had banished Lennox from her mind out of fear that if she allowed herself to remember him, she would go mad, fall into a ravine with no desire to climb out. She would miss him, crave him, wonder about him incessantly.

Even now, from across the room, she smelled him—cedarwood, rain and firewood, salt water and sugar. She tasted tea. Felt Lennox's hands gripping her legs, his stubble on her neck, his breath on her hair.

June's mother coughed again.

One last confession.

"If my brother, Josh, were here," June began, "he'd say, 'Give them something to remember, that way they'll never forget me.' He was such an attention hog."

June's parents chuckled, along with everyone else.

"Most of you remember Josh as a football star," she continued. "In fact, that's why you're here, spending your time and your money. You probably remember his injury during his junior year of high school. You might even have been at the game. Some of you sent flowers and balloons and lots of casseroles. Nancy wouldn't want me telling you this, but I'm pretty sure some of them are still in the freezer. There's only so much lasagna a family can eat." Another laugh from the crowd. "Josh would be happy to know that so many people came tonight to support a worthy cause. He would also be happy to know that, because of your generosity, some lucky athlete will get to go to a college they didn't think they could afford. He would want to say thank you. And since he can't do that, I will. But before I do, I want you to know something.

The boy you remember, the boy who entertained you on the football field, who came to your pancake breakfasts and smiled at pep rallies and shook your hand after a hard win, that's not who Josh was. And I'm here to set the record straight."

Nancy and Phil braced themselves.

"Josh never cleaned his toothpaste out of the sink," June said. "He never hung up a wet towel. He drank milk with his pizza. I mean, who does that? One time, I caught him running down the street with an open umbrella because he thought if he ran fast enough and jumped at just the right time, the wind would pick him up and he could fly. Needless to say, Josh wasn't always the sharpest tool in the box. But he had a great imagination. He could make up a game with a simple tennis ball. He collected boxes of baseball cards, which he was sure would make him millions of dollars one day. He sang musicals in the shower. I swear he knew every word to *Cats*. He told me once he wanted to try acting, or possibly be a mechanic, or the guy who hangs the Christmas lights downtown." June took a breath. "Football wasn't Josh's life. He was so much more than that. To remember only one part of him would be a lie. I want to remember all of him." She looked to her parents. "Josh's death has taught me that it's never too late to reimagine your life. My brother won't ever get that chance, so the best way I can honor him is to do that for myself, and I hope that whoever receives his scholarship will do the same."

She thanked the audience and left the stage to applause. She had carried Josh's death in her body for months, allowing it to consume her, but last night, when her mother told her to tell the truth, June had had an epiphany. She was letting Josh's life be defined by his death, and that wasn't fair. She didn't need to admit how he died. She just needed to tell the truth about how he lived. And now that she had, June felt as though she could finally move on.

She felt a rush of adrenaline. People crowded her as she pushed her way toward the back of the room. She politely dodged them, worried that if she didn't get to Lennox fast enough, he would disappear. But he was still there when June finally broke through the crowd. She stopped in front of him, her body aching to be this close to him again. But nothing had changed. June still wouldn't let Lennox risk his sobriety on her, as much as she wanted to dart into his arms.

"I just came to bring you this." Lennox held out the camera. "I thought you might need it."

"I bought a new one," June said. "It's digital."

"I see." Lennox dropped his arm. He was beyond handsome in his suit, regal and yet still rough and rugged, the material hugging his body deliciously. June tried to control herself, but it felt as if a rubber band was looped around them both, pulling her closer. "I understand. I'm sorry I ruined your night."

Lennox turned to walk away. He was going to get back on a plane to Scotland and never see her again. Good. That was exactly what he was supposed to do. Finally, June would have her ending. Eva and David would be satisfied.

Or would they? Hadn't they once told June that happily ever after never happens when people do what they're supposed to do? It's when they deviate that the plot really gets interesting.

"I love you," June blurted at Lennox's back. He spun on his heel. "But I won't let you risk your sobriety on me."

"Is that why you left?"

June couldn't meet his eye. "I'd give up anything if it meant that my brother was still alive and healthy. And I'd do the same for you."

"Peanut." Lennox stood in front of June, just a breath between their bodies. June steeled herself. "Do you trust me with your life?"

There was no one on earth she trusted more than Lennox Gordon.

"Then trust me with my own," Lennox insisted. "Can you do that? I promise I'll save myself, every damn day, if it means I get to have you." He inched closer. And then closer still. Then he leaned down, rested his forehead on hers, and whispered, "Please say yes, Peanut, because I'm dying without you. And you look too damn good in that red dress. I'm about to take it off you with my teeth."

June flung herself on him then. Lennox stumbled back at the force of the collision. She stuffed her face into his neck, breathing him in, feeling his whole body.

Lennox wasn't just June's person. He was her destination, her anchor.

"Can we go home now?" he asked.

But June was already home with him. Wherever they went, as long as they were together, that place would simply be the next setting in their love story.

EPILOGUE

The February evening was cold and cloudy as Nancy, Phil, and June waited on the hill overlooking the crowd gathered for Up Helly Aa. June felt more nervous this year. She pulled a flask from her pocket and took a sip of whisky. Then she handed it to her parents, who drank without hesitation.

Nancy and Phil had arrived in the Highlands two days ago and were staying at the newly remodeled inn, now an artists' retreat center and residency under the new name the Art of Living. When David and Eva had approached Lennox and Amelia about the venture soon after the fire, the Gordon siblings had gladly handed the property over to new management. Now booked through the summer, the inn hosted artists who came to Knockmoral to join some of the best most-fucking-brilliant nobodies from around the globe.

When Phil Merriweather heard about the residency, he immediately applied. Josh's bedroom now contained an easel in the corner by the window, Phil's canvases stacked against the wall, surrounded by buckets and bins full of paints and brushes. Nancy had indeed been right: they opened the room up for change, and it had taken seed in the form of Phil's art. He had packed more brushes and paint than clothes for his two-week stay at the Art of Living.

One month after the fire, Amelia left for Thailand on a one-way ticket. Last June, when Lennox had heard from her, she was staying with monks at a Buddhist monastery in Chiang Rai, with no intention of coming home soon.

And last night at Anderson's Pub, with everyone gathered for music—a new Thursday tradition started by a group of local musicians, including Lennox—Angus had surprised them all with an announcement of his own. He came trudging through the pub wearing shorts, a tank top, and mala beads and lugging a large backpack.

"Yoga retreat?" David asked.

"Fuck off." Angus stood at the table, panting. "I can't take it anymore. I'm going after her."

"Are you sure you want to do that, mate?" Lennox said as he tuned his guitar. "Amelia said that if you followed her, she'd kick you in the balls until they turned purple."

"Better than the blue balls I have every night, now that she's gone."

"Mom and Dad," June said with a blush. "This is Angus."

"It's best to ignore him," David whispered across the table.

Angus picked up David's half-drunk pint and downed the contents. "That bloody woman cursed me. I haven't been able to shag a single girl since she left. She took my penis with her, and I want it back. I just came to say goodbye."

"Do you even know where Chiang Rai is?" Eva asked.

"No, but I'll find her," Angus said confidently. He took Phil's beer from his hands and finished it, then smacked June's father on the back. "Cheers, mate. Wish me luck."

And with that, Angus MacGowan left for Thailand in search of Amelia Gordon.

"He's a dead man," Lennox stated. "No way he survives."

"I'll toast to that," David said happily.

But Eva had a glint in her eye that June had seen before. "I know that look," June said. "No more plot twists."

"It's not that . . ." Eva pondered. "I hadn't considered a sequel before, but I think this story might just have one."

"Amelia and Angus?" Lennox asked. "Are you planning a horror story? Because Amelia will kill him if he ever finds her."

Eva smiled. "We'll have to wait and see, won't we?"

Now a night later, at the Up Helly Aa celebration, the wind picked up, carrying the smell of fire and a cold that burned June's cheeks. After this night, June and Lennox would take the train down to Edinburgh to deliver more pictures to Ronan's gallery in Leith. Since her work had sold well the prior summer, Ronan had offered June another spot, in his winter exhibit. Her wedding photography was picking up as well, as word got around by way of Ivan's gushing praise of her work.

"Here they come," Phil said, pointing to the flames emerging around the corner.

"I hope this works," Nancy said.

"Don't worry. Hamish is the Guizer Jarl. He promised me it would be OK," June said. "Lennox put the urn in the galley himself. No one will find him."

The tacky football urn had been swapped out months ago for a simple wooden box that Phil and Nancy had brought with them to Scotland. On its top, the words *To thine own self be true* were written in pyrography.

The procession wove through town, torches glowing. The Merriweathers stood, arms wrapped around each other, watching the spectacle that just one year earlier had been foreign to them all. But the beautiful agony of life is in the unexpected turn, the unforeseen swerve that leads a person with an urn to an airport, where she buys a one-way ticket to her future.

"It's remarkable," Nancy said. "Josh would have loved this."

June hugged her parents close as the costumed men circled the galley. Soon the boat was engulfed in flames, glowing brighter and brighter. And as the men began to sing "The Norseman's Home," June smiled upward at the stars, lifted her whisky, and said, "Now, *this* is something to remember."

ACKNOWLEDGMENTS

It is hard enough to create a piece of art in steady times, but during a pandemic, when fear and uncertainty lurk constantly, it is an almost insurmountable feat. *Almost.* I want to acknowledge every artist who stubbornly persisted during this time. I need you. I celebrate you. I am in awe of you. I thank you.

To my agent, Renee Nyen, and my editor, Jason Kirk—once again, we did it. The whisky is on me.

To Carmen Johnson and the entire Amazon Publishing team—you give artists the greatest gift they can receive: a home. Thank you.

To my friend Lori, who graciously offered me her story years ago. I'm sorry it took me so damn long to write it, and I'm sorry for that time in college when I ran over a dead deer in the middle of the road and ruined your car. You'll always be my sister. This one's for TJ.

ABOUT THE AUTHOR

Photo © 2018 Kate Testerman Photography

Rebekah Crane is the author of several critically acclaimed young adult novels, including *Only the Pretty Lies*, *Postcards for a Songbird*, *The Infinite Pieces of Us*, *The Upside of Falling Down*, *The Odds of Loving Grover Cleveland*, *Aspen*, and *Playing Nice*. A former high school English teacher, Crane now lives in the foothills of the Rocky Mountains, where the altitude only enhances the writing experience. For more information about the author and her work, visit www.rebekahcrane.com.